Prai

"Put on your summer
your beach bag. It's an irresistible journey."

—Susan Wiggs, *New York Times* bestselling author

"Hannah McKinnon returns with her latest juicy, unputdown-able read about an exclusive New England enclave—and a summer that will change everything. Don't miss this delectable summer treat that is as enjoyable as, well, a day at the beach!"

—Kristy Woodson Harvey, *New York Times* bestselling author

"I couldn't put the book down, and the ending had me surprised and moved to tears."

—Nancy Thayer, *New York Times* bestselling author

Praise for *The Darlings*

"A perfect beach read! I loved it."

—Pamela Kelley, *USA Today* bestselling author of *The Restaurant*

"Part delectable family drama, part testament to the various ways in which love blooms, Hannah McKinnon's *The Darlings* is an absolute treasure of a novel . . . Slip this one in your beach bag and share a copy with a friend."

—Kristy Woodson Harvey, *New York Times* bestselling author of *The Wedding Veil*

"In the vein of J. Courtney Sullivan, Elin Hilderbrand, and Jennifer Close, and contrasting picturesque coastal perfection with the messiness of real life, this multigenerational saga sets familial obligations against the freedom of new opportunities, all wrapped up in a heartwarming bow."

—*Booklist*

The
Sandy Page
Bookshop

A Novel

HANNAH McKINNON

EMILY BESTLER BOOKS

ATRIA

New York   Amsterdam/Antwerp   London
Toronto   Sydney/Melbourne   New Delhi

EMILY
BESTLER
BOOKS

ATRIA

An Imprint of Simon & Schuster, LLC
1230 Avenue of the Americas
New York, NY 10020

For Aunt Alice & Uncle Bruce,
who shared the Cape Cod summers from the beginning.
Those splendid memories still linger at the shore.

The
Sandy Page
Bookshop

Leah

As she crossed the Sagamore Bridge, Leah Powell did not look down. It was a childhood game she used to play with her little brother James, sitting in the back seat of the family car: who could make it the farthest across the span of the bridge without looking down. The bridge was precariously high, the steep views of the Cape Cod Canal below both breathtaking and alarming. Thirty-five-year-old Leah had bigger concerns.

Despite the surrounding cars teeming with luggage carriers and bicycles and colorful kayaks, Leah was not Cape bound for family fun. Nor was she a visitor. But could she even call herself a local if the only time she'd been back in ten years was when her mother was dying? As her car landed safely on the Cape side of the bridge, she realized it did not matter. Leah Powell was headed back to Chatham, Massachusetts, because this summer there was simply nowhere else for her to go.

At Exit 85 she put on her indicator and let out a shaky breath. She was home, if you could call it that anymore. Only no one was waiting for her back at the gray shingled cottage she'd grown up in. Not her father, who had found it too hard to stay after her mother died and rented it out to zealous vacationers, before moving to New Jersey with his second wife. Nor her brother, James, who lived in a tidy saltbox in Duxbury with his tidy wife and matching towheaded children. The only thing waiting for her at the old family cottage were dust motes and memories.

Until that morning, Leah's home was in Back Bay with her ex-fiancé, Greg. She'd moved in right after he proposed, three long years ago. At first, it was perfect in too many ways to count, which should have been her first warning. Leah worked downtown in publishing and Greg around the corner in the Prudential Center. Her salary was paltry by comparison to his, and it would never have afforded her the Victorian brownstone on its own. "Don't worry, we're in this together!" Greg had said, as he helped her haul boxes of all her belongings from her trusty little Honda Accord, parked at the curb. Still, she had felt funny, moving into his place. After all, Greg had bought it years earlier, before they met. And it was much grander, the neighborhood tonier, than what she'd moved from. Even though he insisted he was happy to pay the mortgage if she covered costs, Leah always had the impermanent feeling that she was a roommate in someone else's place.

For three years they lived happily, in that dreamy early adulthood state, each working their jobs during the day and hurrying home to order Thai food or whip something up together in the gleaming kitchen for dinner each night. Weekends they tried new restaurants on Newbury Street with friends and went out to the bars. In good weather they wandered the Public Garden and watch the Swan Boats or strolled along the waterfront. On rainy days they perused galleries and museums, lingered in cafés. Boston was vibrant, their options of entertainment endless, and after years of sharing a cramped apartment with three roommates in Somerville, Leah couldn't believe that Back Bay was her neighborhood; that this was her new life. But as the years went on and the wedding date kept getting pushed back, doubts crept in. Part of it was her fault. Leah was still grieving for her mother and wasn't ready to celebrate a fresh new marriage with such a fresh loss. Part of it was Greg's fault. Though she initially appreciated his patience, as the months rolled on and no date was set, he seemed fine to continue to coast. He didn't worry when other coupled friends, who'd gotten engaged after they did, celebrated first and second anniversaries. Or when they had their first child. He seemed content to be a forever-fiancé, and Leah began to wonder if she might be, too.

The other issue was that each of them was already married to their job. Publishing was just as tough an industry to survive in as it was to survive on. Leah toiled in her career, starting at the bottom as an editorial assistant her first year out of college at UMass, barely earning enough to survive. Two years later she was promoted to assistant editor where she had a stroke of luck editing a debut bestseller. Her work on that project earned her the title of associate editor to Lindsay "Bestseller" Boyer, who had her own imprint. Lindsay was legendary, rumored to have the magic ear for discovering bestselling debuts. For the next few years, Leah felt simultaneously thrilled and intimidated to be part of Lindsay's team. Her increasingly postponed nuptials didn't concern her nearly as much as establishing herself at Morgan Press.

Don't worry, she'd tell herself in moments of doubt. One of these days you're going to make it to editor. But she knew that to distinguish herself at Morgan, she needed to discover new talent, which is why she always kept her eye out for fresh manuscripts. Unlike others in her office who stuck to assigned projects, Leah trolled the slush pile of unsolicited submissions. That was where she'd stumbled across Luna Hoya, a new voice with an edgy pitch for a memoir. It was so compelling she'd stayed late at work in her tiny cubicle, so late that Greg had texted, asking if she were alright.

"I think I've found something!" she'd gushed into the phone. "This writer. Her opening, I can't put it down."

Greg had laughed. "Can you tell me the rest over takeout?"

It's exactly what she'd done, and even Greg, who wasn't much of a reader outside of the odd John Grisham, had to admit he found Luna's story absorbing. Over fried rice and dumplings Leah read the first twenty-five pages aloud, and then more at bedtime. "You should show it to Lindsay," he said, before he turned out his light. "First thing tomorrow," Leah agreed.

Two things had happened the next morning. Lindsay, who was initially reserved about Luna's sample pages, finally relented. "Well, Leah, you've been looking for a passion project. If your gut is telling you this is it, go ahead and ask the author for the rest of the manuscript."

Leah was thrilled by the greenlight. Lindsay didn't offer them liberally.

The second thing to happen that day was Greg's old girlfriend, Rebekah, reached out to him from out of the blue. "She's back in town and asked to meet for a drink, that is if you don't mind," Greg said sheepishly that night.

"Oh. Rebekah." Leah knew all about her. Greg and Rebekah had dated as undergrads at BC, and maturely, because that's how Greg described her, decided to part ways for graduate school. The last Leah had heard was that she was living in New York and never attended reunions. Which was perfectly fine with Leah. Greg was a good-looking guy, but from the old college photos Leah had stumbled across in a box in the hallway closet, Rebekah looked like she'd been plucked from a prep-school brochure: blond, confident, pearls.

"She's new in town, and I think she's feeling out of sorts." Leah did not point out that Rebekah had gone to BC and therefore knew Boston like the back of her manicured hand.

"I don't know," she said, not wanting to make a big deal out of it but unable to ignore the stirring of anxiety. "Is it just a drink?"

Greg nodded vehemently. "Just one. Just as friends." Then, "You should join us."

Leah declined. She was tired from the adrenaline rush of her workday, and she trusted Greg. "Go ahead," she'd told Greg. "No harm in one drink." It had been such a good day, nothing could touch it.

Six months later, Luna's manuscript had shaken Lindsay

Boyer's imprint and the rest of her publishing house to its very foundation with a scandal that made national news. The debut story that had landed on every major most-anticipated list was still deserving of the acclaim: the problem was, it wasn't Luna's. She'd stolen it from someone else.

"It's a real shame," Lindsay said when she let Leah go. "You're a talented editor, Leah, but you should've vetted her more carefully. There must have been some red flags along the way that you missed." After nine years at Morgan Press, Leah was jobless.

If that seismic blast wasn't enough, it was followed days later by a miserable-looking Greg calling her into the living room one. "I don't know how to say this," he'd begun.

Leah already knew what bomb was about to be dropped. "Just say it," she'd managed, lowering herself onto the couch.

"It's about the marriage."

She'd sunk into the depth of the cushions, staring past his handsome profile at the clouds forming outside as if on cue. "You mean the wedding."

"I mean the marriage. Who are we kidding? We've been engaged three years and haven't been able to pick a date, let alone a venue. Have you even narrowed down a dress?"

She had not. But that was on both of them. "Have you picked out a suit?"

He sat down beside her. "Neither one of us seems invested anymore. And now, with everything that happened at Morgan . . ." At least he'd had the decency to tear up. "I'm sorry, Leah. I really am. But I don't see a path forward for us. Things are just too uncertain."

"My joblessness or your feelings about Rebekah?" she'd pressed, hot tears streaming down her cheeks. Greg didn't answer.

When she shared the news with her father, he swiftly removed the Cape house from the Realtor's summer rental listing. "Come home," he'd said.

Leah really did not want to scoop her tail between her legs and run away, but she didn't have any other option. Her friends were Greg's friends, her job was gone, and she had little savings outside her severance.

"How about I drive up from New Jersey and help you settle in at the cottage?" her father had offered softly over the phone. He was still shy with both her and James, acting almost guilty since he'd remarried.

"Thanks, Dad," she told him, "But I could use some time on my own." To be fair, Leah didn't know if that was true. From where she sat, a whole future of aloneness awaited her.

Now, she parked in the narrow seashell driveway and surveyed the house. The lawn was overgrown in that scrubby coastal way that was wind-worn and salt-blown; rugged more than unloved. The scraggly beach pines surrounding the house appeared taller, casting the small patch of yard in shadow, but the blue hydrangeas that flanked the front door were vibrant, bursting with hope. Leah smiled sadly. How many years ago had her mother planted those? She had not been back since her mother's funeral, and staring at the flowers now was bittersweet. Perhaps someone was here to welcome her home, after all.

Leah found the key under the giant clamshell tucked among the hydrangea; the same spot they'd hidden it since she was a child. When she opened the front door, the air inside was hot and stale. Leah paused on the threshold, wondering if she'd walked into the wrong house. The pine paneling had been painted white, reportedly at her brother's wife's urging when her father decided to rent the house out to summer vacationers, and for a beat she missed the warm honey-tone of the wood she'd grown up with. An unfamiliar slipcovered sofa sat where the comfy old plaid sectional had been, two impractical wicker chairs tucked at its elbows. To the right, the kitchen had also received a coat of paint, the wood cabinets were now a deep nautical blue and the old appliances had been replaced. Leah was relieved to see the butcher block countertops remained, though she doubted it was because her father realized they'd come back into vogue. He was a practical man, if nothing else. When she opened the fridge, she was almost surprised not to see the package of bologna and the six-pack of Budweiser her father always kept on the bottom shelf. Leah had to admit, as sparse as the house was, it did look charming if not completely familiar.

After throwing open the doors and windows she tackled the car. It was full of everything she could cram into it from Boston, from clothes and books and toiletries to an antique brass reading lamp and a box of framed artwork, vintage New England prints she'd collected. Greg surely wouldn't miss those; he was probably already hanging his Red Sox paraphernalia on the exposed nails she'd left stuck in their brownstone walls. She hung towels in the bathroom and made a quick grocery list on an old notepad she found in a kitchen drawer, wondering if the local market still closed at seven. *Eggs, Coffee, Yogurt, Blueberries,*

Sourdough, Tomatoes, Cheddar. By then, the sky was turning a burnished apricot and her stomach was growling mad.

As she was hiding the key beneath the clamshell in her mother's hydrangea, she heard the rumble of a truck coming down the narrow lane. Standing, she shoved her sad shopping-list-for-one into her back shorts pocket, barely registering the faded blue Ford that slowed as it passed her driveway. If the man behind the wheel leaned out his truck window to stare at her, Leah Powell was too exhausted to notice.

Lucy

Lucy!" her mother's voice called up the stairs. "We don't want to be late for your sister."

Late was a stretch, given that her eighteen-year-old sister, Ella, did not keep time. That she had no idea what day it was. And, as Lucy feared in private moments, might never keep time again.

"Coming," she called back, obediently.

She could hear her mother's impatient sigh all the way up the stairs, and it grated on her nerves. But Lucy did not let on. Not like she would have a few weeks ago, groaning audibly, pushing back against being dragged out somewhere she did not want to go. That was then.

Now, Lucy kept her thoughts and feelings to herself. Always. Since that night, there were so many feelings roiling in the Hart house on Bay Street that Lucy sometimes feared the walls would blow out, or the roof might cartwheel into the sky from the force of it all. So where there were plenty feelings, there were few words.

She brushed her teeth quickly, knowing her father was already waiting in the car, his face grim. It was the only expression he wore nowadays, leaving Lucy and her mother to discern his thoughts, though it was not hard. Since that night, the heartache was shared silently among the three of them like airborne particles, breathed in and out each night in slumber, swallowed with morning coffee, choked down with whatever they threw together for dinner if someone remembered to shop. Some days the air was so thick with it that Lucy struggled to breathe, even as she forced a smile at anyone she bumped into in town, especially when they asked how her family was doing. The well-meaning inquiries were the worst, the uncertain expressions and awkward consolations offered little comfort. Lucy never repeated these conversations to her parents.

Lucy dragged a brush roughly through her hair and considered her reflection. It was still startling how unchanged she appeared on the outside, when her heart had basically been torn out of her ribs. There were the same large brown eyes, unlike Ella, who was the only member of the family to inherit their grandfather's sea-glass green eyes. There was her ordinary face, (also unlike Ella), and the same long dark hair pulled back in a ponytail so tight it was perhaps the only thing holding her head together. Long ago Lucy had decided she was neither pretty nor ugly, which landed her in the safe if wholly forgettable zone as far as looks went in their high school hallway. She had never kissed a boy, never kicked a winning soccer goal, though she'd come close, but also never failed a test in her life. As her grandmother liked to say, Lucy was dependable as the sun in summer. She'd meant it as a compliment. But how Lucy yearned to be interesting. Impulsive. Wild, like Ella.

Today, just like yesterday and the day before, they were making the drive to Spaulding Rehabilitation in East Sandwich to visit her. But was it really Ella who lay in that bed? Lucy was not convinced.

Her mother was. "We have to talk to her," she urged, in the small breathless voice she'd acquired since that night. "Ella needs to know we are here. It may make all the difference." Her mother's eyes, brown and deep and sorrowful like Lucy's, would widen with emphasis and Lucy would try to do as she was asked. As such, she brought books to her sister's bedside, books that she knew Ella loved, just as dearly as she did. The well-read dog-eared pages were probably the only thing the sisters still shared in full. They were favorites from childhood, before Ella grew up and away from all of them, busy with soccer and her popular friends, and most recently, her boyfriend. Ella was older by only three years, but lately it had seemed light-years. And though there had still been glints of Ella's old self, like when she tackled Lucy playfully from behind in the kitchen to steal her ice cream bar or slipped into her bed late at night for girl-talk, their foreheads almost touching as they whispered so their parents wouldn't hear, those moments seemed few and far between. Lucy loved her big sister, obviously. But there were also moments she felt betrayed by the leggy and vocal young woman who strode confidently through their front door and seemed to draw the whole family out of whatever separate rooms they were in, like a magnet. The same as she did in the high school cafeteria or the swanky boutique she worked in on weekends or the one party Ella had convinced Lucy to go to, where she danced on Mason Farrell's kitchen island and sang "American Pie" at the top of her lungs before showing Lucy how to climb up the rose trellis to sneak back in the house after curfew. The sisters had grown up in the same quiet house with the same loving, if serious, parents. They shared the same bloodlines. So why hadn't the glittery aura that enveloped Ella ever hovered over Lucy?

A few weeks before that night, Ella had graduated from their tiny coastal high school. She was getting off the Cape, would be attending Tufts, in Boston. The whole community was proud of her. Now they were pulling for her. It wasn't fair. It wasn't possible.

It had been just over two weeks since the accident. Two weeks since the police banged on the front door so hard that all three of them tumbled out of their beds to see what was the matter. Two weeks of numbly registering texts and calls from worried well-wishers. Two weeks of digging forks through tasteless casseroles and tearing open the pastel envelopes of get-well cards. Now, Lucy dragged the brush through her ponytail so hard it hurt. If she opened one more card with flowers on the front of it again she would set it on fire.

"Lucy!" her mother called more shrilly. "Be a good girl and hurry."

"I'm getting the book."

She snagged the old copy of *Anne of Green Gables* from her bed and raced down the stairs and out the door and into the back seat of the car. As an ordinary summer day swept by the car window, Lucy gripped the book. Today, once more, she would pull up a chair beside Ella's bed and open the book to the page marked. Lucy understood she was the only person who could perform this task. Her voice did not shake like her mother's. Nor was it mute, like her father's. It rang loud and clear and bright, a sound Lucy could not believe came from her own chest. But that was the power of the page.

While Lucy read aloud it gave her mother permission; permission to let slip the silent tears that streaked her cheeks. To still her hands and steady her breath, things she did not otherwise allow herself to do anymore. Her father, too, was affected. His gaze would swing to the window overlooking the woods and soften, if just a little. Lucy was not sure if she read more for Ella or her parents, but it was clear that the act of reading aloud was as vital as oxygen to each of them.

Whether Anne of Green Gables was sitting in her schoolhouse or sharing her lonely thoughts from the dusty hayloft of the barn, it was an escape hatch for them all. The words, belonging to someone else, allowed the Harts to feel the things they could not express. These were not the words of their sudden tragic story. Or from the inside of a get-well card. They were not words of any heartache that belonged to them. But there they were, nonetheless, and the three of them hovered close every afternoon by Ella's bed while Lucy's voice spoke them aloud.

Eudora

There is no such thing as a bad dog." Eudora Shipman made a small noise of approval in her throat as she read the meme on her Facebook thread. "Just bad *people*," she muttered to herself.

Eudora was not in the habit of hating people, exactly. No, hate was too strong a word. *Loathe* applied. *Despise* did, too. Let's be clear, this was not aimed at all people. Just the ones who earned it, and as a woman who volunteered (*toiled*) in canine rescue, there was ample opportunity.

Just that morning she'd received a message from the head of the Texas-based dog rescue group, Kathy, informing the volunteers of an abandoned dog and her litter of puppies. Kathy was a saint. Dumped mothers and puppies were sadly nothing new, and though each time Eudora tried to steel herself, it was just not possible. That morning's rescue was a scruffy terrier mix (Eudora's favorite! Even though she swore she did not have one) that had been left behind, locked in a house suddenly vacated by its no-good renters. A Good Samaritan neighbor had heard the barking and whining, peered through a window and called the police. Eudora scrolled through the photos Kathy shared. The little cinnamon-colored dog was matted, filthy, and emaciated. But she was alive, as were all five of her multicolored pups, thank God. Kathy had taken the whole family to her vet and would be updating the group later. Eudora closed her laptop and rubbed her eyes. So many lovely dogs, so many awful people.

"Mom, I'm starting to worry about you," her daughter, Caroline, had said on her visit a few weeks ago. Caroline was Eudora's only child and now lived in Delaware with her two children and husband. They had two scruffy rescue dogs, facilitated by Eudora. "You spend so much time on your rescue work, and so little out of the house these days." *These days.* Code for since Dad died.

Caroline's father, and the love of Eudora's life, Milton, had passed away two years ago. In some ways it did not seem possible. It often felt as if Milton was just here having coffee with Eudora in their little cottage kitchen. But other times it felt like an eternity since she'd heard Milton's hearty laugh. Felt his knobby-knuckled hand in her own. Rolled over against his comforting bulk beside her in the night. Oh, how empty her house and her heart had become without Milton. It was one of the reasons she'd gotten involved with dog rescue.

Her therapist, Maeve, whom Caroline had insisted she see, came up with the idea. "It might be healing for you to get involved in something outside of your usual routine," Maeve had said. "Something outside of the home where you're reminded of your grief."

Eudora had prickled. At that time all she wanted was to work in the garden and cook and read books at home. *That* was healing.

"I know it feels daunting to try something new when you suffer anxiety, Eudora. But I promise, it can introduce you to new people and opportunities that can bring comfort."

The last thing Eudora wanted in her life was new people. The joy of her life had passed away, left her swiftly and silently in the middle of the night with a cardiac episode so discreet that it didn't even rouse her from sleep. It was *so* Milton, slipping gently out of her life as if he'd just left the room to fetch a snack. No emergency fall. No drawn out disease or hospice, like her poor friend Mary whose husband had suffered deeply through pancreatic cancer right to the end. Still, despite his elegant exit, Milton was gone and Eudora was bereft. And mad. She would have liked a little warning. She would have liked one last walk to the pier, one last sunset dinner on their little back porch. So, no! to Maeve's suggestion to meet new people. Eudora had lost the best person of all.

"What about animals?" Maeve asked. "You've mentioned you like dogs. Maybe visiting the local shelter and taking a dog for a walk would be a good place to start."

Dogs. Maeve was not stupid. Eudora loved dogs, always had. But later in life Milton developed a sudden allergy to them, and when their last dog, Barkley, passed away they could not have another. Eudora was not stupid, either. She knew Maeve was not so interested in dogs as she was in getting Eudora out of her house and interacting with people. She was just as maddening as Caroline. But the pressure to do something from both was a teakettle at near boil. As it was, Caroline was hinting more and more that Eudora should leave Cape Cod behind and move down to Delaware, near them. As much as she loved her grandkids, Eudora also loved her house full of memories here on the Cape. She did not want to *leave it behind*. "Fine," she'd relented. "I'll check out the local shelter."

The drive there gave her an anxiety attack that took her breath away and made her have to pull over twice, but oh, the dogs! Their wagging tails and sad faces! The big dogs were a bit boisterous for her to manage at her age, but the smaller ones she enjoyed immensely. The trouble was the driving. Getting out of the house was not like it used to be when she worked as a guidance counselor at the high school and sailed out the door ready for whatever the day threw her way. These days, at seventy-five, Eudora was afraid of so very many things.

That's how she stumbled across Kathy's online rescue group. Shaggy Dogs specialized in small, scruffy mutts, and they were always on the lookout for people in the northeast willing to foster dogs as they awaited their forever homes. Eudora jumped at the chance. First she fostered Matilda, who was potty-trained and shy and just needed a loving touch. Then along came Spanky, who was wild and silly and not potty-trained, but one new area rug later—all set! The third foster was the failure. Little Alfred, with his whiskery downturned mouth and crooked tail. His expression was fixed in judgment, and so was he, it turned out. Alfred would not eat, did not care to socialize with other dogs, and preferred the comforts of home. On his daily jaunts, he hit the brakes if he saw anyone coming the other way and dragged her swiftly back to the safety of the house. It was a match made in heaven. Now Eudora knit, cooked chicken and rice for Alfred's meals, and they avoided the neighbors each day together.

This just did not cut it for Caroline, however. "Mom, it's unhealthy to stay home with the dog. I worry you don't socialize with *actual humans*."

"I know plenty of humans," Eudora countered. She was about to list names, but when she thought about it, aside from Mary who'd moved to Florida, the only people she talked to were Caroline, her postwoman, and Maeve.

"What about a book group?" Caroline suggested. "You love to read. I saw online that the Eldredge Library has a monthly group."

Eudora sighed. If her daughter had already done this much sleuthing there was slim chance of getting out of it.

"The library is so close you can walk. All you have to do is sign up and go."

"Fine," Eudora said. She would go to the library group.

She was not happy. She was still thinking about it that evening when she took Alfred for a walk. Eudora's neighborhood was modest, neatly tucked away from beach traffic and Main Street, a little rabbit warren of narrow lanes with wooden signs that had kept its simple old Cape charm. It was an older neighborhood, built in the thirties and forties, formerly comprised of local schoolteachers and fishermen. The houses were situated snugly, with tidy front yards and picket fences swallowed by hydrangea at this time of summer. Unlike the neighborhoods close to the beaches and lighthouse, hers had not been completely overtaken by summer people who scooped up all the smaller homes, adding on to them in every possible direction to accommodate open floor plans and hulking marble islands, all the better to entertain weekend guests. Still, many of her original neighbors had sold and moved on, their houses now belonging to seasonal families who crammed the narrow seashell driveways with their Range Rovers and oversized SUVs. Despite the fact Eudora did not *socialize*, as per Caroline, no longer knowing the names of the people who shared her street did make her feel sad.

"Come on, Alfred," she said, as they crossed. Alfred was refusing to go potty, taking his time to sniff mailboxes and stalk bunnies hiding in the hedges, when she heard the rumble of a truck. A pale blue Ford pickup was rolling their way. Probably some contractor looking for directions. Town was full of them this time of year, locals hired by wash-ashores to improve on their summer homes. It was another reason she kept to the side streets.

The truck pulled up alongside her. "Mrs. Shipman!"

Eudora stopped and peered in the window. "Well hello, Luke Nickerson."

It had been so long since she'd seen him, she'd almost forgotten how handsome the young man was. It always took her breath away. "How's everything at your place?" he asked.

"Fine, fine," she said, nodding. In addition to being a former student of hers, Luke was also a talented craftsman. He had redone their back deck the year before Milton passed away. It had been his idea to also build a small pergola for the climbing hydrangea she'd mentioned wanting. Both the deck and pergola turned out beautifully. Unfortunately, the hydrangea planting had proved too challenging for Milton's back. On his last day on the job, Luke offered to do the digging, but Milton, stubborn as he was proud, declined. The next morning Eudora had been standing at the kitchen window sipping coffee when she looked out and saw all six hydrangea plants settled into the earth around the pergola, neatly covered with fresh mulch. Luke never cashed the check she'd sent him for the extra work.

Now Luke leaned out his truck window, his blue eyes soft. "I haven't seen you in a while, but I was very sorry to hear about Milton," he said.

"Thank you," Eudora said, surprised by the tears that sprung to her eyes.

"If you ever need help around the house, no matter how small the job, I'm here." Luke's gaze was so earnest. Such a good man. How he remained single was a mystery. Not her business, she thought, swatting that thought away.

"Alright. I'll leave you and . . . " He leaned out the truck window to look down at Alfred.

"Alfred," she said. She'd forgotten all about him at the end of the leash! Alfred glared up at Luke like he'd rather he did not exist. At the mention of his name he lifted his lip and flashed one tiny white canine.

"Great name. I'll leave you two to your walk."

As she watched his truck pull away, Eudora thought about the list of people Caroline had asked her to name. *Well*, she thought, smugly, *there's a name you can add!*

Leah

On the third day, Leah found herself with no more excuses to avoid the lump in her throat she'd been ignoring. She knew exactly which beach she'd go to, exactly what spot she'd sit in to cry it all out.

Since coming back, she'd not allowed her limbs or mind a second of rest. She'd aired out the house, swept cobwebs from corners, mopped floors up and down. The refrigerator was stocked, the kitchen cupboards organized. She'd even driven into town and spent way too much money at Chatham's Cook's Nook on a beautiful All-Clad French skillet. The kitchenware her father stocked for the renters was tinny and well-used. The discovery of her mother's old cast-iron pan in a box in the basement was both happy and heartbreaking. She'd since oiled and seasoned it, nesting it with its pricey new companion. Leah was not planning to stay for long on the Cape, but she needed to eat, she reasoned.

It was a strangely comforting and sad thing to move into one's old childhood bedroom. Leah's room was smaller than she recalled. Although all personal memorabilia had been removed for summer renters, the view outside her window of the old neighborhood had not changed. Nor had the old ceiling light she'd spend hours staring at as a teen while lying on her bed listening to John Mayer and the Fray, plotting her big, bright future.

She'd left her ex, Greg, the six-hundred-thread-count Egyptian cotton bedding for their California king. Here she threw her old Laura Ashley quilt—set aside in storage likely by her mother—back on the bed. It was as though her mom had known she'd return, sleeping alone in a single bed again, and left something familiar and comforting to wrap herself in. Staring at its cabbage rose pattern only cemented the feeling her life was going in reverse, but there wasn't time for self-pity. Instead, she filled her childhood dresser with her grown-up clothes and placed her favorite books in a friendly stack on the bedside table. Lastly, she washed and dried the household linens on the old clothesline she was inexplicably happy to discover still strung across the backyard between two pines. The drying took ages, but how luxurious the scent of sun and salt air when she pulled her sheets from the line at the end of the day.

As a last ditch effort to make the rental house a home again, she addressed the wall art. Someone (her brother, James's wife, Lexi, she imagined) had redecorated in a tacky mass-produced beach motif. The framed signage felt bossier than calming: *Beach, Sleep, Repeat* and *Have the Sunniest Day!* She pried them from their pegs, replacing them with framed watercolors and vintage botanical prints of her own, pushing thoughts of Greg and their Back Bay brownstone away as she did. She wondered how long it would be before Rebekah helped him fill in the empty spaces on the walls.

When there was nothing left to attack indoors, Leah tackled the yard. She drove to Agway and loaded her back seat with bags of dark, earthy-smelling mulch, splurging on red geraniums for the flowerpots by the front door. It took all day, and she almost succeeded in eradicating the thoughts of Greg and Luna and Morgan Press and Boston. Covered in dirt, mulch, and sweat, she sprawled on the front steps to consider her work. It was only midday, but there were no further distractions to be had. She'd have to go to the beach.

Chatham boasted some of the most beautiful beaches in New England. As a teenager, midday had been the prime time to go. She'd hang out with friends who worked the snack shack at Ridgevale Beach or lifeguarded at Harding's Beach. One summer she had worked the little booth in the parking lot at Cockle Cove, checking beach stickers of incoming vacationers. Since coming back she'd avoided all of it; she needed to be alone, not surrounded by happy sunburnt families.

The problem was, Leah also needed the ocean. Saltwater ran in her veins, her father used to tell her. Their whole lives were spent here on the Cape. She knew where sunsets were best viewed and where riptides were worst, to exit the water if she saw seals (sharks would be right behind). She knew how to float on her back without moving, surrendering to the buoyancy of the salt: for her that simple practice was as spiritual and healing as faith or drugs were for others. The ocean was Leah's place of calm. She'd come back to the Cape in search of that feeling.

By evening it was time. She waited until six o'clock, when the throngs of vacationers with their unwieldy umbrellas and beach chairs would have vacated the sand, when the guards would have jumped down from their tall white stands, and the parking attendants would have left their little booths for the day. Up in her room, she tugged on her faded blue one-piece, threw on an oversized T-shirt, and grabbed a fresh towel from the closet. On the way to Harding's Beach, she stopped at Mac's Seafood and ordered a cold lobster roll, aghast at the number of people. The once pint-size seafood shop where her father bought fresh clams had burgeoned, taking over adjacent shop space. It now offered catering and dining beneath cheerful red umbrellas. When did that happen? She ordered a cold beer while she waited, thinking how much busier the town seemed, and how much of an outsider she felt after so many years away. But when she pulled into Harding's Beach, that outsider feeling lifted.

Here she was home. She left her car unlocked, like a local, and grabbed her bag. She jogged across the sand, still warm, to the water's edge. The water was brisk, the sound of the incoming tide lulling. For the first time in ages she felt herself exhale.

To her right the beach stretched its arm up to a rock jetty that arced into the sea. The summer houses lining the seawall were already turning a dusty pink. To her left the view was more rugged, the grassy dunes looming over the shoreline. It reached a point so distant she had to squint to see the end of it. Instinctively, she turned that way. Climbing the dunes, she found herself a little hollow and sat. A handful of people walked on the beach below. Up here she was protected and out of sight, the call of gulls overhead and the surf beneath her only companions.

The lobster roll was fresh and cold, and she found herself wolfing it down, surprised by how hungry she suddenly felt. Lately, she'd had little appetite, but now, with the lobster roll gone, she licked her fingers hungrily. As the sky grew dusky peach, then orange, Leah wrapped her arms around her knees and stared out to sea, at the light dancing off the surface. Her mother had loved to climb the dunes with her when she was little, and they'd sit side by side, digging their toes through the sun-baked layers of sand until they reached the colder depths below. She could not remember the last time she'd climbed these dunes. Or the last time she'd come to the beach with her mother, before she died. For the past decade her whole life had been Boston and publishing and then Greg. Now she had nothing for herself, and nowhere but here to go.

A soft cry emanated through the dune grass, and Leah realized with a start that it was her own. A sob lodged in her throat. She missed her mother. And her job. She even missed Greg. In all the sleepless nights since she left they'd spoken only twice, about things she'd left behind. There was a fresh formality to their conversations. They were being polite, tiptoeing around the hurt that was still too fresh to examine, and besides, what was the point? It was over between them; their future together was as boxed up and shipped off as Leah's personal belongings. Before they hung up the last time, Greg had wished her luck settling in. She had bitten her tongue, refusing to ask if he'd seen Rebekah since she'd left, though the effort almost killed her. Sitting in the dunes, now, she let her thoughts go there.

It was just the start of her favorite season, but already it felt like the summer of goodbyes. Lindsay, her boss at Morgan Press, would not be reaching out again, either. Leah had been quietly *let go* with an impersonal letter of recommendation, a joke. Everyone in publishing knew about the Luna scandal. There would be no work for her at any house after that. Leah was not sure there was much of anything left for her in Boston, either. Their friends, mostly Greg's from the beginning, had quietly slipped out of touch.

Now, Leah stood up and strode down the steep dunes. Her feet sank into the sand, and her muscles pumped satisfyingly with effort. She stopped once, to shed her T-shirt. When she reached the water and waded in, Leah's breath caught happily in her chest. The water was brisk, reminding her that she was still alive. She waded out to waist deep and sank below the surface. Into the darkness and rippling chorus and cold she sank until she was submerged. Under water, Leah was not afraid. Nor was she alone. The ocean was a life force, a tidal universe of its own. It welcomed her back like an old friend.

When she couldn't hold her breath a moment longer she burst to the surface. The horizon stretched out before her like mercury. She imagined the ocean tasting the sadness on her skin and laughing. Here, she was so small. Just another small human taking up her small space in the water that parted to make room for her. And yet it held her up and let her float until her limbs shivered with cold and the sunset turned dusky and she was ready to climb out.

On the way home, Leah rolled down the windows. Her hair was sticky with salt, her skin tingled like she'd had a good scrub. On a whim she drove past her turnoff on Old Queen Anne

Road and continued to Main Street, taking in the bright store-fronts and well-heeled summer people. Young couples pushed strollers. Grandparents trailed, holding the hands of wiggly tod-dlers and melting ice-cream cones. Clusters of kids congregated outside the pink awning of the Chatham Candy Manor. At least some things did not change, she thought. She passed the Ben Franklin five-and-dime that had been there forever, the historic Eldredge Library with its stately wooden doors, the Wayside Inn. The famed Chatham Squire restaurant and tavern, a line already out the door. So much of Main Street seemed frozen in time, a bygone era of summertime Americana preserved like a postcard. The flower boxes, the shingled storefronts, the flags and awnings, all of it a coastal smorgasbord for the lucky vaca-tioner's senses.

At the end of Main the storefronts grew more staggered and the crowds thinned, as the street gave way to stately houses and private summer dwellings. At the stop sign, Leah turned right toward Chatham Light. It was a favorite scenic stretch along Chatham Bar with an overlook across from the lighthouse. Leah slowed, to savor it. When she spied a coveted parking space along the street, she pulled in. It was a beautiful night; she'd walk over and take in the view.

She did not make it to the lookout, however. She was too dis-tracted by the big white house she'd parked in front of. *Captain Harding*, the placard by the front door said. It was faded and peeling, not unlike the old house itself. Both were wholly differ-ent from the other homes that bookended it. Leah looked up at the large picture windows, the wavy glass panes that rippled like the harbor across the way. It appeared old and empty. A gloominess came over her that anchored her there on the sidewalk.

When she was young, Leah recalled the historic house had been beautifully kept. Over the years it had changed hands and uses, the last Leah remembered it had been a general store and later an art gallery. Now, the old beauty appeared vacant and in need of upkeep. The shingles were as weathered as its facade and the building looked tired. A large sign in one of the front windows read: *For Rent.*

The steps creaked as she walked up. Leah peered in one of the front windows. Despite the dim lighting, she could make out the large open space of the first floor. Even from the outside Leah could sense the layers of dust. There was a folding table shoved against one wall. An ornate old fireplace dominated another, an emblem of dignity amidst the decline. An old bucket and a few paint cans littered the edges of the room. The walls were heavily adorned with hooks, and a few holes, probably remnants of the long vanished art gallery. Other than that the space was barren and Leah was hit by a wave of loneliness so visceral that she wondered if it were coming from the house itself.

Leah empathized. Everything she'd built her life on had just crumbled beneath her, leaving her adrift. Her career at Morgan Press. Her relationship with Greg. The future they'd mapped out in Boston, all of it gone. After so many years filled with the noise of purpose and plans, the strange new silence that followed was deafening.

As she stood at the window, Leah's heart ached, just as she imagined the house's old chestnut floorboards creaked. Her nights back in Chatham were as forlorn as the empty bedrooms she imagined inside, wide open and waiting. In the old house she recognized a piece of herself.

Unable to help it, she tried the door handle. Of course it was locked. Still curious, she peered again through the smudged windows, and as she did Leah felt an unexpected plume of hope rise within. The ceilings were high and the windows large. Even at that late hour, the remains of daylight spilled into the space, highlighting the detailed moldings and trim work. It was a grand old house, and no amount of age or emptiness could diminish its elegant bones.

Something about the house was calling to her. She knew it was ridiculous, and yet she stood at the window staring at the *For Rent* sign. She could not begin to imagine what it would cost to rent a building of this size in this location. Nor could she fathom the amount of work it needed. Too much for one person. Too much for one person with a small severance and no job to speak of.

Knowing all of this did not change the quick pulse of hope through her veins. Leah took out her phone. Suddenly, she knew what she needed to do.

Lucy

The smell at Spaulding Rehab was different from the hospital's smell, but not by much. As the sliding doors whooshed open, welcoming them into the lobby's frigid interior, Lucy blinked beneath the fluorescent lighting. "Did you bring the book?" her mother asked again.

She held it up.

"Oh good!" her mother chirped. Her father said nothing.

It had been almost three weeks since the accident and just days since Ella had been transferred to Spaulding Rehab. The rehabilitation center was located on the Cape, in East Sandwich, closer to home and less foreboding than the dark beeping corridors of the hospital unit in Boston.

"She's ready to go," Dr. Kapoor had told the family, the day Ella was transferred. He'd smiled reassuringly, something he'd not done in the early days that followed the accident.

From the first frenzied visit to the ER, Lucy's parents had allowed her in each room. They let her listen in on all the conversations with the doctors, nurses and specialists, ask whatever questions she had. On the one hand there was no way they could have kept her out, but on the other hand it was a dubious privilege. Perhaps there was such a thing as knowing too much. Because then you didn't just know what to hope for, you knew what was at stake.

The pounding on the front door had begun at one-thirty in the morning. It was followed by the sound of her parents' voices and a commotion in the hallway. Her mother appeared, illuminated by a slice of light from the doorway kneeling beside her bed. "Baby, your father and I have to go."

"Where? It's late."

"It's Ella."

She did not need to hear anything more. "I'm coming," Lucy had insisted, slipping into shorts, tugging a T-shirt over her head. There was no time to argue.

There had been an accident. On the eternal drive to the hospital in Hyannis, her parents whispered in urgent tones, like she wasn't sitting right there in the back seat. Like she couldn't hear them. But she did. The car accident was on Shore Road. The car belonged to a boy named Jep Parsons. Ella was with him in the car and had been taken to Hyannis.

As she watched the dark scrubby brush flash by along Route 6, all Lucy could think of was the way Ella had looked when she went out that night. Radiant, like she was certain the night ahead held something special. "Jep and I are going to Aly's party," she'd gushed, ruffling Lucy's hair before sailing out the door. There had been so many graduation parties that summer already. Their parents, normally strict through high school, had given up the fight. Ella was eighteen, thriving, headed to Tufts in the fall. They'd all made it. Or so they had thought.

Striding through Cape Cod Hospital's ER doors, there was no sign of Jep or his family. The nurse at the front desk kept asking Lucy's father to please sit down. Finally, a doctor ushered them back and into a dark room that did not contain the one person they were desperate to lay eyes on.

"Where is she?" Lucy's parents kept begging. The doctor's words were no comfort. *CAT scan. Subdural hematoma. Boston MedFlight.*

They would not be seeing Ella; she was already being prepped for air ambulance transfer.

"Comatose is a somewhat misleading term," Dr. Kapoor had explained, what seemed like a lifetime later in the ICU at Boston. "It may be more helpful to think of the patient as hovering between conscious states." While her parents tried to take comfort in this medical explanation, Lucy did not. Staring at her sister's tanned motionless arms against the white sheets, she saw no hovering. Every bright element of Ella's being had been frozen, paused. Her long dark hair fanned around her lovely face like an angel's halo. But beyond the sight of her, where was Ella?

That was three weeks ago. Three mind-numbing weeks. During that time, Ella had been moved from ICU to acute care to rehabilitation at Mass General in Boston. Only now had she returned once more to the Cape; but it was still not home.

Lucy and her parents had trailed her from facility to facility, room to room in a distraught pilgrimage. Along the way the status of urgency changed, as did the faces of the doctors and caregivers.

Eventually Ella's responsiveness did, too. After a week, she began to make small noises in her throat and could squeeze your fingers, if weakly, when you held her hand. The first time it happened, the family was there. Lucy was reading aloud, her parents beside her. "Here," her mother said, rising from her chair to stretch at one point. They'd been sitting for hours. "Hold her hand," she told Lucy's father. Lucy had looked up from the page as they switched seats, her father's face as expressionless as Ella's. It irked Lucy, and it felt unfair, as if he were leaving the burden of all the feelings to her and her mother. Her mother had gone to the window to look out, and Lucy had resumed reading. It took a moment before she heard the strange sound beside her and realized where it was coming from. When she turned, she saw the tears streaming down her father's cheeks. She followed his startled gaze to his hand, gripping Ella's. His voice was hoarse with lack of use, but her mother spun around from the window as if knowing.

"She's awake," her father cried. "I felt her squeeze my hand." A couple days later Ella's eyelids began to flutter and open for brief periods. One rainy afternoon the nurses called them at home: Ella had begun tracking people with her eyes.

Her mother had actually cried and kissed Dr. Kapoor on the cheek when they left Mass General a week later. "She's ready," the doctor assured them. "She's recovering as well as we could hope." Try as she might, Lucy did not share his belief. Despite the time passing and the purported states of consciousness Ella moved through, Lucy did not see the huge progress they proclaimed. It felt like her sister was never really coming back.

Today, the occupational therapist was in the room when they arrived. "Oh, hello!" Judy looked like she had just graduated from college, and her constant good cheer grated on Lucy's nerves. She'd have made a great kindergarten teacher. "Ella and I are just finishing up. She had a super session."

Different hospital, same lies. Lucy stared at Ella, lying in the bed, eyes closed. Even though they fluttered open these days, it made no difference. The doctors had assured the family that Ella was *emerging* and had become responsive. More lies. Not once had Ella looked at any one of them with recognition. Not one word had she uttered.

Lucy dropped the book on the table and fell into a chair as Judy updated her parents. Outside the bank of windows the sky was cloudless, bright; the perfect summer day. Normally both parents would be at the Shoreline Suites, the little motel the family owned and operated. Summer was high season. Some nights her father slept there, in a cramped office behind the reception area, because guests needed things at all hours. Her parents took turns working reception. Her father managed the property, and her mother cleaned the rooms. It was hard work, the kind of job people called a burnout business because it was day and night, seven days a week. Her parents were worn to the bone, but neither ever complained. Nor did they let their daughters work there.

"Dad, I don't mind. I need the money," Ella had told her father.

"No. Go into town. Pick a gallery. A shop. A nice restaurant. Something else." Their father didn't even like them coming by the motel to drop off lunch or say hello.

"What's the big deal? Is he ashamed of us or something?" Ella had joked.

"He's not ashamed," their mother whispered to Ella later. "Of the motel or you girls. It's because he inherited it from his parents and felt he had to take it on. He wants more for you."

Secretly, Lucy was relieved their parents didn't want the girls working at the motel. It was spotless and well kept and comfortable, but there was a sadness about it, too. It was low-slung and dark, set off the side of Route 28; the kind of place you could drive right past without noticing. Most people preferred the fancier inns on Main Street, or the resort on Shore Road.

Ella had the most fun job of them all lined up that summer, working at one of the boutiques in town where she got to wear all the cute shop dresses in bright coastal prints. Otherwise the sisters would be at one of the beaches, meeting up with friends and soaking up the sun. At fifteen, it was the first summer Lucy planned to get a job of her own. But now all that had changed.

Lucy watched Judy go over the exercises with Ella from across the room. Ella's limbs were like a rag doll's as Judy gently manipulated them, exclaiming all the time about how much progress Ella was making. Who were they kidding? There would be no running down the beach or diving into the surf. There would be no afternoons of boogie boarding that they'd looked forward to all winter. Ella was unable to sit up, to lift her arm, to bend her leg. Lucy wanted to scream at them all: What are you talking about? She's *not* getting better.

Her father, too, had a hard time watching when the specialists came in. Now he excused himself to go get a coffee. But her mother seemed to relish it, somehow, as though the mere presence of whatever staff was doing whatever therapy was proof that they believed like she did. "Look how strong you are, darling!" she murmured softly. Lucy had to look away.

Judy was just finishing up when there came a scuffle and raised voices from out in the hallway. All three women's heads turned. "Stay here," Judy said, hurrying for the door. Lucy peered around her for a better look. Two men were in a heated discussion at the nurse's station in the hall. It was then that Lucy realized one of the men was her father.

"How dare you show your face here!" he shouted. A male orderly intervened, positioning himself between the two of them. Right away Lucy knew who the other person was.

"What's happening out there?" her mother asked, still standing by Ella's bed as if on guard. But Lucy was too fixated on the unreal scene before her to answer.

Jep Parsons faced her father head-on, but he looked more ready to receive a blow than to throw one. Lucy watched him push a flop of dark hair out of his sad brown eyes, shoulders squared.

Jep was one of the beautiful people in the hallways at high school. But he was otherwise completely unlike Ella's other friends. Jep was quiet, he kept to himself rather than running at the front of the crowd like the other guys. He was built like an athlete, but you wouldn't find him at the pep rallies or the football games. Instead he hung out in the art room and worked at his father's mechanic shop on weekends. He wore Converse sneakers and black hoodies, but he wasn't a stoner or a loser or a nerd. Jep wasn't a guy you could put your finger on. When Ella whispered one night in Lucy's bed that she had a crush on him, Lucy wasn't surprised—almost every girl did. But when they secretly started dating, Lucy wondered. They could not have been more different. Maybe that was one of the reasons Ella had kept their relationship a secret from the family. Their strict father was the other.

Jep Parsons represented everything their parents feared. It wasn't his fault. Both her parents were lifelong locals (*lifers*, her father joked without smiling) who'd grown up in working-class families. They'd never gotten off the Cape. They'd never achieved the upward mobility they so often talked about with their girls at the dinner table. There was a time, however, when Lucy's father had had the chance: a full scholarship to Princeton, for wrestling. Maybe that was why he was so quiet. Maybe that was why he was so strict. Years ago, Martin Hart was poised to be the first in his family to go to college, and to an Ivy, no less. It was what he'd worked hard for and he was so close, he could taste it. Until the all-states tournament his senior year, when he blew out his knee in his first match. Despite two surgeries and six months of recovery, Martin's wrestling days were over. So, too, was Princeton. Without the scholarship, his family simply could not afford the cost. Resigned, Martin remained on the Cape, took classes at the community college and eventually took over Shoreline Suites from his father. It was something he never spoke of; what Lucy and Ella knew about it came from their mother, in private whispered moments. But it cast a hard shadow across his outlook, a veil that hung over both his kids, whether he intended it or not.

All Martin wanted was for his daughters to make a better life for themselves than the 24/7 grind of running a local motel. Dating was frowned upon: it would distract them from their schoolwork. Dating a kid from another lifer family, who skipped classes and had his sights set on becoming a local mechanic, was out of the question. The fact that Jep Parsons had been driving drunk and had stolen a bright future from his daughter filled Martin Hart with fresh rage. It didn't matter that Jep had been arrested. It didn't matter that his blood alcohol level was borderline while Ella's was well over the legal limit, or that Jep had been kept overnight in jail. Nor did it matter that his pretrial conference loomed in the coming weeks. There was no justice that could satisfy Lucy and Ella's parents that summer.

Now, in the hallway, Lucy's father puffed his chest out and leaned in like he might rush Jep. Lucy could see the old wrestler in him come alive. It was as heartbreaking as it was alarming.

"Mom!" Lucy cried.

Her mother turned but would not leave Ella's side. "Martin, no!" she called out to her husband. The orderly reached for Jep. By then, two nurses had stepped in, too.

"Kid, you have to go," the orderly barked, placing his hands on Jep's shoulders and steering him swiftly away from Ella's door. "Now!"

Jep didn't fight. "I just wanted to see her," he begged. His voice was full of desperation. "Please . . . let me see Ella."

As the nurses tried to calm him down, Lucy's father roared in reply. "You stay away from her! You will never see my daughter again."

Lucy felt her mother go rigid beside her. "It's alright, honey," her mother cooed to Ella, eyes still trained on the hallway. "Everything is alright now."

But it wasn't alright. As the shouting in the hall dissipated, there came a sudden scratching sound in the room. Lucy glanced back at her sister. Ella's fingers spasmed on the sheets. "Mama, look." She pointed. "What if . . . "

As if reading her mind, her mother's head snapped in her direction. *No,* she mouthed, eyes wild.

In the hallway, Lucy's father had collapsed into a chair, head in his hands. A nurse was talking softly to him. Jep Parsons was being escorted out and away, but his voice carried down the hall. "Please don't do this," he cried. "I just want one minute!"

Meanwhile Ella's fingers scratched away at the sheets, like an animal in distress. Lucy went to her and placed her hand atop her sister's.

"Now, now," her mother cooed, stroking Ella's head. "The noise is over. Let's calm down and try a few pages of our book."

Lucy ignored her mother's words, hanging on to her sister's hand instead. Ella's green eyes opened and locked on hers. She squeezed Lucy's finger, and fighting tears Lucy squeezed back.

Ella *was* coming back to them. She was fighting her way back. And it wasn't just for them, Lucy realized with a start.

The fresh silence in the hall was palpable. Jep Parsons was gone.

Eudora

The heavy oak library doors creaked as Eudora let herself into the vestibule. Eldredge Library was such an architectural treasure, it took her breath away each time. From the rich quarter oak panels and cornices to the bronze finishes to the stained glass windows and ornamental fireplace, stepping into the Romanesque revival–style library always made Eudora feel like she was stepping back in time. But today there was another pressing matter taking her breath away: the anxiety she'd walked with here since she left Alfred and her house. All because of what she'd promised her daughter, Caroline, she would do: the book club meeting.

That morning, she'd woken with dread in her stomach. It wasn't about the reading; she'd gotten the book and finished it well in advance. Kristin Hannah's *The Women* had proven a compelling selection. The dread came from having to attend the meeting.

Her whole life Eudora had not been a particularly shy person. Anxiety was a term oft overused in her opinion. Everyone had anxiety these days, it seemed. Financial anxiety. Political anxiety. Body-image anxiety. Social anxiety. Lord knew, there were plenty of good reasons for it in this crazy world Eudora often felt she no longer recognized.

When her anxiety began, she initially chalked it up to a preference for her own company and the comforts of home. She'd lost her husband. She was of a certain age. Those seemed like explanations enough. Eudora was retired, having put in a good thirty-seven years in the local high school as a guidance counselor. She knew what real anxiety was, having spent all those years counseling teens experiencing some of the worst life events. Broken homes. Body dysmorphia. Substance abuse. That was just skimming the surface. As her career progressed, so too, did the issues her students dealt with. By the time she retired, it could not have come soon enough. Eudora hung on as long as she did because she loved those kids so much. They needed her, and she would not turn her back. But she began to feel ill-equipped to help them. Their struggles were so much sharper, the stakes so much higher. When she'd started as a school counselor, bullying meant someone taking your lunch money or teasing you in the back of the bus. By the time she'd retired, bullying meant someone anonymously altering your image online and sending it out in a mass pornographic text to every kid in the school. It was unfathomable the things kids these days had to contend with. It was too much for her students. It ended up being too much for her, too.

Now, standing in the library as she had promised Caroline, Eudora tried to steady the pounding of her heart and headed for the circulation desk. A pleasant woman directed her to the reading room in the rear. "Aren't you lucky," she said, nodding at the book in Eudora's hand. "I wish I could join this meeting! What did you think of it?"

"Exceptional," Eudora said, clutching the book more tightly.

It was early, and every chair in the semicircle was empty. How she wished there were rows so she could sit in the back. Eudora chose a seat in the middle and fixed her gaze on the high ceilings and beautiful stained glass windows. Something about being here made her think of the high school. It had been eight years since she'd retired. She couldn't remember the last time she'd spoken to any of her old colleagues. Such a strange thing after thirty-seven years on the job.

At first she used to get together with all the other retirees for lunch. They'd always meet at the same spot, the Wayside Inn on Main Street. It was fun, trading stories about what everyone was up to: new grandchildren, European travel. One of the men, Albert, a retired math teacher, had shocked them all by opening one of those axe-throwing bars with his son outside Boston. It was exciting seeing everyone outside of the faculty lounge, once their *natural habitat*. Who knew that Arlene Burnett, the unsmiling gym teacher, would join a karaoke club? Or that shy Sheldon Smith, the history teacher, would publish a juicy romance novel? At times it seemed like a competition to see who was living retirement to the fullest. For her part, Eudora and Milton had taken an Alaskan cruise and toured the battlefields of Gettysburg. They'd visited his sister, Blanche, in Dallas and welcomed two grandchildren. But she never felt like her stories were half as riveting as others', and it made her wonder if she was doing retirement wrong. Eventually the retiree lunches thinned out. Some of her colleagues moved south. Some got sick. One passed away. Eudora didn't love the reminders of their increasing age; the men got fat, the women shrank. The longer they were away from the high school, the less Eudora felt she had in common with any of them. But there was one former student that kept her bound to the group: Shelby Smalls.

Shelby Smalls first came to Eudora's attention through Art Halloran. As her world history teacher, Art noticed that Shelby was missing classes and reported this. On the occasions when she did show up, he said she seemed on edge. Arlene, the gym teacher, once caught Shelby hiding in the defunct shower stalls in the girl's locker room during lunch. Calls were placed home and Shelby ended up sitting across from Eudora one rainy spring afternoon.

All of the kids Eudora saw in her counseling office had some level of risk assigned to them, whether it was academic or otherwise. As far as she could tell, Shelby was exceptionally bright; as evidenced by her high standardized test scores. There did not appear to be any substance use going on. No obvious domestic disturbances at home. But looking across her desk that day as the rain played against the window, Eudora thought Shelby looked like one of the most worrying cases ever to come through her door. Her eyes were full of a sadness Eudora had not seen before. The girl actually looked frightened.

At first she did not want to talk to Eudora. Her replies to questions were one word: No, she did not belong to any clubs or sports teams. No, she did not have a favorite class. When Eudora asked Shelby about her friends, she could not name a single one. The only interest she seemed to have was sketching in her notebook and avoiding eye contact. When Eudora stole a peek at her page, it was clear the girl was remarkably talented.

"Can I go now?" Shelby asked, finally.

Eudora had one more question. "Honey, I can see you aren't comfortable talking to me. And I can tell you really don't want to be here."

Shelby made a face and kept sketching. Eudora could not give in. Teachers were concerned. Eudora was concerned. If she was going to help the girl she needed to learn *something* about Shelby.

She paused, trying to think of a question that might shed some light. "Where would you rather be right now?"

For the first time Shelby looked Eudora straight in the eye. "Dead," she said.

In the end, Shelby Smalls would leave her teachers, counselors, and school administrators asking themselves for the rest of their careers what they could have done differently. It was the main reason Eudora had stayed in touch with her colleagues after retiring. Despite the painful reminder each time she saw them, she held on to hope that one of them might have a scrap of information—some small crumb of evidence that all these years later Shelby was okay. Because to this day, what happened to Shelby Smalls was a weight they carried together.

The door to the reading room opened, startling Eudora from her memories. It was time for the book club meeting to start. Eudora recognized none of the attendees. She smiled at the red-haired woman who took a seat beside her, but she was too busy talking to someone to notice. The woman was dressed in a brightly printed pink seashell top and white capri pants, very fresh and summery. Eudora glanced down at her sensible white sneakers worn out from walks with Albert. Then at her faded jeans and brown top. Perhaps she should have picked out something nicer.

"I'm telling you," the red-haired woman went on, "she's planning to open in just two weeks. Can you imagine? Given the state that place is in?" She was addressing another woman, dressed in similar attire with a blue-and-white turtle print. (What did Caroline call it? Coastal Grandma?) "But you gotta give it to her, it took chutzpah to call the owner and get him to agree to it. Captain Harding's house has been a town wart for *years*."

Eudora perked up. The captain's house, as it was fondly still called by locals, was a source of much community upset. The antique beauty was located on a scenic street in town that ran along Chatham Harbor and Lighthouse Beach. Though it was surrounded by stately neighborhood homes, the poor house had been falling into disrepair for years. It had long been one of Eudora and Milton's favorite places, back when it was an inn. They celebrated many anniversary dinners by the dining room fireplace and attended more than a few Christmas parties there over the years. For them, there were many memories tucked in those rooms. "If we only had a million dollars," Milton used to say.

"More like five million," Eudora used to correct him. It was true, but they held out hope someone with a big heart and deep pockets would resurrect the sad old place.

Now, the blue-and-white turtle woman sat down beside the seashell woman. "I heard she got a one year lease! That poor girl doesn't realize it's going to take that long just to get the place up and running."

"She's in over her head."

"I heard the historic district is getting involved."

"She'll have her hands full with zoning."

"I heard the neighbors are not happy."

"The location is lovely, but it's hardly commercial," the seashell woman went on.

"Not exactly walking distance from Main Street."

"She'll never get foot traffic."

"Or locals. There's no parking."

"That's why the art gallery died."

"And the general store, before it."

"Mm-hmm. Won't last."

Eudora was intrigued. Someone was looking to take on the house!

Originally, the Captain Harding house had been a sea captain's lavish home, built for his wife and five daughters. After his death, as local legend had it, the wife and daughters were left penniless and turned it into a bed-and-breakfast to survive. In later years, it was sold to a family who ran a general store on the first floor. The proprietor passed it down to his grandson who later moved out of the area, renting it out to various retail tenants who came and went. The most recent owner was reportedly a global marketing manager from Los Angeles who'd hoped to tear it down and rebuild a summer house, but the historic commission and zoning boards had forbidden it. He'd given up the fight and apparently lost interest. According to the rumor mill he had so many other vacation properties across the country, it was no dent in his purse. And so Captain Harding's house sat empty and unmaintained year after year. The historical society and community were helpless to try to raise the funds to purchase it, as the property alone was worth so much. But as the town held their breath waiting for someone to save it, the front porch sank. The paint peeled. Neighbors claimed they could see racoons scuttling through the parlor room windows at dusk like they were attending a party.

"Excuse me," Eudora said, praying she didn't seem like an eavesdropper, but really, the redhead was a human megaphone. "I couldn't help but overhear you mentioning Captain Harding's house?"

Both women's heads snapped in her direction like they were surprised to see her. "Did you hear? Some out-of-towner wants to open a shop."

"How wonderful!" Eudora said, before thinking.

Both women made a face.

"I've always loved that house," Eudora admitted. "It's such a community gem. Maybe this woman will bring it back to life."

The turtle lady shrugged. "Maybe, but . . . "

"It's been tried before," the seashell lady interrupted. "Too much work. Too much capital. Too many restrictions."

Eudora kept her mouth shut. The historic commission restrictions were the only thing saving that house, despite its poor condition.

"Personally, I think the town should've let the new owner do what he wanted. The poor neighbors in their beautiful homes have to look at that monstrosity. Tear it down. Start fresh."

The book club librarian had joined them and was just taking her seat, as the seashell and turtle ladies continued their banter in strained whispers. Eudora didn't hear what else they had to say. Her heart was pounding too hard. Only this time, it wasn't a panic attack. Book tucked under her arm, she'd already left the reading room. By the time the book club was underway, Eudora Shipman was halfway down Main Street.

Leah

The paint color she'd chosen was all wrong. Leah stepped back for a better look at the sample she'd brushed onto the wall. When the light hit it, the gray-green hue she'd hoped for looked more like puke. She groaned. The local hardware store had limited options, and she was on a tight budget. Still, she was grateful for the paint and the wall, puke colored or not.

The night Leah saw the *For Rent* sign in the window of the old house, she made two calls right from the front steps. The first was to the Realtor. The second was to her father. "I know this is crazy," she began. "But I want to open a beach bookstore. I found the perfect spot." Her father had only one question. "What will you call it?"

The name had come to her right there on the steps. "The Sandy Page."

The idea was the easy part. All night she reviewed her bank statements and crunched the numbers. Between her small savings and her even smaller severance package, her idea wasn't quite financially feasible. Undeterred, she holed up in the cottage and researched. She placed a call to her favorite indie bookstore back in Boston and talked to the owner. Then she worked through the night to create a business plan. The next day, heart pounding, Leah walked through the double doors at the local bank and presented her idea to the small business loan officer. Before they'd even finished reviewing her assets, the loan officer took off his glasses and gave her a sympathetic look. She was too high risk to qualify for a loan.

Crushed, she drove the long way home, avoiding the old captain's house so she wouldn't add salt to the wound. When her father called to ask how the bank meeting went, she let it go to voicemail. Moments later, he called again.

"I'm sorry, Dad, but I'm too upset to talk about it right now. The bank denied me."

"Hang on," he told her. "I have an idea of my own."

Long ago her parents had set aside savings for her future wedding. Leah knew it couldn't have been easy for them, but it was something her mother had insisted on doing. "I want you to use the wedding money to open your store."

At first Leah had been unable to speak. "What if it fails?" Risking her own money was one thing. Using savings that her mother, now gone, had helped to set aside for a very different purpose felt unthinkable.

"Then at least you know you tried," her father said. "I'd rather you invest in yourself than some fiancé." What he said next sealed her decision. "It would have made your mother happy."

Now, every penny mattered even more. Leah examined the fresh paint from a different angle. Maybe if she cocked her head just so in the right light, it would look less like puke. No such luck.

"Hello?" The front door opened, and a young man poked his head inside. "I'm Brad. The one who called about the job?"

"Yes!" Leah had posted a bookseller position online. "Please come in," she said, sizing him up.

Brad was dressed smartly in a gingham button-down and tailored chinos. She watched as he navigated the canvas tarps and painting supplies strewn about the floor. "Sorry about the mess."

Brad surveyed the scene warily. "Uh, I was under the impression this was a bookstore?"

"It will be! Very soon." Then, seeing the look on his face: "It's bad, isn't it?"

"Well." He narrowed his eyes at the paint sample on the wall. "I might say *ambitious*."

At least he had a sense of humor. "Optimism. I like that."

Besides the inspector and the plumber, Brad was the first person who'd come inside since she'd met with the Realtor and signed the lease. The house's owner, Stefan, lived on the West Coast and apparently hadn't laid eyes on the house in years. It took the Realtor and Leah a few days to convince him that the property was not worth the exorbitant rent he was asking and, in fact, required improvements. In the end, he'd agreed to reduce the rent and cover only necessary repairs: the rest were on her. "I know it looks like a lot, but we had it inspected," Leah tried to assure Brad. "Aside from a little plumbing hiccup, it just needs a fresh coat of paint. And some new boards on the front steps."

"And maybe some books?" Brad suggested. He tried the light switch on the wall by the fireplace, but nothing happened.

"Yes, but I'm getting the place for a song!" she added brightly.

The look on Brad's face was doubtful. "You must have quite the vocals." He glanced around. "The advertisement said book-seller wanted."

"I know what you're thinking. It's a bookstore without shelves." Leah sighed as she followed his gaze around the room. "Or stock."

"Or working light fixtures," Brad said, his big brown eyes swinging to the dusty old-fashioned schoolhouse pendants hanging from the high ceilings.

Any sense of accomplishment she had over the million little things she'd done in the past week vaporized. It was one thing to apply for the necessary business permits and licenses at town hall, which was a headache in itself. And to clear out the dirt and debris that had accumulated over the years, which was thick as soot; to sweep out cobwebs and mop floors and scrub windows. The smells were mostly gone! The antique pine floors gleamed. But now, standing here with Brad and seeing it through his eyes, she couldn't deny the facts.

"The thing is, I need to start a job as soon as possible," Brad said, interrupting her thoughts. "I'm a PhD economics student at BU. I'm only here for the summer, staying at my grandmother's, and I really need the money for next semester."

"Oh, you can start right away!" Leah said, pushing back the rising swell of doubt.

"But . . ."

"I do have a few questions, though," Leah went on. This was an interview, after all. And Brad had not yet been hired. "Can you paint, Brad?"

Brad squinted at her. "Paint? I took a watercolor class at school . . ."

"No matter. Can you clean? Carry boxes? Do office work?"

He glanced around in confusion. "Is there an office I'm missing?"

"Here's the thing, Brad. You need money for school, right? You're in a pinch if you don't start earning soon."

"Correct."

"Turns out, I'm in a bit of a pinch, too. You see, I used to have a job in publishing back in Boston." Here her voice faltered, but she pressed on. "And I used to be engaged. Then things kind of fell apart. As in, blew up." A small crazy laugh escaped her. "And I lost all of it."

Brad was staring at her like he was watching a car wreck unfold, but she kept going.

"So, here I am back home, like you, this summer. Only, unlike you, I don't have another place to be this fall." Leah held up her arms. "This is it. This store is it for me."

"Wow, that's a lot . . ."

"It is a lot," Leah agreed. "I've got some money to get this place going. But it's become clear to me that it's going to take more than that."

To her relief, Brad had not yet run away.

"What I need now are hands. And heart."

Brad shifted uncomfortably, saying nothing. He was either on board or off, but at least he knew what he was getting into.

"So, last interview question: Have you got that in you, Brad? Because that's all I really need to know."

By the end of the day, they'd made three trips to the hardware store. Brad, who'd somehow managed to stay completely crisp and clean, had assembled a rough office desk out of two saw-horses and a sheet of plywood, and was sitting on an overturned bucket staring at his laptop. "The internet guy is coming out in two days."

"Two days?"

"Best I could do. I begged. Said you were elderly and living here alone with no phone service."

"Brad!"

He threw her a look. "Still want to open in two weeks?"

Leah kept her mouth shut.

"I've scanned Facebook Marketplace. With your budget this is what you're looking at for furniture." He turned his laptop screen in her direction.

"A purple couch?" She leaned closer, for a better look. "What is that stain on the cushion?"

Brad closed his eyes. "Something I will *not* be sitting on."

"Okay, scrap the couch for now. What else have you got?"

Luckily he'd found a handful of better options. "Now, none of this matches, but you said you wanted that homespun mis-match aesthetic . . . What did you call it?"

"Eclectic."

Brad made a small face. "Check."

Ignoring this, Leah scrolled through the options he'd found. "Not bad. Look, this cute red pedestal table could go right in front, for new releases and beach reads! And the low pine table could go in the back for the kids' section." There were assorted chairs for reading, a Victorian settee in emerald velvet, and an antique sideboard. "What's that for?"

"I was thinking that could be the checkout counter. It's wide and deep, and it's got that beautiful scrollwork on the legs that people will see when they first come in." He gestured toward the ceiling. "It complements the trim and molding, I think."

Leah looked at him with new appreciation. "You've got an eye for this. Bravo."

For the first time all day, Brad appeared to relax. "I do what I can."

For the next two days they taped, tarped, and primed the walls. It took some effort for Brad to dig up "old clothes" to wear to work. "You say you're on a student budget," she teased, "but you don't dress like it!"

"Sale racks," he said, matter-of-factly dusting the front of his button-down. "Conscious consumerism."

Between paint coats drying, they measured and planned the store layout, hit salvage stores and trolled yard sale listings. Up in the attic they discovered an old oil painting in a gilded frame and hauled it downstairs. When they dusted it off, the faces of five young women appeared, each one dressed in period clothing. All had matching auburn hair.

"Creepy," Brad said.

"These must be the captain's daughters!" Leah said. She was ecstatic. "It's an old family portrait. It's been buried under all that garbage. We should hang it up."

Brad shivered. "Or bury it in the backyard." He stepped left, then right. "Look! Their spooky eyes follow you."

"I'm going to hang it up."

They stored the painting, along with their salvage finds, in a back room with beautiful tray ceilings and faded damask wallpaper that had probably once been the dining room. "We should think about a use for this space," Leah said, her imagination already pumping.

"Focus," Brad cautioned.

Despite the headway they made, it became clear that the old house still had problems that paint and furniture could not fix.

"We need more help," Brad said on a lunch break one day. They were sitting on the front steps, eating chicken salad sandwiches and drinking iced coffee from Chatham Perk.

Leah appreciated Brad's directness: it was as reliable as the starch in his shirt collars. "I have you. What more do I need?"

"Professional help." He smiled. "Of the contracting variety. I feel like we're kind of friends, so I can speak frankly," he added for good measure. It was true. Crawling into the bowels of an old fireplace together to clean out racoon poop was undeniably bonding.

"Take these steps," Brad said, pushing down on a board that was curling up and away from its nails.

Leah considered the squishy section of wood rot. "We

could make a trip to the lumberyard and replace a few of the boards."

Brad made a face. "You can slap a painting smock on me or send me up a ladder after cobwebs, but I'm no builder. If someone steps in the wrong spot on these steps, game over."

"I know, but funds are tight." Stefan, the house owner, had made it clear in his last email that he was done funding improvements. Leah glanced across the street, between the tidy cottages on the other side, and at the cerulean blue stretch of Chatham Harbor beyond them. *Breathe*, she told herself.

"Surely you have investors you can turn to?" Brad asked hopefully.

Leah almost choked on her chicken salad.

"No?" Brad's eyes widened in disbelief. "Is this all on you?"

Somehow she managed to swallow the chicken along with the fresh lump in her throat. "Go big or go home?"

"Oh dear," Brad exhaled. "You already came home."

"I have a small severance from work. And my wedding money."

"Wedding money." Thankfully, Brad knew better than to ask. "Is it enough?"

"I guess we'll find out."

Brad said nothing.

"Look, I know this must seem crazy, especially to an economics student. But I know books and readers. I also know this town. There's no bookstore in a ten-mile radius. And hundreds of tourists stroll these sidewalks every day."

"I get it. Tourist season is only so long, so you need to open fast."

"That's not even it," Leah said. Brad was proving a good sport and a huge help, but she needed him to understand her vision. Or maybe she still needed to convince herself. "It's also this place. This old house is one of the last remaining of its kind. She was built by a sea captain for his family. And when they fell on hard times, the daughters united and turned it into an inn to keep it going."

"Historic girl power. Impressive."

"Yes," Leah agreed. "Later, it became a general store. And after that an art gallery." She paused. "When I think of all the stories this house could tell about the people who've lived within these walls, it makes me feel like they're still here. Counting on us. Opening this store gives the captain's house a second chance." She did not say that it was hers, too.

Brad looked at her sympathetically. "Well, hell." They finished their lunch in silence. "Let's do what we can and try and get this haunted house open, I guess."

"It's not haunted."

"Oh, I hear things. Someone is clomping around."

Leah laughed. "Probably just raccoons."

"Probably those Harding sisters." Brad waved heartily at a pair of older women pointing at them from across the street. The women quickly moved on. "One thing is for sure: you've got people talking."

"Yeah, well. Talk like that can go either way in a small town."

After opening up to Brad, Leah noticed he started showing up earlier and staying later. He printed out a calendar of to-do items and taped it to the inside of the front door, which they'd painted a chipper coastal blue. They drove to Harwich and Dennis and Orleans to pick up the furniture finds from their online sleuthing. On those trips, Brad was most chatty.

"So we've established your fresh singlehood," he said, as they headed down Route 28 toward Harwich. "What do you do around here for fun?"

"I don't have time for fun, Brad."

He made a small noise. "Pity. These are our young and pretty years. Plus, it's summer."

She turned to him. "What's your excuse?" Brad could be dramatic.

"I live with my grandmother," he reminded her.

"You must have friends. A love interest?"

"My friends are in Boston. The love interest ended last spring when he graduated and moved to Chicago." Brad didn't appear to be reeling from the breakup, but she sensed he was lonely. "It's hard to meet someone."

It was one of Leah's worst fears, that, after Greg, anyone remotely compatible was already married with kids and a Goldendoodle. "I can't even think about dating yet," she confided. "And I don't like my chances out here on the Cape."

"Oh, please. All those men in their Nantucket reds?" Brad teased.

"All married. Or old. And the ones that aren't are only here on vacation. No, thanks." She steered quickly through a roundabout and hit the gas. "The odds are against me."

"Narrow that pool down to single gay men, and then we'll

talk odds. And don't forget to throw in a traditional Portuguese grandmother."

She couldn't help but laugh. "I can't imagine there's much privacy in that scenario."

"Privacy isn't the problem," Brad said more seriously.

Leah glanced over at him in the passenger seat. "Brad, does your grandma not know you're gay?"

He swiveled to look at her. "You mean the woman who asks me every day if I've met a nice Catholic girl yet? She even asked about *you*."

Leah almost swerved. "Oh my God."

"Yeah, oh my God."

"But your parents know, right?"

"My parents have known for years. They met my last boyfriend, Arty. They even invited him to visit over Christmas. But when my grandmother joined us for dinner, they cautioned me to introduce him as my roommate." He looked at Leah. "I know how it sounds, but it's not because they're ashamed. They're just trying to protect me."

Despite the mess her life was, Leah had never had to worry that her family would reject her. "Brad, that must take a toll on you."

"There are times I've thought about telling her, but then I see the way she reacts when there's a gay person on TV or a mention of sexuality on the news." He made a face. "She turns the channel in disgust. She won't even read a book with a gay character."

It was a heartbreaking revelation. "I'm so sorry," she told him.

"Here." He reached into the small bag on the floor of the

passenger seat. "She baked these this morning." He unwrapped a small foil package and handed it to her.

Leah peered down at the decadent egg custard pastry. Despite the bad taste his revelation had left in her mouth, it looked delicious.

"Pastel de nata," Brad said before she could ask.

"How are you not three hundred pounds?" she asked, shoving the still-warm decadence into her mouth.

Brad watched her finish it off. "She's an excellent baker for a homophobe."

"Brad."

"Kidding. I love her."

Leah glanced over at him. "This tastes like love to me." She noticed he only had a few bites of his own. "Do you mind . . . ?"

"Just take it," he said, handing over the rest.

As the week unfolded, things picked up. Stock began arriving in large cardboard boxes from book warehouses in the Midwest. The shelving units Leah had purchased should have been delivered by then. "I don't understand," she said, scrolling through her emails. "There's still no tracking on the bookshelves."

When she finally got through to the company, the news was not good. The bookshelves were all backordered. "But I have proof of payment," Leah insisted. "My bank account is down thousands of dollars."

"I'm sorry, ma'am," the woman on the other line said. "We're experiencing production delays. I can credit your account, though, don't worry."

Leah *was* worried. The sun was low in the sky as she surveyed the storefront. Book boxes spilled across the floor. She needed shelving units in order to open. She needed to pay Brad by the end of the week. There was nothing to suggest this unfinished room was anything other than a bad idea. Leah sank to her haunches in the middle of the floor, and this time she didn't try to fight the tears. She was crying so hard at first she did not hear the rapping sound at the front door.

Leah looked up. In the shadow of the setting sun she could make out a woman outside the door. Leah scooted back against the fireplace hoping she was out of sight, but the woman did not leave. Instead she pressed her face to the glass and peered inside. "Hello? Is it okay if I come in?"

"Damn it." Leah wiped her face with the edge of her dirty T-shirt and stood. "Sorry, but we're closed," she called loudly.

"I have something for you." The woman held up her hand. Whoever she was, this person was pushy. "Please?" she added.

Leah opened the door just enough to peek out. "Apologies, but we're not open to the public yet," she explained. To her dismay, a small white dog popped out behind the woman and started yapping at her. Leah hopped back.

"Oh, don't mind Alfred. He's all bluff."

Alfred did not look like he was bluffing. "Could you please hold him back? I had a bad dog experience as a kid," Leah added, stepping farther back into the shop.

"Oh, goodness. I'm so sorry," the woman said, reining Alfred in. "What happened?"

The woman had a neat bob of silvery hair and a figure that was plush in the way of a storybook grandmother; her expression filled with such warmth and concern that suddenly Leah found herself explaining the whole incident through the crack in the door. "It was an accident. I was in second grade and was visiting my friend when I tripped over her old dog. He got scared and bit my cheek." One eye on Alfred, she leaned closer, pointing to a small scar on the side of her face. "Seven stitches."

"How awful for both of you," the woman cooed sympathetically.

"It wasn't the dog's fault, but I'm kind of afraid of them now."

The woman nodded. "I'll take Alfred straight home, but before I do I have something for you." She thrust a folded piece of paper through the door. "My name is Eudora, by the way. Did you know this used to be the penny candy store?"

Leah looked down at the paper then up at Eudora. "Excuse me?"

"This house. My late husband, Milton, grew up here in Chatham. He had such fond memories of when he was a little boy and this place had a penny candy counter. The root beer lollies? *Those* were his favorite." She smiled like she was rolling one of the root beer candies across her tongue right then.

"Oh. That's a sweet story." Confused, Leah glanced down at the paper. A phone number was written on it. That was all.

"I heard you're opening a bookstore, and I think it's wonderful." Something about the woman was oddly familiar, but Leah couldn't place her. "This is a special house, and it broke my heart to see it empty all these years. My Milton's heart, too. Anyway, that's my friend Luke. You should call him."

"Luke?" None of this was making sense, not the penny candy memories or the phone number this tiny woman insisted on giving her.

"The phone number. You should call him."

"I'm sorry, I don't understand."

"Luke is a carpenter. Well, more of a master craftsman, though he's too modest to admit it. I overheard some women at the library book club talking about your opening date." She squinted past Leah, though not unkindly. "You look like you could use some help."

Luke

Luke had a long list of jobs backed up, as was customary during the summer months. It was his busy season, and though he tried to stagger the custom woodworking projects he took on, it was nearly impossible from Memorial Day to Labor Day. He wasn't complaining.

During the economic fall in 2008, when everything in construction and real estate screeched to a halt, Luke had just graduated high school. He'd tried college for a year, at his parent's insistence, but his heart had always been in working with his hands, like his father. After a year of wasted tuition, he'd convinced his dad to let him take a gap year and apprentice with him. The timing could not have been worse for residential construction. There was little work to be had, and his father's business was feeling the strain. Luke watched his father part ways with workers who'd been with him for years. Suddenly his dad was home most days instead of rising at dawn to hurry to a job site.

When he was in high school, Luke's favorite class was a woodworking elective. His woodshop teacher taught him the basics of jointing and planing, how to turn a lathe and other specialty skills. Luke took to the detailed work, from scrollwork to finishing. His first project was a small stool that his mother still kept in her kitchen. That slow first year with his father he dabbled in tables and cabinets in the family's garage workshop. His father admired his handiwork and started bringing Luke out on small projects, constructing built-ins for mudrooms and butler's pantries, all the rage in interior renovation at the time. Houses may not have been turning over like they used to, but residential owners still desired improvements.

Despite the national turn, the Chatham area was a niche market. Their client base were the owners of hedge funds and summer homes, so while the locals may have taken a hit in the market, most seasonal residents still had plenty of money in the bank to coast through. There were custom kitchens that needed new cabinetry. Living areas that demanded built-in entertainment centers, pool houses whose ceilings needed to be vaulted, carriage houses that required small kitchenettes for weekend guests. Luke had long admired the historic coastal homes in his small town; he knew the merit of cedar shake siding, appreciated the clean lines of a traditional Cape Codder. With sparkling water views and natural light as focal points of design space, Luke understood that less was more when it came to cabinet faces and trim work. During that period Luke made a name for himself with his customization. Word got around and he amassed a small but impressive portfolio. Soon,

Saltwater Woodworks was an LLC. Ever since, there had been no looking back.

Despite the steady workflow, Luke kept the business small and project selection tight. It was an intentional balance, not unlike the one he utilized in his designs. Luke did not want to live to work. He did not want the years of physical labor to bow his body and gnarl his fingers as he had watched it do to his father. Life on the Cape was naturally abundant; who needed more than a sunset over Ridgevale Beach or a paddle across Little Pleasant Bay? As such, he lived in a small house on Oyster Pond River and ran the business out of an old boathouse in the rear of the property as a one-man show. Keep it simple and solid, his father used to say.

When Eudora Shipman called him last night, he was surprised. He'd just seen her a few days earlier walking her cantankerous little dog. It had been almost two years since he'd wrapped up a project on her house, and her husband passed away shortly thereafter. Luke had gone to the funeral; they were good people.

"Eudora, to what do I owe the pleasure?" he'd asked.

"I may have a job for you," she said, sounding a little unsure.

"Alright. I'm happy to come by. How's Wednesday?"

"Actually, it's not really my job. Or my house. So I can't guarantee the work, but I know you're the right man for it."

Confused, Luke had set his mug down on the coffee table. From the time he knew her as a guidance counselor at his old high school to the time he'd done some work on the house for her and Milton, she'd always had a sharp mind. He sure hoped it was not slipping; he'd heard loneliness and loss could do that to a person. "So, let me understand, this job is not at your place?"

"You know the captain's house?" she asked brightly.

"You mean the white Greek Revival off of Shore Road?" It was sometimes hard to keep up with all the nicknames the locals ascribed to some of the older properties. As it was with small towns, everyone had their own claim to memories in just about every corner and on every street. It was even more so with historic towns. Memory talked in a town as old as Chatham.

"Yes! That's the one. It's being brought back to life as a bookstore."

"A bookstore?" Luke usually had his ear to the ground for local news, but when the summer residents poured in and work picked up, he tended to fall out of earshot. The days were long, the bars and restaurants where he normally picked up news were clogged with tourists, and by evening all he wanted to do was park his truck in his own driveway and put his feet up. Or take his kayak out to a quiet spot on Oyster Pond with his dog, Scout. Like most locals, during tourist season Luke tended to avoid town. "I must have missed that news," Luke allowed, and instantly his mind flashed to the woman with the blond ponytail he'd seen at the Powell cottage almost two weeks ago. The Powell family was long gone, but when he'd driven by that day he'd had the crazy thought that the woman in the front yard might be Leah Powell. But that was just memory talking.

"The poor woman who is trying open it seems to be in way over her head. She thinks she can open in a matter of weeks, but the place is in such disrepair."

"That's a shame," Luke told Eudora, but he still didn't understand what any of this had to do with him. After he wrapped up his current project at Stage Harbor he had another he was already behind on.

"That's why I'm calling," Eudora went on, as if reading his mind. "Would you please stop by the place tomorrow and take a look?"

"You mean at the Greek Revival?" It was still unclear where this job was located. Or what the job might be. He had no time to help a wash-ashore with her new business.

"Yes, the old captain's house. She needs help."

Luke exhaled. "And you are affiliated with the bookstore owner how?"

"I'm not."

Eudora may well have lost a few marbles, Luke realized with a pang of regret. "Eudora, it's very nice of you to want to help this woman, but I'm very busy at the moment. Even if she were looking to hire, the soonest I could go is next week sometime. Besides, it sounds like she isn't really looking for help."

"Leah."

"Excuse me?"

"Leah Powell. She's the small business owner."

Luke's breath caught in his chest. "She's the one opening the bookstore?"

"Trying to. But at this rate, I don't see how she can. The house is rotting. The front steps are broken. Lord only knows what's going on inside, but I overheard that it will never pass inspection. She probably has no idea how strict commercial regulations are. And this historic district, well, we know how fussy they can be . . . "

He'd stopped listening as soon as he heard the name. "I'll go over first thing after work tomorrow."

"Really?" Eudora let out an ecstatic gasp and somewhere in the background Alfred barked. "Oh, thank you, Luke! You're a good egg, you know that?"

He didn't know anything about that, but he did know one thing: Leah Powell was not a wash-ashore.

When he left his job on Stage Harbor Road, it was already four-thirty and Route 28 through town was a traffic jam. Luke tried not to count all the Connecticut and New York plates, but they outnumbered the Massachusetts ones by a long shot. Just as the Land Rovers outnumbered the pickup trucks this time every year. But every seaside town depended on summer tourism. From the shops and restaurants to the Chatham Bars and Wayside inns, right down to the ice cream truck that ran laps between Ridgevale, Harding's, and Cockle Cove beaches, this time of year was most challenging and most income-earning for all the locals. Come September, the town and the beaches would be theirs again. And Luke's wallet would be full if his body sore.

His current job was in the final stages, and it was one he'd enjoyed. The family was doing a full kitchen reno and had hired Luke to craft their island and cabinetry, as well as that of the butler's pantry. He liked the family, and he liked their taste when it came to the wood elements of the design: they'd chosen classic Shaker-style panels and doors that would be painted in cloud-gray. The focal piece, however, was a large hearth-style hood over the eight-burner Viking range. The butler's pantry would have a striped butcher block counter. The custom order had taken months, but they were finally at the installation phase which was always exciting to him. Once he was done, though, there was another project waiting for him in South Chatham. He didn't know what Eudora expected him to do with Leah Powell and her bookstore plans. From what little he'd heard, Leah was just a tenant in the house, renting out the retail space downstairs. Any carpentry work was up to the owner, not the renter. Besides, the work he did was expensive. Tenants didn't invest in rental spaces. Still, his curiosity had gotten the better of him. He looked down now at his shirt and smoothed the front. Much as he'd hated to admit it, he'd taken care to pick out a blue chambray that he knew complemented his eyes.

As he waited in traffic, he tried to focus on work stuff instead of the growing butterflies in his stomach. It was silly. He hadn't seen Leah Powell since high school, since he was friends with her younger brother, James, and used to go by the Powell house to hang out after soccer practice. She'd paid very little attention to him, though he couldn't quite blame her. Back then he was an awkward, skinny teen who got tongue-tied around attractive girls. Last he'd heard, she'd stayed in Boston after college. James had at least come home a few times over the years for the odd high school reunion or to visit in summer, but not Leah. He hadn't seen her in more than a decade.

Beside him on the seat, Scout had his nose pressed against the window. "Almost there," Luke said. Scout was too intent watching other dogs on the sidewalk to bother flicking an ear in his direction.

It was a surprise to find a parking spot along the street outside the house. Luke cut the truck engine and glanced at the building. From there it looked a bit unloved; the paint was peeling and one shutter hung crooked. Eudora wasn't wrong about the front steps buckling; that would certainly need to be addressed before customers could tromp up and down them. But the house had good bones, as did most of the historic gems in town, and so far this one seemed no different. He rolled the windows down lower, and a salty breeze blew in from the channel across the way. "Stay," he told Scout. "I'll be quick."

The front doors were glass paneled, so Luke could easily see inside. The place looked empty for a store about to host a grand opening—no real furniture, no books. There was also no sign of Leah. There was, however, a young man unpacking boxes. Luke rapped on the door before poking his head in.

"I'm sorry, but we're not quite open yet," the man said. He seemed flustered, and Luke noticed stacks of boxes lined behind the ones he was working on. "We'll be posting an opening date soon!" he added, but his expression didn't match the forced cheer in his voice.

"Sorry for dropping in," Luke said. "My name is Luke Nickerson. I'm looking for Leah Powell?"

The young man gave him a more thorough once-over, hands on hips. "Brad," he said, coming over and extending a hand. "Is she expecting you?"

It was unclear what Brad's relationship was in terms of Leah or the bookstore, but Luke had to smile at the protectiveness in his demeanor.

"No, I can't imagine she is. I'm an old friend," he added for good measure.

And just like that Leah appeared in the doorway that led to the back rooms. She was talking on the phone, looking more exasperated than Brad. "No, I'm sorry but that does not work at all. We need these shelves immediately."

She did not seem to notice Brad or Luke and instead paced back and forth through a narrow path between stacks of boxes as the phone call continued.

"She's a little . . . preoccupied," Brad said, watching her with concern. When the phone call and pacing continued, Brad turned to him. "Is there anything I can help you with?"

Luke looked around. "That's actually why I'm here. A friend said you had a lot of work left to do and suggested I come by and offer my services. I'm a contractor."

Brad's doubtful expression washed clean like an Etch A Sketch screen. "A contractor? You don't say." He smiled like this was the best news he'd ever heard, and to Luke's shock he slipped an arm in his. "It's not up to me, of course," he said, lowering his voice and leading Luke away from Leah and her pacing, "but we do, in fact, need help. Like, a lot."

Luke was still out on the porch with Brad inspecting the steps when the front door swung open. Both men looked up. "What's going on?" Leah asked, eyes glancing briefly off Luke and landing on the steps.

"Good news!" Brad began, but Leah cut him off.

"Are you an inspector?"

For the first time her eyes locked on his, and Luke felt a familiar ripple go through him. Despite the years that had passed, remnants of the teenage girl he remembered were still very much in front of him and easy to piece together, her green eyes just as inquisitive. "Because no one from town hall gave me any warning. We aren't ready for an inspection yet."

Luke raised himself to full height and laughed. She had no idea who he was. "Then I guess it's a good thing I'm not the inspector."

"Wait." She stared at him, eyes tracing his face before giving him a full once-over. "Do I know you?"

"Once upon a time you did." He smiled, waiting for the other shoe to drop. Wondering if he really did look that much different, and hoping that it was a good thing if he did.

Brad's head swiveled between them as if watching a tennis match. "Leah, this is . . . "

"Lucas Nickerson?" she cried. A familiar laugh escaped her. "Wow! Hi. I'm sorry I didn't recognize you at first. You look so different!" Her whole demeanor softened. "I can't remember the last time I saw you."

"Actually, it's Luke. And I think it was your high school graduation party," he offered. But that wasn't true. The last time he'd seen Leah Powell he'd sat in the church pew behind her, at her mother's funeral. She was with her boyfriend, and Luke had spent the better part of the service staring at the elegant line of the back of her neck. Afterward, at the reception, he'd paid his respects to James and Mr. Powell but hadn't been able to find her in the crowd. The last he saw was of her walking out of the church, hand in hand with the boyfriend. He doubted she even knew he had come.

Her reaction now confirmed as much. "Graduation. That was ages ago! And you go by Luke now." She smiled. "I guess I'll always think of you as Lucas."

He didn't have the heart to tell her that no one had ever really called him that, except her and his mother. Which was just another reminder of how little attention she'd paid him when they were kids.

"So, you still live in the area?"

"Never left," Luke said, realizing how provincial that sounded. "I went to college but came home to start my own business."

"Guess what he does?" Brad interrupted enthusiastically. "Luke is a *carpenter*."

Leah nodded. "That's great."

"Isn't it? He came by to offer us his help."

"Oh." As if a switch had flipped, Leah crossed her arms. "That's very kind, Luke but we don't need any help."

"We don't?" Brad said flatly.

"We don't," Leah confirmed. She looked around uneasily. "There are a few things left to do, but we're getting to them."

"The *steps*," Brad reminded her.

"Sure, the steps are kind of wonky."

"Rotten," Luke said, gently. "Rotten right through, in some spots." He pressed the toe of his work boot against a board. They all watched the corner of it crumple like dirt.

"True," Leah admitted, "but that's a quick fix with a new board."

She ignored Brad's look of disbelief.

"And the railing," Luke added, wiggling it gently. The whole thing rocked back and forth before separating. The three of them watched a spindle drop off and roll into the sidewalk.

"Like I said," Leah said, "there are still some things I need to get to."

"What about the soffit?" Luke asked, pointing to the ceiling overhead.

All three heads turned skyward. "What about it?" Leah said grimly.

"It's coming away from the siding, see that?" Luke gestured to a section of wood that appeared water-stained. "The good news is it looks superficial. Wouldn't know for sure though, until I looked beneath it."

"Right." Leah jammed her hands in her pockets. "I'll add that to the list."

Luke held her gaze. She looked good. And she looked just as stubborn as he remembered her, like when she'd argue with James about sharing the car or refuse to let them tag along at a beach bonfire party. Aside from swapping out her high school ponytail, Leah Powell had not changed one bit. And she did not want his help, no matter how badly she seemed to need it. "Well, as long as you've got a list, I guess you've got it under control," he said, finally.

"Good to see you," she said. There was that smile again. "Maybe we'll bump into each other."

"Maybe." Luke shook Brad's hand. "Nice to meet you, Brad. Leah, good luck with the store. I'll have to come by when it opens."

He was halfway to his truck when Brad cried out in exasperation. "Oh come on!" When he turned, Brad was pleading with Leah. "There is no way we can fix these steps. Or that railing. Or that soffit thing!"

"But . . ."

"But nothing!" Brad went on. "This is your old friend. Who showed up out of the blue. *Who just happens to be a builder*. This is what we call serendipity."

Luke held his breath, eyes on Leah. It was her call.

"I don't have much left in the budget," she admitted. Her voice was small, but he knew the admission was not. So that was the problem.

"I'm sure we can work something out," Luke said. It was a terrible idea. But there it was.

"There's more," she added, turning glumly toward the door. Luke had the sense she wanted him to follow, so he did. "Even worse than the rotten entryway." When they stepped inside the house she looked about ready to cry.

"Actually, it's not so bad in here," Luke said, strolling through the room. He ran a hand along the doorframes, looked beneath the paper on the floorboards, checked the window seals. "It's an old house, but the interior seems remarkably tight."

"This is the problem," she said, gesturing to the walls on one side of the room and then the other. They seemed freshly painted; not perfect but not horrible.

Her lip trembled, but she didn't cry. "I can't sell books without shelves."

"That's not a problem," Luke reassured her. "Custom woodwork happens to be my thing." Leah brightened visibly, as he went on. "For your purposes, what you need is heavy-duty shelving that's secured to the walls so they can support all that weight and don't tip over on anyone. I'd measure for book heights and keep the design simple. Trim work is optional."

The look on Leah's face was pure relief. "Great! I have one condition. Can you build them by the end of this week?"

Luke coughed back a laugh. "*This* week? No, I'm afraid it's just not possible." It was almost humorous, if it weren't so outrageous.

"But I want to open in ten days. That's my *only* condition."

"Ten days! That's your only condition?" This time he did laugh. She had no idea what she was asking.

Leah gestured to all the boxes of books piled in the corners. "How else do I display all my stock?"

"I was wondering the same thing." He realized he sounded exasperated, but it was beginning to feel like Leah's problems were becoming his. "I'm not in retail, but isn't it customary to secure the display units before you purchase the merchandise?"

Her green eyes flashed in defiance. "I'm not an idiot."

"And I'm not a miracle worker."

Brad's head swiveled between them. "We did place an order for shelves," he rushed to explain, "but there was a problem with it."

"That's unfortunate, but I have a waiting list of clients," Luke said. "Besides, even the simplest design takes time. You've got to measure, cut the support frame, drill each panel, and paint. That's before attaching any of it. And that's assuming the lumberyard has what you want."

Leah held out her hands. "Please understand, I didn't go into this without a plan, but I also didn't realize the scope of the work. The Realtor assured me the house was sound. And the owner isn't local; he's not responding to my requests for repair help."

Hearing this made Luke annoyed on her behalf. It was well-known locally that this place had been empty and in disrepair for years; he wondered who the Realtor was. "That's not right. You should go back to the Realtor."

"I have. In the meantime, we scoured and painted this place top to bottom. We bought furniture and books. I secured all the necessary permits. Now I need this store to open so I can make rent. And I need shelves to make that happen."

Brad was nodding along like his life depended on it. "What she needs is a miracle."

Luke looked between the two of them. Their expressions were an infuriating mix of desperation and determination. They had no idea what they were doing. How had their mess landed on his plate? He should never have agreed to Eudora's request.

"Leah, we go way back. I love that you're trying to resurrect this old house and turn it into something for the community. And I would love to help you do that. But your timeline is downright unrealistic."

"Okay." He watched her gaze fall to the floor, and something inside him dropped, too.

Okay? After all the backstory and pleading and demands, she was going to give up that easily? "If you could work with me on timing, then maybe . . . "

"No." She shook her head adamantly. "I wish I could, but I can't. Too much is riding on this. I'll figure something else out, don't worry."

He wasn't worried. Not really. "There aren't enough days for what you want to do."

"Like you said." She was saying the words, but she didn't believe them. Here he was, stopping by to offer help, and it wasn't enough.

"It's unicorns and rainbows," Luke added. "And I don't have a magic wand." He waited but Leah said nothing.

Luke went to one of the windows and looked across the way where the deep blue of Chatham Harbor flickered earnestly against the sky. It was a shame; he could see the amount of work she'd done, and he knew it couldn't have been easy. The place was so old. Still, there was something special about it. There was an undeniable energy humming within the walls. He wasn't sure if the energy emanated from Leah and her crazy ideas or the Harding family ghosts. Whatever it was, it rooted him there in the paint fumes and the dust and the disappointment on Leah Powell's pretty face.

"I really wish I could help you."

She blinked. "I don't recall asking you for help, Luke."

God, she was bold. And stubborn. But it was also the truth. And he knew in that very moment there was no way he was walking away.

"I'll get my measuring tape."

"What?" She followed him outside, Brad trailing closely, too.

"Don't question the man!" Brad hissed. "I think he's helping."

"Really?" Leah brightened. "Luke, I can't thank you enough!" She hurried after him. "We can start first thing tomorrow morning."

Annoyed and invigorated, Luke ignored them both and went to his truck. Scout barked happily from the front seat, and Luke opened the truck door and let him out.

"Wait. You have a dog?" Leah stood at the top of the steps, a funny look on her face as she eyed Scout who was wagging and wiggling about.

"His name is Scout. He comes to work with me. That's *my* condition."

"Oh."

"Leah *loves* dogs," Brad chirped, but Luke could tell from the look on her face that this was not the case. It didn't matter. She had her conditions, and he had his.

Luke lowered the tailgate of his truck with a bang and grabbed his toolbox. "You may want to place a dinner order at the Squire."

"Why?" Leah asked, keeping a wary watch on Scout.

"Because we're not starting tomorrow," he said. "We're starting right now."

Lucy

What had Jep Parsons been thinking showing up in the rehab hospital like that? Lucy couldn't stop replaying his surprise visit. Her father's loud confrontation in the hall when Jep showed up, her mother's basic denial of him being there at all. Her parents' reactions could not have been more different. But it was the effect it had on Ella that had shaken Lucy most. Lucy knew her sister had heard Jep's voice in the hallway. And his impact on her was undeniable.

Of course no one talked about it. Not after the fact, when Jep had been hauled off by the staff. Not on the long, silent car ride home where her mother commented endlessly on the scenery and her father stared straight ahead at the road. When they pulled into the driveway, Lucy thought her head would explode. So she did something she'd avoided doing all summer.

She waited until they were safe inside, before either of them retreated to their usual corners of the house, before she asked the question. "Mom, Dad—what is the plan with Jep?"

Her father's head snapped in her direction like he'd been stung by a wasp. Her mother froze on her way to the kitchen.

Lucy took a deep breath. "Ella heard him. Her hands went crazy on the bed. I think she wanted him there."

"What did you just say?" her father hissed. Lucy flinched. Her father had always been a reserved man, even-tempered and thoughtful. The expression on his face was unrecognizable.

"We do not speak his name in this house," her father went on, his eyes lighting up like electricity itself was coursing through his limbs. "Not ever!"

Her mother came to her defense. "Martin, please. She didn't mean anything by it."

"Didn't mean anything?" He stared wildly between them and Lucy wished she had kept her mouth shut. His silent rage was better than this. "You two want to pretend this is not his fault? That he did not almost kill our daughter? That boy is a *monster*. I hope the next time we see him will be in court."

Every fiber in her being told Lucy to let it go, but her mind flashed back to the squeeze of Ella's fingers around her own. The desperation in her green eyes. Her hand tingled at the memory. "Dad, I know it was Jep's fault. But Ella reacted to him. She knew he was there. It was like she needed him."

"Needed him? She's afraid of him!" her father barked.

It took every ounce of courage she had left, but Lucy had to say it. For Ella's sake, if not her own. "You didn't see her, Dad. It wasn't fear." She paused, waiting for the ceiling to come down, the sky to fall. Instead, her father stormed up the stairs. A moment later her parents' bedroom door slammed.

"Lucy." Her mother came to her and placed her hands on either side of Lucy's cheeks, like she used to when she was very little. Her eyes were wide and soft and sad. "Your father cannot handle this. He's right—Jep is the one who hurt your sister. He was drunk. He was selfish and drunk and irresponsible. And we could have lost her." Her eyes bore into Lucy as if trying to impart the gravity of this, but what her parents always failed to realize was that she was already well acquainted with it.

"It's not about Jep," Lucy said. "It's about Ella. What if seeing him helps her? What if it makes the difference?"

Her mother shook her head. "Ella is coming out of it on her own. She is. She just needs time."

The words made sense, but Lucy did not believe them. She knew her sister as well as any of them. Probably better. Still, there was no way she was going to convince them to even consider letting Jep Parsons anywhere near Ella.

Lucy went out the kitchen door to the small patch of backyard. She flopped on the one of the recliners, the one Ella had sunned herself on every day up to graduation. Maybe her parents were right.

But as she stared at the cloudless sky, Lucy felt nothing but dread.

Unlike Ella, Lucy did not have an endless lineup of friends. What she did have was one best friend, Reya. Like her, Reya was skeptical of the popular kids in the hallways and more concerned with her class rank than her social rank. If quiet by nature, she was vocal about her opinions, mostly about her favorite authors and which bubble tea flavor was the best. The two had been best friends since fourth grade when they were paired up for a project on the founding fathers. They had been assigned John Adams. "We will be focusing on Abigail Adams," Reya informed Lucy, when they met in the library.

"But the assignment was for her husband," Lucy reminded her. "He was president."

Reya pushed a library book across the desk. "Read for yourself. There's a reason people dubbed her Mrs. President."

Though everyone knew about what happened the night of the accident, it was Reya who was constant. Who showed up the morning after and reached out every day since. Today was no different.

I'm done with camp at three. Want to meet in town for ice cream?

Lucy wished she'd applied to be a junior camp counselor at the boys and girls club, like Reya had. At the time she'd claimed there was no chance she would waste her summer chasing bratty kids around the beach with sunscreen and juice boxes. Now she'd give anything to get out of her house. *Sure* she texted back. *Meet me at Buffy's.* Maybe she'd pick up an application while she was there. Scooping ice cream would be easy enough.

At 3:05 Lucy leaned her bike against the side of Buffy's and let herself in the creaky screen door. The line was long and loud, teeming with weary parents and noisy toddlers. Lucy couldn't help but notice the four teenagers who worked the counter looked exhausted. She politely made her way to the front and when there was a pause between orders for double scoops and shakes, she asked one of the girls at the counter if they were hiring. The girl adjusted her pink baseball hat and blinked. "Sorry. My boss filled all the spots back in April."

Lucy groaned. She knew from living in a resort town that these jobs were coveted. She also knew a lot of them were scooped up by out-of-town college kids who came for the summer, or whose parents had summer homes. It was a common local grievance to be elbowed out of the way by the summer people, even when it came to work.

"Try somewhere else," Reya suggested, as they sat at one of the picnic tables with their cones. Reya had ordered black raspberry Oreo; she always tried something different. Lucy stuck to peach. She'd had enough change this summer.

"Like where?" she asked, catching a trail of melted peach ice cream with her tongue before it ran down her wrist. "All the good jobs are taken. At least here on Main Street. And I need someplace close enough to bike."

She didn't add that she couldn't bother her parents with driving her back and forth since every free moment they had was spent with Ella. Reya understood. "Hang on, did you hear about the new bookstore?" When Lucy shook her head, she went on, "I passed it on my way here, over by the lighthouse. There's a sign in the window that says grand opening."

At the end of the commercial strip of Main Street, they swung their bikes right at the stop sign. There were houses on both sides of the street, but the left boasted a mercurial strip of blue sea just beyond the rooftops. Up ahead, Chatham Light loomed against a cloudless sky. Midway along the stretch sat the old captain's house. Sure enough, when the girls pulled up on their bikes, there was a large hand-printed sign in one of the front windows: *Help Wanted.*

They propped their bikes up at the bottom of the steps, which were roped off with yellow tape. A small sign affixed to the tape said: *Fresh Paint! Deliveries, please use side door.* Below it in parentheses: *Not Open for Business Yet.*

"Geez, that's a lot of signage," Reya said.

Lucy let her gaze travel from the still-wet steps to the windows, covered in brown paper. "Looks like no one's here." She reached for her bike.

"Not so fast." Reya grabbed her by the hand and tugged her toward the rear. "The sign says go around to the side."

"For deliveries," Lucy reminded her.

"Well, I'm delivering you," Reya puffed, pulling her around the side yard to the door. "You'll thank me later."

Lucy was about to object just as the door flew open. A woman, not young and not old, stared back at them in surprise. Her blond hair was tied back in a red bandana. "Oh! Hello. Can I help you?"

Reya elbowed her. "Hi," Lucy said. "You have a sign in the window for help wanted?" It came out as a question, which was not the way she'd hoped to introduce herself.

The woman smiled. "Yes, I know. I put it there." She seemed to be lighthearted, and something about her made Lucy smile back with relief. "Are you looking for a job?"

Lucy nodded. "I'm Lucy Hart."

"Did you say Hart?"

Lucy nodded again.

"Brad!" the woman called over her shoulder into the house. The room she was coming out of seemed to be some kind of old kitchen, and there was a decent amount of noise emanating from within. A saw purred in the background, as well as music.

A young man appeared. "Did you call me?"

The woman stuck out her hand and Lucy shook it. "Brad, you'll never believe who showed up. *This* is Miss Hart."

An hour later, Lucy was pedaling home fast, Reya puffing to keep up behind her. Her heart pounded, though she wasn't sure if it was with excitement or fear that she'd just made a very big mistake.

"I can't believe she hired you because of your last name," Reya called out.

"I don't think that's the only reason," Lucy called back over her shoulder. Reya surged up alongside her.

"She said she was looking for heart. That you were a sign."

"Whatever. I think she was just being nice."

"Or crazy."

"Or that," Lucy admitted. They pulled their bikes to a stop at the sign and paused to catch their breath. "I don't know. She seemed nice. And it's a *bookstore*."

Both of them loved bookstores and were used to having to drive all the way to Hyannis for the Barnes & Noble. Now they'd have one in their own town.

"I just hope she actually opens," Lucy said, realizing that she really wanted this job.

The interview, if it could even be called that, had consisted of Lucy and Reya being invited inside. The first thing that happened after introductions was Leah inviting them inside and shouting for someone named Brad. "You'll have to excuse Leah," Brad said, rolling his eyes sympathetically. "She's been looking for two things to make this store happen. Hands." Here he pointed to a good-looking guy walking by in construction attire. "And heart. Which, kiddo, seems to be you."

"Lucy, do you live in Chatham?" Leah had asked.

When Lucy told her she'd grown up there, Leah seemed overjoyed. "I grew up here, too. So you know this old captain's house has been around a long time."

Lucy couldn't say she remembered the old house as anything other than an eyesore. "It's always been empty," she said, trying to be polite.

"Exactly. Which is why we are bringing it back to life. Follow me." Lucy wondered at the word *we*, but Reya was as entranced as she was nosy, so she followed Leah like a puppy, leaving Lucy no choice but to do the same.

While the back of the first floor was divided into tiny old rooms, the front was completely open. And huge. And for the first time, Lucy believed it was actually going to be a bookstore.

The floors were brightly polished. Old schoolhouse lanterns cast a dreamy glow overhead. Even with the paper covering the windows, sunlight slipped in over the tops highlighting row after row of tall wooden bookshelves. The source of the machinelike sound turned out to be a drill that the so-called *hands* of the operation was using to affix the last of a series of floor-to-ceiling shelves. The front shelves, nearest to the store's front door, were already lined with books. A pedestal table set up at the entrance held an array of new releases. An old-fashioned school desk boasted stacks of beach reads. Right in front of the double wooden doors, the floor was a mosaic of blue-and-white check-ered tile. "That's a remnant from the fifties, when it used to be a general store," Leah said proudly. She pointed to a beautiful wooden mantel over the fireplace Lucy hadn't noticed. "And that was added when it returned to an inn."

"And now it's a bookstore," Reya said. Leah looked at her like she could hug her.

"That's the plan." She turned to Lucy. "I assume you're a book lover?"

Lucy was busy walking between the small tables of books, each one a different color and style, adding to the mismatched magic. She stopped at a table of classics and ran her finger along the spine of a leather-bound *Anne of Green Gables* and swallowed.

"She lives for books," Reya said breezily, and Lucy threw her friend a warning look.

"I read a lot," she told Leah.

"Excellent. We could use someone to help with YA literature recommendations."

Lucy didn't know why, but suddenly she couldn't speak. Standing in that sun-spilled room teeming with freshly unboxed books was too much. It was a world away from the strained quiet and pulled shades of Bay Street.

"Are you okay?" Leah asked. She was intuitive and pretty. Lucy would have to keep her guard up. In that moment, she de-cided that if Leah hired her, she didn't want to bring Bay Street with her here.

"Yes, I'm just happy I stopped here," she admitted. It was the truth. She could not recall the last time she felt happy about anything.

"Well, I'm happy you did, too." Leah put her hands on her hips. "We open this weekend. Think you can handle a cash register?"

Now, as they pedaled single file along the tourist-clogged stretch of Shore Road, Lucy felt her chest open up. At the crest by the Chatham Bars Inn, they swung left and zigzagged their way through the neat grid of streets, down Seaview and onto Old Harbor Road, the large summer cottages with sprawling yards and ocean views giving way to slightly less grand houses as they moved away from the shoreline. They coasted by the old elementary school playground and the Chatham Fire & Rescue Department and down Tip Cart Drive where the houses were snug, the yards mere postage stamps. These were local neighborhoods, the homes separated by the occasional boat marina or bike rental outfit. The Cape Cod Rail Trail snaked throughout, a scenic bike path surrounded by wetlands, parks, and fields.

"Want to come over?" Lucy shouted over her shoulder. Reya's house was only a couple streets away from her own.

"You sure your parents won't mind?"

After the initial onslaught of casseroles and get-well bouquets, it seemed everyone was giving the Hart family a wide berth. "They'll be fine," Lucy said.

Spirits buoyed by her new job, Lucy was excited to share the news with her parents. They were almost home when they approached Parsons's Garage. How could she have forgotten? Since the accident, she'd gone out of her way to take side streets to avoid it. Lucy slowed, a pit of dread filling her stomach.

Jep Parsons's father was a mechanic, and the auto repair shop had been in the family forever. Lucy knew that Jep worked there. That was common knowledge. What was not common knowledge was that Jep's father, as a graduation present to his son, had gifted him part of the business. Ella had slipped into Lucy's room one night after graduation. "Can you believe it? Jep is half owner now!" For a girl going to Tufts in the fall, she was not at all put off by the fact that her secret boyfriend was not college bound himself. She was happy for Jep.

Now, without realizing it, Lucy stopped her bike along the roadside abruptly.

"Whoa, what're you doing?" Reya cried out, narrowly avoiding crashing into Lucy and skidding past her to a halt. "Some warning would be nice." But when Reya looked up at the garage, she understood.

Lucy stared at the gray shingled building, the two open bays where cars were up on lifts. Through the office window someone was talking to a client, but it wasn't Jep.

"What're we doing here, Lucy?" Reya whispered.

But Lucy couldn't answer. Her eyes had traveled to the side of the shop, where a bunch of cars were lined up. At the end of the row, tucked neatly against the wall of the building, was a vehicle nearly covered in a dark green tarp. The red nose of the car peeked out from beneath the edge of the tarp, the chrome Mustang motif sparkling in the afternoon sun.

Lucy sucked in her breath, her hands shaking on the handlebars.

"Shit," Reya said under her breath. "Is that the car?"

There was a clang of metal on pavement. Jep Parsons emerged from one of the garage bays, and bent to scoop up a spanner that he'd dropped. When he stood, his eyes landed on the girls.

"Let's get out of here," Lucy said, jerking her bike back toward the road.

"He's coming over . . . " Reya began, but Lucy was already pedaling off as fast as her legs would pump.

She didn't stop until she sailed into her driveway, her quads like lead and her lungs on fire.

Leah

It was opening day. Leah was up before the sun had even risen, staring out the window at the pink dusting of sunrise peeking over the edge of the horizon. All signs were pointing to exactly the kind of day she'd hoped for: sun-filled, blue sky, the perfect Cape summer day.

It still seemed impossible that she'd pulled it off. Even after they'd stayed late putting the finishing touches on the interior and filling the flowerpots by the door last night. Even after Luke had surprised her with one final job.

It was late, and he'd found her in the office, posting her last grand opening announcement online. "I have a little something for you," he'd said, somewhat sheepishly.

"For me?" Leah had looked up from her laptop. It was still a wonder to her that the man filling her doorframe in faded jeans and his Saltwater Woodworks T-shirt was the same bucktoothed kid who'd run around the backyard with her brother, James, all those years ago. For the life of her she could not remember the name of the nice older woman who'd stopped by to hand her the scrap of paper with Luke's name and number scribbled across it, but Leah wanted to thank her. Not that she'd called him; Leah had been too stubborn. And not that any of it had clicked with her at the time: the woman had not included Luke's last name, and Leah had always remembered him as *Lucas*. Never mind that Leah had not even recognized him when he still managed to show up. That fact still made her blush with embarrassment. Now the whole thing seemed serendipitous, a kind of small-town magical realism she read about in romance novels. Despite all of it, somehow Luke Nickerson had found her anyway.

When she thought back to their childhood, Luke had been a skinny, shy kid Leah pretty much ignored, except to yell at her brother and him to keep it down when they played late-night video games. Or to ask him to move his bike when he left it lying in the driveway behind her car. Long gone was that scraggly kid she'd caught more than once staring at her across a bowl of Cheerios at the kitchen table the morning after he and James had a sleepover—who blushed each time she made eye contact. No, the man standing in her doorway now was broad shouldered and compelling, his ease as sure as the humorous glint in his blue eyes. It was Leah who now felt a little unsettled every time she looked at him.

After Luke had swung by the shop to offer his help, she'd called her brother, James. "You won't believe who came by the other day."

"No kidding," James had said, when she told him. "His business is pretty successful. Did you know *Architectural Digest* did a piece on a kitchen reno he did for one of the Shore Road houses?"

"I had no idea," Leah replied in wonder. Since he began working with her, Luke had come in and gotten straight to work each day, saying little about his business or his life, even when she inquired. In fact, he'd made the store such a priority the past week that she assumed the other jobs he'd mentioned had slowed down. "He said summer was his busy season, but he makes it seem like he's basically a handyman."

James had laughed. "Yeah, a handyman none of us could ever afford. I'm surprised he has time to give you. Our old friend Scott just inherited his parents' house and wanted to update it. Apparently, Luke is so booked out he can't even start until next year."

"He's been here every day," she told her brother, wondering how that was possible. True to his word, Luke had finished the shelves, often coming in at odd times. One morning he showed up looking exhausted with several freshly sanded and painted units, ready to be installed. "Did you stay up late to finish those?" she'd pressed. She didn't believe him when he shook his head, no.

"Sounds like he's doing you quite a favor," James said.

Leah's mind flashed back to the "agreement" they'd struck. Luke had assured her they'd work something out, insisting he was happy to wait until she had some dependable revenue coming in. Leah had insisted he at least provide an estimate before starting. Despite some initial balking, he'd finally handed her a figure that even she knew was too low. Now she realized with chagrin that he was practically working for her for free.

She'd have to find a way to pay him back. At least one thing was sure: Luke Nickerson wasn't going anywhere. He was as local as the haul that came off the fishing boats each morning at Chatham Fish Pier.

The clincher was the *little something* he wanted to show her the night before. Leah had braced herself, assuming he'd found something dire. Like when he'd shored up the front steps, and found the frame wasn't up to code. Or when he'd had to replace the wood over the entryway since the water stains had proven to be dry rot. When she followed him outside Brad was waiting, too, a goofy look on his face. "What's going on?" Leah asked, immediately suspicious.

Luke pointed overhead. Leah's eyes swung skyward and she gasped. A beautiful wooden sign hung over the door, the lettering etched in gold trim.

THE SANDY PAGE BOOKSHOP

Leah gasped. "Luke! When did you find the time?"

"It's nothing," he said, already waving away the fuss she was making.

"It's not nothing!" She could not believe how beautiful it was, both the gesture and the craftsmanship.

His eyes crinkled shyly. "You can't have a shop without a sign."

"Thank you," she managed, pulling him in for a hug. Standing on the sidewalk between Brad and Luke, Leah felt for the first time like everything might actually be okay.

Now, leaning against her kitchen sink, she could still recall Luke's scent of pine and soap and something else . . . freshly cut wood, she realized. She smiled wistfully. But there was no time to think about Luke or anything else this morning. It was opening day!

On the drive to work Leah ticked off the remaining to-do items on her list. Brad was picking up flowers. Lucy would finish hanging twinkle lights in the children's area. Doors would open at noon.

For the past two weeks she'd basically taken up residence in the store. Her days began early and ended late. There was setup and display, final book orders to be inventoried and stocked. Training for Lucy and Brad. An interview with the local paper. Development of her website and social media platforms, which had quickly been designated to Brad; he had a knack for these things and the patience she did not. There was a debate over whether or not to serve coffee. Lucy didn't drink it. Brad thought coffee would draw customers but worried the retail space was crowded with Leah's flea-market finds; Leah didn't want spills on her merchandise but was determined to find a use for the vintage Formica table she'd snuck into the shop when Brad wasn't looking. (They both won. There would be a trial run of a Cape Cod French roast on the red table.) Leah had spent so much time out of the house that her refrigerator was empty, her laundry basket spilled over. But it would all have to wait. Today was the day.

At that early hour the street was quiet, and the captain's house was still and dark. Leah paused on the threshold, imagining she was a new customer walking through the door for the first time. The smell of fresh paint lent that sense of new-beginnings promise. Inside the doorway a colorful collection of beach reads greeted customers on the antique pedestal table like a bouquet. She flicked on the wall switch and the school-house lanterns cast a dreamy glow over the store. Leah smiled, a welling of pride rising up within her. Luke's floor-to-ceiling bookcases lined the walls, teeming with crisp hardcovers and trade paperbacks. Throughout, carefully curated display tables stood like clusters of guests at a dinner party; each one held a different genre: thrillers, romance, new releases. A pair of love-worn leather armchairs she'd found in a moving sale were set up in front of a window, just inviting readers to sit down. Over the fireplace, the portrait of the Harding sisters hung, each red-haired young woman gazing back at her. "Big day today, girls!" she told them.

Leah strolled quietly between the book displays, running her hands over the sleek covers. There were small personal touches everywhere: on a stand-alone shelf housing cook-books, her mother's old cast-iron skillet hung from a nail on the end. By the self-help books, a tiny table of assorted tea tins and handmade mugs commissioned from a local ceramicist in Sandwich. In the back corner, where a tall, spinning wire rack held local history books, two old wooden buoys were strung from the top. Curating these small local finds had taken time, but they told a story. From the day she'd seen the *For Rent* sign in the window of the captain's house, Leah had wanted this place to share its own story. It was the perfect backdrop for her vision, and she'd worked hard to create a space humming with the town's seaside culture and history. Now it was time to open its doors to Chatham.

Minutes before ten, Brad sailed through the front door, a bag of his grandmother's breakfast pastries tucked under his arm. He found Leah in the old dining room in the back, which they'd set up as a temporary office space. "Figured you were running on fumes," he said, handing the pastries over.

Leah shook her head "You've got to stop."

"Try telling that to my grandmother. Pushing food is what she does."

"Well, she's a little too good at it," Leah said, before scarfing down a buttery breakfast roll.

Lucy Hart strolled in at eleven, her expression set in its usual serious fashion. Leah still was not sure what to make of the girl. So far she'd shown up on time and seemed game for whatever strange job she was handed. She trimmed the front hedges under the hot sun without complaint, mopped floors, and hauled furniture. She was also living up to her last name. When they caught mice in the catch-and-release traps Leah had insisted on, Lucy named each one and spoke to it gently before releasing it outside. When they shelved incoming stock, Leah noticed she handled each book like it was a delicate piece of art. But thanks to the occasional scratching and rattling noises heard overhead, Lucy balked at going upstairs.

"You sure this old house isn't haunted?"

Brad had done the sign of the cross and looked up at the ceiling. "Racoons in the attic," he whispered, though it was not clear if that was reassurance or a prayer.

But there was something about Lucy that Leah could not put her finger on. An air of sadness that seemed to follow her from room to room. When Leah asked about her family, Lucy had paled. "I have a sister," she'd said, "but she's away." It was clear she did not want to say more.

Now, as Lucy finished touches on the children's area, Leah joined her. "The kids are going to love this, Lucy. Thank you." It was true. There were tiny chairs around a white table with a play tea set, a stack of picture books in the middle. Lucy had arranged two stuffed frogs on the classics shelf, right next to the *Frog and Toad* and *Wind in the Willows* series.

Ten minutes before the doors opened, Brad ran the vacuum one last time. The bakery delivered the pastries and Leah arranged a neat platter by the coffee. The three of them looked around the room and then at each other. "Five minutes," Leah said, glancing nervously toward the door. "I think I may pass out."

"Please don't," Brad said.

"Whatever happens today," Leah said, trying to sound like the calm leader they all needed, "just remember two things: smile. And offer to help customers find what they need. We want everyone to feel welcome.

"Okay, stack of hands." Leah motioned them to huddle and stuck her hand in the middle. Brad and Lucy stared at her, expressions blank. "Haven't you guys been on a sports team?"

Brad adjusted his bow tie, which Leah was touched to see he'd worn to work that day. "The debate team."

"Lucy?"

She shook her head. "Dance class."

"I have a better idea." Brad disappeared in the back and returned with three champagne flutes.

"Where did these come from?" Leah asked.

"Borrowed from my grandmother." He set them carefully on the cash register counter, along with a bottle of sparkling cider. "I could use the real stuff, but it's a workday, so . . . "

Brad uncorked the bottle with a festive *pop* and passed the glasses around. "To Leah, our intrepid bookseller," he said, raising his glass.

"To the Sandy Page," Lucy added, smiling brightly for the first time since she'd been hired.

When she tugged the doors open at noon, Leah walked outside. There wasn't a single soul waiting. Across the way, cars were pulling into Lighthouse Beach parking lot but as they emptied the passengers made off in the opposite direction, toward the view finders. On the front sidewalk a woman with a stroller and two kids pushed by, without even glancing up. A cyclist raced past on the street.

Brad appeared at Leah's elbow. "Oh dear."

"It's okay," she said, feeling anything but okay. "We advertised. We have signs in the window. People will come."

But for the first eternal hour no one did. Finally, someone appeared in the doorway. All three of them leapt to attention. "Welcome to the Sandy Page!" Leah said, rushing to greet him.

The man looked around. "Do you have a restroom?"

By one o'clock, only two potential customers had shown up. Both browsed the shop and exclaimed how lovely it was, but neither bought a single book. Leah deflated.

"It's only the first day," Brad said.

Both he and Lucy seemed eager to find something to do, but

Leah couldn't think of a thing. Pacing the old creaky floorboards was driving her crazy. "I'll be right back," she said.

Outside the weather was as perfect as the sunrise that morning had promised. For the life of her, Leah couldn't understand why no one was showing up. After the local newspaper write-up and the online marketing they'd done, she'd expected a line at the door. At least a handful of people on the sidewalk.

Feeling low, she crossed the street to the Lighthouse Beach parking lot. There were certainly plenty of people here, enjoying the view and taking photos. Some were making their way down the long staircase to the sandy stretch of beach. Leah was tempted to approach them, to point out the store, invite them to come check it out—but it felt like a desperate move and she was too embarrassed.

Instead she joined the view seekers, like any other tourist. Looking out over Chatham Bay, Leah wondered if she'd made a terrible mistake. Coming home was one thing. Dumping all her savings into a historic old house she didn't own and trying to start up a small business was another. Maybe she'd been too distraught from the loss of her publishing job and the breakup of her engagement to think clearly. Maybe she'd lost her mind. Her father would be calling that night asking how it went. James would be, too.

For the first time in days, Leah checked her phone for missed calls. She knew what she was looking for, even if she was ashamed to admit it. To help her move on, Leah had blocked Greg's calls. Prior to that, they'd talked a few times: he called about a coat he'd found in the closet that he would ship. Then he'd texted asking for her forwarding address. Just the other morning, Google had about done her in when a series of photo memories popped up on her phone. They were of a trip the two had taken to Hawaii. One in particular, of them sipping piña coladas on the beach, had gotten to her. It was the same beach they'd talked about returning to for their honeymoon. It sent her spiraling back to what could have been and wondering if he was seeing *Rebekah*.

When she checked her phone, there was not a single message or missed call from Greg.

Leah jammed the phone in her back pocket. Why did it matter? A clean break was for the best. Her life was here now. She turned and stared across the street at the old captain's house. *My bookstore*, she reminded herself. This was her job now, this was her home now. Jaw set, she stalked back across the street and pounded up the front steps, so strong from Luke's repairs that there was nary a creak nor a give. She pulled the front door open roughly, about to call Brad and Lucy out, to brainstorm a better publicity effort when she stopped in her tracks. There were people! Not a crowd, but a handful. A small grateful laugh escaped her.

Lucy was in the back children's area, kneeling by the table with two little boys and a girl, while their mother scanned the picture book selections. Two older women surveyed the new fiction table. On one of the leather armchairs by the window a man was bent over a book, lost in reading. At the counter, Brad was about to check someone out. Just then he saw her, waving her over excitedly. "Leah! You do the honors."

"Honors?" she asked.

Brad nodded toward the woman at the cash register. "Our first official sale."

Tears sprang to her eyes as Leah understood. "Oh!" She smiled at the woman, who was holding three paperbacks, and hurried over to her. "Yes, of course."

"I just love what you've done here," the woman said, handing the titles over. "This house has always caught my eye, the architecture is just so different from everything else in town, you know?"

"Greek Revival," Brad said, as if he'd designed it himself.

"It was looking so sad and run down. And now it's home to a bookstore!"

"I'm so glad you came in today," Leah said.

"So am I," the woman said. "And I get to be the first customer!" She reached for a tin of mints, and grabbed a seashell-printed bookmark by the register. "I'll take these, too."

When the woman handed over her credit card, Lucy called over from the children's section.

"Wait!" Lucy held up her phone. "Want me to take a photo?"

She did want that. Unable to speak, Leah managed a nod. Their first customer leaned in smiling and Leah followed suit.

"Smile!" Lucy said.

By the end of the day, Leah and Brad sprawled on the armchairs. "Why am I so exhausted?" Brad asked. "It wasn't like it was Filene's Basement Annual wedding dress sale."

"How do you know about that?" Leah asked, unable to hide her smile. "That was way ahead of your time."

Brad shrugged nonchalantly. "The stuff of fashion lore."

"We're tired because of the last two weeks," Leah said, rubbing her neck. "And the hype. And the worry."

"Well, it was a solid start, I think. Word will get out. Foot traffic will steer our way."

Leah appreciated Brad's enthusiasm. She glanced to the back, where Lucy was tidying up.

"Alright, you two. Home you go. We get to do this all over again tomorrow."

As she was locking up, her phone dinged. Probably her dad checking in to see how the big day went. She pulled her phone out of her pocket. To her delight it wasn't her dad.

Hope today was all you wanted it to be! Sorry I couldn't make it over- got stuck on this job.

It was Luke. The fact that he'd thought to reach out buoyed her spirits. *Day was great,* she texted. *Thank you for all you did to make it possible.*

There was a long pause before he replied. Then, *Okay if I swing by tomorrow? Want to check the paint on that last shelf. It wasn't quite dry.*

Leah sat down on the top step. The paint was fine, long dried and set. *It was a little sticky,* she lied. *May need a touch up.*

Eudora

Eudora could not believe she'd missed the opening day for Leah Powell's new bookstore. After all, she was the one who sent Luke Nickerson to help that poor girl to begin with. As it turned out, Leah had not recognized her the day she showed up and poked her head in the door, but that was perfectly fine with Eudora—better, even. She didn't want to get into any discussion about their old high school, where Eudora had been a guidance counselor. Not after what happened with Shelby Smalls and Eudora's swift retirement thereafter. Shelby had been sent to Eudora for help, but despite her due diligence Eudora had not uncovered what was going on with the poor girl. It did not seem to be anything at home. They could not pinpoint anything at school. What Eudora did was invite her in to her office every week for lunch. It didn't matter that she mostly doodled or sketched the entirety of those lunches. Eudora was happy to talk. Eventually, her patience paid off and it was Eudora's chance to listen. Shelby talked about her golden retriever at home. About her hope to go to art school. Once she mentioned a boy she had a crush on. For a brief while Eudora felt that Shelby seemed lighter and more relaxed, that perhaps Eudora was making a difference.

Shelby began showing up unannounced. Sometimes she just poked her head in to say hello. Sometimes she even shared a drawing she was working on in that notepad of hers. Never once, however, did Shelby give away the source of her suffering. It was another girl in her class, named Anna Meyer. Anna was the kind of bully that even the most tuned-in teacher might overlook. She was unremarkable academically and socially, an average student who blended into the backdrop of the high school hallways and classrooms with no overt signs of inappropriate behavior. That was because Anna Meyer conducted all of it online.

What later came to light was a smear campaign that would make Hollywood publicity firms shudder. All because Anna's boyfriend had taken a liking to shy, quiet Shelby one evening at a party. The resulting cyberbullying involved rumors, social media attacks, and manipulated photos of a pornographic nature that circulated the phones and communications of just about every student at the high school. Right beneath Eudora's and the administration's noses, Shelby Smalls was tormented for months. Until one morning when her mother found her lying in the bathroom beside an empty bottle of pills.

Though the ambulance got her to the ER in time, where Shelby was intubated and put on a ventilator, she never returned to school. Afterward, she was transferred to a psychiatric facility, and much later, her family moved quickly and quietly out of the area, leaving only the lawsuits they filed in their wake.

It didn't matter that Eudora was not found to be liable in any way. She felt the guilt in her veins. It haunted her in her sleep. Each day she went to school and passed Shelby's locker, Eudora felt a panic grip her chest. Shelby had trusted her. She was the one person the young woman had turned to. And Eudora had failed her. There was nothing she could do but quit.

While Eudora had long suffered the tourist-filled summers in Chatham, since her departure from the high school she now took comfort in them on the rare occasion she left the house. It was easier to be among strangers. Eudora could get lost in the crowds, just another face in line at the market or the pharmacy. None of the tourists recognized her as the counselor who testified in the cyberbullying trial that made all the local and Boston news that fateful summer.

Yesterday, however, she'd felt pulled to the bookstore opening. She'd even marked the date on her calendar in red marker. Something about this new shop in the old captain's house had captured a little piece of her heart. For the first time in a long time, Eudora felt reconnected to her little community. When it came time to go, however, there was her anxiety waiting for her at the front door. It had turned into a full-blown panic attack that caused her to take to her bed for the rest of the day.

Today was a new day. She would not allow her anxiety to keep her home again. Alfred danced about her feet when she dangled his leash.

Twenty minutes later, (because Alfred had to sniff every telephone pole, mailbox, and shrub) they climbed the bookstore's front steps. She was tickled to see they'd been shorn up and freshly painted. That Luke: she'd known he would take the job. It wasn't easy to turn down someone you grew up with in a small town.

To her delight, the front door was painted a lovely coastal blue. Eudora pushed it open, met instantly by a feast for the senses. Everywhere she turned the bright covers of book jackets faced her, from tabletops and floor-to-ceiling bookshelves and artfully arranged stacks on little curio tables. It was like drifting into a book lover's paradise and someone's cozy coastal living room, all at the same time. Eudora stood in the doorway with Alfred, completely forgetting the bouquet of dahlias she'd picked from her front garden and tied with a raffia bow that morning.

All throughout the lovingly appointed space were people: people reading in armchairs, people gazing up at shelves, people scrutinizing the backs of paperbacks or picking through baskets of vintage wallpaper bookmarks with tiny seashells strung to their tops with silk ribbon (how clever!). It was not crowded, but satisfyingly busy, and what Eudora loved most was that everyone was so focused on their browsing that the only sound was the tinkle of soft music and the occasional murmur of satisfaction when a reader met a good title.

"Welcome!" A young man in a pink button-down sailed out from behind the antique sideboard she was pleased to see was being used as a checkout counter. "My name is Brad. What beautiful flowers!"

Friendly, not pushy, she decided. Eudora smiled appreciatively back at him. "These are for the owner," she said, holding out the flowers. A low rumble at the end of her leash reminded her; she'd nearly forgotten all about Alfred! "Oh dear. Is it alright if he comes in?"

Brad looked adoringly at Alfred who showed one tiny white tooth in return, then stepped back. "Our contractor's dog comes in all the time."

Ah! "Yes, you must mean Luke."

"You know him?" Brad leaned in. He wanted details, she could tell.

"Small town." She would not take credit for sending him over.

"You must be local." He winked, conspiratorially. "We have to stick together."

"You live in town, too?" She tried to hide the fact it gave her a start. Eudora did not recognize him from high school, but from the looks of him he would've graduated about the time she retired.

"My grandmother does. I visit her every summer." He glanced about the shop. "Let me find Leah for you."

While she waited, Eudora looked around. Whatever coffee they were serving smelled divine, and she had to stop herself from getting a cup. She'd had her fill that day; too much caffeine had led to some rather unpleasant online interactions with people looking to unload their dogs. Alas.

Leah Powell came out of a rear door and headed for Eudora, a light of recognition on her face. "I owe you a tremendous thank you!" she said, happily. "I have to admit, Luke came by before I called him, but you were right. We needed help." She looked about the store. "I never would have opened without him."

Eudora realized Leah only recognized her from the day she'd poked her head in the door. She extended the flowers. "Congratulations on the shop!"

"Thank you! These are just stunning," Leah said, with far more gratitude than Eudora expected. Yes, her garden was lovely, but they were just a handful of dahlias. She watched as Leah swiped at the corner of her eye. Was she crying?

"It's been a roller coaster," Leah admitted. "On opening day, at first no one showed up. But now word is getting out, and everyone has been so appreciative."

Eudora needed to introduce herself properly. "I'm not sure you remember me," she said, "but I used to be a guidance counselor at your old high school."

Leah cocked her head, eyes narrowing. "Mrs. Shipman? Gosh, I'm sorry! I thought you looked familiar the first time you came in."

"I take it Luke didn't tell you?"

She smiled knowingly. "He seems good at keeping secrets."

"Yes, he doesn't poke his nose in where it doesn't belong. I like that about him," Eudora admitted. "He's helped me a lot over the years, first when my husband was sick, and then after. I figured he might do the same for you." She gestured about her. "I just love what you've done. You've brought the place back to life with books!"

"Well, I'm glad you came back. I was hoping you would. Please make yourself at home, and feel free to linger."

Eudora watched as Leah headed to the children's section. As much as she hated to leave the house for too long, being here felt different. Somehow familiar to her. Even Alfred seemed to agree. She glanced down to see he'd curled up at her feet, on the edge of an area rug. Perhaps she would stay a while, as Leah suggested. At the very least, buy a copy of Louise Penny's latest.

After strolling about and perusing the shelves, Eudora found what she was looking for and was paging through a French pastry book when she noticed a young girl standing behind the check-out counter. Probably a sophomore in high school, she guessed; very pretty but likely unaware of that fact, based on her body language. Eudora had seen it too many times in her years in the high school hallways, the slight hunch of shoulders, the shy tuck of a chin when someone spoke to her. How Eudora wanted to give those girls a hug and tell them not to be so afraid to take up their space in the world!

She headed for the checkout counter. The Sandy Page was so lovely she was tempted to stay longer, but Alfred had made a few grumbles and she didn't want him wearing out his welcome. Eudora set both books down on the counter—the profiterole recipe had sold her on the cookbook, too. "Did you find everything you were looking for?" the girl asked. *Lucy,* her nametag read.

"Yes, thank you, Lucy. You must be so happy to work here."

Lucy threw her an unexpectedly bright smile. "I am," she said, softly. "It's the best place ever." Eudora could tell she meant it.

"I'll take one of these, too," Eudora said, adding one of the vintage wallpaper bookmarks to her pile. "And one of these." She grabbed a small bag of saltwater taffy from a basket.

"The Candy Manor made those special for us," Lucy said,

pointing to the pink label: *Sandy Page Saltwater*. Eudora knew the Candy Manor. Just as every child in every corner of the Cape knew it.

"Leah really thought of everything!" Eudora said, taking another. She'd send one to Caroline and the kids.

"They're too good, if you know what I mean," Lucy warned.

Just then, the bell jangled over the front door and they both turned. A teenage boy stood in the doorway, glancing around uncertainly. Lucy's smile instantly evaporated.

"Here you go, dear," Eudora said, holding out her credit card. But Lucy didn't seem to hear. She was frozen, eyes fixed on the boy. Eudora glanced between the two. Something was wrong.

"Excuse me," Lucy said, abruptly. She left Eudora at the cash register, credit card hanging in the air, and disappeared into the back room. Brad emerged a moment later.

"May I check you out?" he asked. If he'd noticed the boy in the doorway, it did not have the same impact as it had on Lucy.

"Is she alright?" Eudora asked.

"Who?"

"That nice girl, Lucy. She was helping me." Eudora glanced back at the boy. He was just leaving, pulling the door closed behind him. She watched as he turned down the sidewalk, his dark brown hair disappearing from view.

Brad shrugged casually. "Lucy just asked me to take over so she could take her lunch break. Was something wrong with her service?"

"Oh no," Eudora lied. "She mustn't have seen me at the checkout."

When she got outside with Alfred and her two books, Eudora inhaled deeply as if she'd just had the most satisfying meal and was ready for a nap. Caroline would be pleased: she had gone out, socialized, and even reconnected with an old student. And she had two lovely new books to show for it.

But the whole way home she couldn't help but wonder about Lucy and the boy in the doorway. Red flags were waving in her guidance counselor's mind, a thing she'd found she could never turn off, despite retirement.

One thing was for sure, she'd have to go back to the Sandy Page.

Lucy

Why had Jep Parsons shown up at the Sandy Page? And how did he know she worked there? It was only her second day. There was no one connecting the two of them except for Ella, and Ella was in bed at Spaulding Rehab unable to talk to anyone. Lucy feared she knew the answer. He was looking for her.

She felt bad for taking off on her customer, that nice old lady especially, but she could tell from one look at Jep that he was there to say something. Curious as she was, it could not have been a worst time or place. And her parents had forbade her from talking about him, let alone to him. Even mentioning his name wasn't allowed at home. Whatever it was he wanted, it involved Ella, that much she was sure. Showing up like that at her new job, in front of customers, was not okay. She was just glad she could duck away from him into the back office, and that Leah hadn't noticed. Working at the Sandy Page was the only thing keeping Lucy sane this summer, and she wasn't about to risk that. Maybe her parents were right; Jep Parsons was nothing but trouble and she should stay away from him.

But it wasn't that simple. Lucy had seen her sister two times since Jep had shown up at Spaulding Rehab, and neither time did Ella respond to any of them the way she had when Jep was shouting in the hallway begging to see her. Lucy couldn't shake it. Despite the doctors and nurses assuring her family that Ella was making progress, that day was still the most connection she'd felt to her sister, her old sister, since the accident. Ella was now able to sit up. To blink, to communicate. To feed herself and follow simple speech. But she was not back; as far as Lucy was concerned, she was not anywhere back to being Ella Hart. Two months ago she was the high school homecoming queen. A month ago, the valedictorian standing at the graduation podium. Now, she was just a mute girl stuck in a hospital bed with sad eyes. Jep Parsons either knew something or had something that Ella needed. Lucy needed to find out.

After work, Lucy retrieved her bike from where she'd propped it up against the side of the bookstore and rolled it to the sidewalk, looking left and right. She wasn't sure if she was more relieved or disappointed when she didn't see any sign of Jep.

It was a long ride home, but the weather was nice. Commuting by bike was one of the conditions her parents had made when they agreed to let her take the job. At first, Lucy was afraid they wouldn't at all.

"What about your sister?" her mother had asked, as if Lucy were abandoning Ella somehow.

"Mom, it's just a summer job. I need money. And besides, you guys let Ella work at my age." She felt bad the minute the words were out. Any mention of her sister was just another reminder of the uncertainty of Ella's future.

"We can't drive you back and forth every day if we're at the rehab center," her mother explained. "How will you get to work?"

"She's got her bike." Her father, who'd been sitting at the kitchen table without any sign of listening, sounded decided. "Besides, it will be good for her. To be busy."

Lucy had met his gaze across the table; all summer she had felt invisible, around him especially. Perhaps he wanted her out from underfoot. Or perhaps he, too, understood that she could not sit in this house every day, not with the slowly spinning clock or the deafening vacuum Ella had left.

"Alright," her mother relented, finally. "But you still have to see your sister, at least every other day."

Lucy agreed. She'd leave afternoons open three times a week. But she was unsure how to broach that subject with her new boss. Leah Powell was an enigma of sorts. Between a few breadcrumbs from Brad and an article in the local newspaper about the Sandy Page's grand opening, Lucy learned that Leah came from some big publishing gig in Boston. But it didn't make much sense. She was young and pretty and used to live in the city, so why was she back in boring Cape Cod? Sure, she'd had a vision of turning that place into what it was now, but it seemed like a small, lonely life compared to what she had left. Something bad must have happened. Lucy was dying to know what.

But Lucy had her own ghosts to contend with. She did not want to talk about Ella at work. That was what she liked best about the Sandy Page so far, besides the books, of course. As far as she was concerned, Leah was still a newcomer in town. And Brad was visiting his grandma for the summer. Which meant neither one of them had been in town during the accident. And neither seemed to know about it, at least not yet. For the first time in forever Lucy could sail in and out of a door just being Lucy. Without anyone asking how Ella was. Or how her parents were getting on. Or when Ella would come home.

All Leah and Brad wanted to know was what time she was coming in to work, and whether or not she'd pick a side in the coffee debate. It lent her a veil of anonymity Lucy did not have anywhere else in her life, and she planned to keep it that way. Here she could be a high school girl who rode her bike to work and liked to read fantasy books. Until Jep Parsons threatened to blow it all up by showing up like that at the store.

Lucy took the long way home, pedaling along Shore Road and through the back streets across town. It let her avoid the traffic on Main Street, but it was also for another reason. She wanted to ride down Crowell Road again. This time, alone.

It was six o'clock when she left the bookstore, an hour after the garage closed. As she biked closer, Lucy worried that maybe they'd stayed late. Maybe someone had come in last minute needing an oil change or a tire repair. But as she swung her bike into the lot, to her great relief Parsons's Garage was empty, the bays closed for the night and the office windows dark. There was no sign of anyone around.

Lucy dismounted her bike. Parsons's was a small family outfit with an office on one side and three mechanics bays on the other. Parked behind it was a neat row of vehicles waiting to be worked on. Aside from the occasional passing car, there was no sound but for the breeze rustling trees around back.

Warily she scanned the roofline of the building, wondering if they had security cameras. Not that Lucy was doing anything illegal. Well, trespassing after hours maybe. But she doubted anyone would blame her if she were caught doing what she came to do.

She was a little surprised to find Jep's Mustang right where it had been. It was out of line of sight, which she imagined they'd done on purpose for themselves as much as for the inquisitive gazes of customers, but she wondered why they hadn't brought it in for repair yet. Or towed it away to a body shop. From what Ella had shared during their late-night conversations, that vintage Mustang was Jep's pride and joy. He'd saved up his own money working for his dad for years, and together they'd found a junker that they could restore together. By the time he turned sixteen it was done: the body painted cherry red, its chrome polished to a high shine. It was the kind of car people took note of and remembered. Which was one of the reasons Ella took great pains not to be seen in it. Her parents would never have approved of her seeing Jep. Riding around town in his showy classic car was impossible.

But Lucy knew Ella had been in it. At night, they snuck out together. Once, Ella told her she convinced Jep to let her drive it. "You can't believe the sound it makes when you get it going!" she'd shared in urgent whispers, her eyes bright even in the darkness of their room at that late hour. "I love that car."

Lucy had wondered if she also meant she loved Jep.

Now, tucked among the shadows on the far side of the garage, Lucy lifted the front corner of the green tarp. The plastic crinkled and snapped audibly as she peeled it back and away, moving along the side of the car as she did. The red nose of the Mustang jutted through, crumpled and creased. Then the windshield. The sight of the windshield, fractured like crushed ice, stopped Lucy in her tracks. There in the center was a crater, the glass split around it like rays from a crystal sun, save for a red-brown stain at its core. Lucy heaved. Dropping the edge of the tarp, she spun away from the car, holding her stomach and lurching toward a nearby bush. Was it Ella's blood? Both of them had had head injuries, the police had told her parents. But it was only Jep who walked out of the ER the next morning.

Her chest heavy, Lucy bent over waiting for the sickness to rise up and out of her, but instead it settled. Eventually, so did her heart. She straightened, forehead still prickling with sweat. This was not a good idea. She shouldn't have come back without Reya. She shouldn't have come here at all.

Standing away from the car she saw the entirety of its damage for the first time. The front end was done for, pushed into the hood and engine well like a crushed metal box. The driver's door hung ajar, crooked on its hinges. Jep was drunk that night. How could he have driven her sister like that if he cared at all?

Lucy wanted to get out of there, but it was as if the car was calling her back. And even though it scared her just looking at it, Lucy felt compelled to look more closely. She went to the passenger side where Ella had been. The seat sparkled with glass. The floor was empty. Lucy crept around to the driver's seat, unsure what it was she hoped to find but determined to look. The driver's side had the most damage, to her surprise. Like the other side, the seat was covered in glass shards and debris. Lucy rested her hands on the door and peered down to the floor. There, among the glitter of windshield shards, something else sparkled. It was gold. Lucy pulled the open door farther ajar and it protested loudly. Glancing quickly around, she squeezed through the opening, straining to reach the floor mat. With one final heave her fingers reached the object, rescuing it from the glass. Lucy knew right away what it was: Ella's gold chain bracelet. The one her parents had given her for graduation. The dainty emerald birthstones glittered in her palm. She closed her fingers around them.

Standing beside the car, Ella's bracelet practically humming in her palm, Lucy pictured the wreck. Jep staggering out from behind the wheel, onto the roadside. Did he go back for Ella? Had he checked on her first? From what the cops said, both of them were out of the car by the time police arrived. Ella was lying on the grass, unconscious. Jep was holding her.

In his statement Jep swore she'd been awake after the accident. That she'd been hurt, but awake and conscious. He claimed that it was only after he helped her to the side of the road that her eyes fluttered, her head lolled, and she slipped away into unconsciousness. It was in the official accident report, which Lucy had snuck a look at when she'd slipped the folder from her father's desk one night.

Jep's story about that night was the only story they had.

There were no other witnesses, not even Ella, who remembered nothing or at least couldn't communicate it if she did. If there was a story to be told about what really happened that night, Jep Parsons was the sole writer. Jep held all the words in the palms of his hands, and so far he'd never broken from the page.

Luke

Since finishing work at the Sandy Page, he could not get Leah Powell off his mind. He may as well have been fourteen years old again. But he had real jobs to get back to. And as for Leah, he wanted a few days to think. It was hard to do that when he was around her.

It was no easy feat juggling the jobs at the bookstore along with his real jobs. Having finished the kitchen reno in Stage Harbor around the same time he became aware of the fact that Leah was back in town, Luke's next project in line was a custom walk-in closet for a couple on Ridgevale Road. He was still working on it. Though the scale was small, the details of the built-in units, doors, and drawers were intricate. The wife wanted the main wall of the closet to resemble an oversized antique hutch, with double doors. The husband, who Luke gathered would've been just as happy with a rod and metal hangers, was unyielding during their first consultation. "Don't they make some nice laminates these days that look like wood?" he'd asked. Since coming to Luke's workshop and seeing the choices of wood, hardware, and finishes, he'd come around. They settled on cherry wood in a dark Shiraz finish with bamboo-style bronze hardware in champagne. There would be no laminates or plywood in this design. The trouble was, Luke was a week behind on his projects. The day he agreed to work with Leah was the same day he was supposed to start the custom closet job.

Between the two, Luke quickly found himself working sixteen-hour days. Every spare hour found him running between the job at Ridgevale, his workshop, and Leah's shop. There had been no time for kayaking or running Scout along the beach. There was barely time to steal a few hours of sleep.

Somehow, he'd managed to get the bookstore ready in time for opening day. Leah had fretted and fussed about paying him, especially after she saw the sign he'd made her, but he knew things were tight. He also knew from running a small business that it would be a long time before any actual profit came in, but he didn't say so to her. Luckily for him the last few years had been good, and business was booming; as for Leah, they had history. She was good for the money. What mattered most was that the Sandy Page opened its doors, and the look on Leah's face when he surprised her with the sign was payment enough for now.

Working together the last ten days, there were so many things Luke wanted to ask her about. Instead they talked about her brother, James. About his parents, both of whom had relocated to Florida. And about Scout, who'd begun to grow on her. Somehow Luke hadn't realized that Leah was afraid of big dogs—it seemed so inconceivable that a laid-back guy like Scout, who loved everyone, could be seen as threatening. But that's exactly how she saw him.

At first she avoided Scout altogether, staying on the opposite side of the room. "Let me keep him in the truck," Luke offered, as soon as he realized.

"You can't. It's hot out."

"Then I'll take him back home," Luke insisted.

"There's no time. It's fine," she said, even though he could tell she didn't mean it.

"Lie down, buddy," Luke told him. Scout complied, settling quietly onto the rug near Luke.

By the end of the first day, Leah was no longer climbing over furniture to avoid the dog if he was in her path. Nor was she wincing when she held out her hand to give him a biscuit, at Luke's suggestion. Midweek, she was sharing the crusts of her sandwich with Scout at lunch when she thought Luke wasn't looking. When Scout didn't come after Luke called him one evening at quitting time, he found the dog curled up at Leah's feet at one end of the old Victorian couch. Both were sound asleep.

"Well, look at that," Brad mused, standing beside him in the office doorway. "I guess you really are a miracle worker."

There were so many things Luke wanted to know about Leah's life and why she had come back, but he got the sense that beneath the pluck and determination she demonstrated when it came to the bookshop, underneath it all she was fragile. He could see it in moments when she didn't think anyone was looking; the sag of her posture as she reviewed spreadsheets on her laptop at her makeshift desk in the old dining room. The faraway look she got in her eyes in quiet moments. It was in the tone of her voice at the end of the day, when they were still behind schedule (they were almost *always* behind schedule) and she looked about to cry—though she never did. At least not in front of him. Underneath her drive and determination and big ideas there was still the fleeting shadow of the teenage girl he'd spent years admiring from afar. And so he tread carefully. Luke did not ask if she was still engaged. Oh, he wondered. From the moment he heard she was back in town, he had a feeling something must have changed. Why else would she have left Boston where, James had told him, she'd had an important job in publishing, in addition to a fiancé. He hadn't talked to James in ages, and it would seem suspicious to call him up now. Eudora was the one who'd tipped him off about her shop. Later, Mike at the grocery mentioned that he heard Mr. Powell had taken the house off the summer rental market because his daughter had moved back. When those tidbits only scratched the surface of his curiosity, Luke looked online.

Sure enough, Leah's name came up a few times attached to the name of a debut author, Luna Hoya. He'd never heard the name but there were plenty of mentions from a few months ago. According to an article in the *Boston Globe*, Luna had penned one of the most anticipated books of the year. It was the story of her grandmother, who'd been abducted as a young woman by a Mexican cartel and forced into drug manufacturing. The premise was incredible and heartbreaking: the single mother had not only survived and managed to escape, but to connect with federal agents and work as an undercover operator, eventually negotiating her freedom to cross the border to safety with her children. The publishing world was abuzz with the book, especially as told by a third generation immigrant and the granddaughter of the protagonist. Foreign rights had been sold. Streaming networks were lined up to option it for television. Luna's advance was record-breaking, as was the expectation of publication day sales. Only there was one problem: the story was not hers.

It belonged to her longtime boyfriend. As a student, he'd drafted the story for a writing workshop class at NYU. When the two broke up Luna stole his pages and his idea, secretly submitting the work as her own. From what Luke could find in the press coverage, Leah was not only Luna's editor but also the one who discovered her. When the story blew up, so did Leah's career.

Luke was floored. He'd known the Powells his whole life. There was no way Leah would have knowingly been involved. He wondered about the legal fallout, and if she'd been tossed out with the bathwater in the company's rush to distance themselves from the scandal. He wondered if it was over, or if there were still repercussions. But instead of asking, Luke kept all of this to himself. Leah had been through a lot in the last three months. It was her business to share or not. In the meantime, he was glad to see her back home, trying to start over. She had guts, he'd give her that.

Leah's grit only added to his inability to get her off his mind. If he were honest, it was probably why he'd sent her that text offering to come by the shop to check the paint. It was laughable. That paint was long dried, and the shelves were filled with books. But when she said, *Yes,* it was the green light he needed.

Now, as he arrived at the bookstore, Luke actually felt nervous. He was grateful when he pushed the door open and found customers milling about. Leah was at the counter talking with someone. By the time she noticed him, he'd checked the paint that he already knew was fine.

"The place looks great," he told her. "And full of customers!"

She looked pleased and almost relaxed, two things he'd seen little evidence of leading up to the opening. "It's a shock how busy we are," she agreed happily. She jammed her hands in the pockets of her white summer dress and grinned. With the store open, gone were her raggedy denim shorts and faded T-shirts. Her blond hair flowed loosely about her shoulders, and he had to remind himself not to stare.

"That paint dried nicely," he said, quickly. "I didn't find any spots or smudges that need touching up."

She cocked her head coyly. "The paint is perfect. Though there is something else I may need your help with." So, he *was* still needed here. The initial thrill of her admission was accompanied by a rush of dread. Luke was still struggling to catch up on his other jobs.

"Lead the way," he said, anyway.

He followed her to the back of the store, through the dining room-office. It was now more organized, outfitted with a real desk, a filing cabinet, and the green Victorian couch he'd found her sleeping on that one time with Scout. "Do you need shelves in here, too?" he asked.

"This isn't the room I was thinking of," she said, continuing through a set of French doors. "This is."

Luke glanced around what must have been an old parlor room in the captain's house. The ceilings were high with formal dentil trim molding, as in the storefront, but the room was smaller and cozier. An exposed brick chimney ran up the center, typical of historic homes. "What's the plan for in here?" he asked warily.

"A knitting room."

"Knitting?"

"And crafts. And maybe also painting." She spun around, the edges of her white dress flowing alluringly. Luke kept his eyes on hers. "Ultimately, I'd like it to be a studio."

"For you?" he asked, confused.

"No, silly. For customers. We've got all this incredible space that I pay rent for. And the summer crowds will thin out soon. So I was thinking it would be great to turn this into a community gathering space and host some events that go year round. I think tourists and locals alike would come to a Paint and Sip."

Luke was not about to ask what a Paint and Sip was. He was already flummoxed. She'd barely been open a week, and she was already expanding. "Aren't you already working round the clock?"

"Yes, so I may as well offer things in these other rooms while I'm here. Build on the business."

Luke did not suggest that the business was too new to build on, that this would probably necessitate more management and therefore require more hires, which would, of course, affect her bottom line. It was not his business, figuratively or literally. But the thought of his unpaid bill did flash briefly in mind. "How soon are you thinking of doing all that?"

"Right away. It would only require some paint and cleanup, I think. Unless you find something wrong in here."

A brief inspection of the room found no other issues. "It looks sound for what you have in mind. Is that all you need my help with?"

"I have a huge oak dining table in my dad's basement. It was my grandfather's. It's solid and dented and dinged already, so it would be a great gathering space. I figure all I need is that and some chairs, for people to gather and create together."

Luke still couldn't tell what his part would be. "You want me to restore it?"

"No, I like it old. Shows character. As for you, I would love some kind of organizational cubbies for storing art supplies, baskets of wool, that sort of stuff. And maybe a rack to dry canvases on."

"Do you knit?" He was curious now where all this was coming from. "Or paint?"

"No." Leah shook her head, as though this was all beside the point. "But I know someone who does. She's in here all the time, but she seems lonely. You know her, too."

After a beat it hit him. "Eudora Shipman?" When she nodded, Luke laughed. "She agreed to help you open a knitting room?"

"It's not just for knitting. And no . . . not yet, anyway."

"There is no way," Luke said. "Eudora is a lovely person, but she will never do that. Not for you or for me."

Leah made a face like he'd spat in her food. "You're wrong. Remember how caring she was in high school? Everyone went to see her with their problems, even the kids who didn't have her as a counselor."

"Eudora has changed since then," Luke explained. Leah wasn't around when Eudora left the high school. She probably had no awareness of the news stories about the high school student who tried to kill herself because of bullying. Or Eudora's involvement in the trial thereafter. "She doesn't get out very much these days."

"What do you mean? She's been in here every day."

There was no way what Leah was saying could be true. "Are you sure you have the right person? You didn't recognize her at first, you told me yourself."

"Well, I do now. And she's here every day. With her little white dog, Alfred."

He couldn't believe it. Over the years he'd worked with her, Eudora never left her house except to walk her dog. It all became clear one day when he was at the Chatham Market. Luke had stopped in for a sandwich and got to chatting with the owner, Mike. When Mike asked if he was done for the day, Luke said not nearly—he was, in fact, headed to Eudora's house next. At which, Mike piped right up—said he was short-staffed and asked if Luke wouldn't mind dropping off a couple bags of her groceries. "She doesn't come in anymore." He confided that he still delivered groceries to Eudora each week, even though he'd ended the delivery service after Covid. "She's the only one I'd do it for," Mike said sadly. It dawned on Luke that Eudora must be suffering from some kind of agoraphobia or anxiety.

"I can't believe she's been coming here," he told Leah now. "Why?"

It wasn't his place to say. "She's kind of kept to herself since her husband died," he said. "And you're right. I do think she's lonely."

"So can you help with the studio space?" Leah asked. Her voice was hopeful in a way he found hard to turn down, just as the look on her face was.

If Leah's bookstore had gotten Eudora out of the house, he would not stand in the way. "I have to finish a closet job in Ridgevale, but I can swing by tomorrow to take measurements."

His breath caught in his chest when Leah threw her arms around his neck. It was the second time she'd hugged him, the first being the night he surprised her with the Sandy Page sign out front. The vanilla notes of her shampoo filled his nostrils, just as they had the last time.

Leah pulled away, turning her face up brightly to his. For a fleeting foolish second Luke wondered if they might kiss. But of course not. "You're the best," she said, holding out her hand instead.

Luke stared at the check she held out to him. "It's nowhere near all of it, but it's a start. The Realtor finally got through to Stefan, the owner. He agreed to cover the work on the steps and the overhang out front. As you predicted, the shelves are on me."

"I can't," he began, holding up his hands. "You just opened, and I know the expenses of a small business at the start."

But she insisted. "If you don't take it, no knitting room." He laughed at that.

"Not exactly a threat."

She shrugged. "Until you accept payment, I can't work with you. I'll have to hire someone else."

Luke did not say that that *was* a threat. Instead he thanked her and accepted the check. When their hands brushed, he tried not to let it get to him. But the whole ride home his fingertips tingled.

Leah

It wasn't a matter of if, so much as when Mrs. Shipman would show up. Despite a slew of book buyers and a fabulous story hour led by Lucy, who read aloud beautifully to the gaggle of children who came, Leah kept her gaze trained on the front door. She could feel it: Eudora Shipman would be there any minute and she would propose her idea.

Only, Eudora did not come.

Brad, who'd been wary of the knitting club idea, but leapt on board with the Paint and Sip, wasn't convinced they needed her. "She's a sweet old lady, sure. But I could run those programs."

"You knit?" Leah asked. It should not have surprised her; Brad was so good at so many things. But knitting seemed a stretch even for him.

"Not a stitch. But my grandmother, Maria, does. If you're determined to go through with this sewing club, I'll invite her."

"Knitting," she reminded him. "Along with other artsy things."

"Artsy things? Is that how you're going to advertise?"

Brad's skepticism aside, Leah was beginning to have doubts of her own. Perhaps it was a crazy idea to expand into the other rooms of the house. She'd only just opened. On the other hand, she was paying rent for the entire house. And she needed to find a way to keep foot traffic going all year, once the summer tourist rush disappeared at Labor Day. Besides, she was beginning to realize that the captain's house held meaning for so many different people.

There was an older gentleman she'd seen lurking about the front door the last few days. He wore a long sleeve flannel shirt, despite the warm weather, and pants held up by old-fashioned suspenders. Leah guessed he was around seventy-five, maybe eighty. Finally, he came in one day, carrying a large bag. He marched up to the counter and set it there.

"I brought vegetables," he said. Then, "My name is Willet Smith. I live a few houses back."

"Vegetables?" Brad asked, peering in the bag.

"From my garden. Brussels sprouts and tomatoes. Though tomatoes are technically fruit."

Unsure what to do, Brad called Leah. "He brought vegetables?"

Willet looked as grumpy up close as he had through the window, but there he was with an offering. "My father used to work here, when it was a general store."

"Your family has history here, too!" Leah exclaimed.

"I have so many vegetables in my garden, maybe you'd like to sell some. It's just me, now that my wife has died." His expression softened. "I can't possibly eat them all."

"We sell books," Brad said. "May I interest you in one? We have all kinds of new releases."

Leah elbowed him. "Thank you for the vegetables, Willet."

After that, Willet came in every few days. He had yet to buy a book, but Leah, Brad, and even Lucy went home with vegetables.

While most people came for the books (and some to snoop around and see what she'd done with the place), there were others who came in just to see the house and reminisce.

Whether it was dancing at the annual Christmas party held by the former innkeepers or coming for a twenty-five-cent ice cream when it was a general store, being inside the house conjured up memories. Take the customer who came in yesterday with an old photograph of a woman standing beside a painting. "This was taken in this very room," she told Leah. The woman's mother had been a well-known painter who showed her work there, back when the house served as a gallery. "My mother's artist friends from New York came up here each August for a painting retreat," she went on, eyes misting. "Each morning they rose early and traveled the Cape, from Monomoy Island to the wilds of Truro, chasing the summer light and scenery." It gave Leah joy picturing the visiting artists traversing the beaches with their easels.

The old house had been through so many iterations over the years. It made Leah want to harness those memories, to find a way to bring the public through its doors again. Maybe Brad was right. Maybe the captain's daughters who'd turned it into an inn were haunting her thoughts, along with the upstairs halls, compelling her to fill the rooms once more.

It wasn't just the house's history she felt speaking to her. Her customers were voicing requests, as well. Several shoppers had come in looking for knitting books, something she was sorry not to have on hand. That was the first rule of a small-town bookstore: know what your community wants. Quickly she'd ordered several. When she'd later spied the knitting needles poking out of Mrs. Shipman's bag, a seed took root. Her shop was being embraced by the community. Wouldn't it be nice to embrace them back?

The house must have been listening. Whenever Leah left the hum of activity in the front and wandered to the rear quarters, she could swear a sense of melancholy came over her. Back there the walls were stark, the chestnut floors bare. The vacant rooms echoed, practically pleading for the chatter and foot traffic the bustling storefront so enjoyed. Leah understood the hollowness the rooms felt; she'd felt that, too, coming home.

She began to look at the house with fresh eyes. There was the parlor room with a lovely but nonworking fireplace. Off of it was a spacious butler's pantry with an open window that looked into a kitchen, empty save for an old stove and a pump sink that conjured thoughts of *Little House on the Prairie*. Leah decided to start with the parlor. A crafting room would work perfectly; in there she could rotate different activities throughout the week.

That's where Mrs. Shipman and her knitting needles came in. Back in high school, Eudora Shipman was the adult kids turned to. The girl who got pregnant senior year spent a lot of time in her counseling office. As did the girl who got into an Ivy

League college. Eudora maintained an open door and a tray full of cookies. But there was something about Leah's reunion with her that went beyond those memories: a kinship of sorts, when it came to the shop. Mrs. Shipman came in each day and bought something every time, however small, though Leah suspected it was an excuse more than anything. Something about the shop resonated with Eudora beyond the books, beyond her obvious affection for and friendship with Luke. There was a story there, and Leah felt bound to ferret it out. But that day Eudora did not come in.

Happily, the other person Leah was expecting did show up. "Oh good, he's here," she said, spying Luke's truck pulling up. Scout was smiling out the open window.

"Back so soon?" Brad said. It wasn't a question. "Just like your friend, Mrs. Shipman, Luke seems *quite* at home here."

"He's here to do some touch-ups," Leah said, ignoring the smirk on his face.

Brad lowered his voice. "I don't think the house is the only thing he's interested in touching up."

"*Brad,*" she hissed, gesturing toward the customers. "And wipe that smirk off your face."

Unfazed, Brad plowed ahead. "Are you really going to deny it? I know you said the two of you went way back, but that guy is harboring a serious schoolboy crush."

Lucy joined them at the register. "Crush?" Quiet as she was, Lucy was still a teen with big ears. The bell jangled over the door as Luke came in. "Oh. Your miracle worker."

"Not you, too."

"You have to admit, he's textbook leading man material," Brad whispered. "And we are standing by the romance section."

This only delighted Lucy, who whisked a copy of Emily Henry's *Funny Story* from the display.

"You're both insufferable." Leah did not stick around to watch them fist-bump.

She had *never* thought of him like that, not then or now. And he'd certainly given her no sense of any lingering interest since he'd started working with her. But as she followed him back to the parlor room to take measurements, she couldn't deny the obvious. Perhaps he *was* textbook handsome, or whatever it was Brad had said.

When she closed the door behind the last customer, it was just after six o'clock. Besides Brad and Lucy, Luke was the only one still there. "Do you need me for anything else?" Lucy asked.

It was Friday night. Leah supposed she had friends and weekend plans waiting for her. "You came in early today," Leah said appreciatively. "Get out of here and go have some fun."

Clearly she'd misunderstood, because Lucy's expression fell. "There are still some boxes of new inventory I didn't unpack yet," Lucy said.

For some reason, Lucy did not want to go home. Leah made a mental note of it, but she could barely afford payroll as it was. Besides, she wanted to wrap up and go home. It had been an exhausting first week.

"Thanks, but we can tackle those tomorrow," Leah told her.

Leah watched her gather her things and head out. She was

growing fond of Lucy, and also a little concerned. It felt strange that she didn't know that much more about her now than she did the day she'd hired her. Unlike Brad, who was vocal about everything from admiring a pair of shoes a woman wore the other day to lamenting their favorite apricot chicken salad being taken off the menu at Chatham Perk, Lucy rarely spoke unless spoken to.

She found Brad and Luke in the parlor room, measuring the walls in preparation for new craft storage. "Brad, feel free to get out of here," she said.

Unlike Lucy, he looked delighted to hear this. "Good, I've got a date."

Luke glanced over his shoulder but kept working. Leah, however, was not going to pass this opportunity up, even with Luke standing there. "Really?" She sidled up closer to Brad. "Anyone I might know?"

"Remember the guy who came in the other day with the navy and red lobster sweater?"

Leah did remember. The man was probably in his thirties, preppy in that predictable Cape vacationer manner, and handsome. "Yes, you admired his sweater."

"I lied. It was hideous." Brad broke into a wistful smile. "But he wasn't."

"How did it turn into a date?"

"There was small talk about Ina Garten's new memoir. Which led to an inquiry about local restaurants. I recommended the Impudent Oyster. He asked if I would join him."

"Brad!" Leah punched him playfully in the arm. "Why didn't you tell me?"

"I'm telling you now. Anyway, I have to go home and get ready. We're meeting at eight."

Leah did not bring up his grandmother, and neither did Brad. Instead she said, "Have a great time on your date."

"*Hot* date," he said, as he hurried out, leaving her alone with Luke.

Leah wandered around the room as Luke finished his measurements, picturing how she'd arrange the space. Outside the windows, the light was shifting from gold to pink.

"So, no hot date for *you* tonight?" The words flew out of her mouth before she could stop herself. "I'm just joking," she rushed to add.

Luke looked up from where he was kneeling on the floor marking points along the wall with a pencil, then back down at his work. "No." Then, "That would be tomorrow night."

"Oh." So the joke was on her. "Well." She would not ask with whom. Or where. Neither was any of her business. But suddenly she was dying to know both.

Luke stood, tucking the pencil behind his ear. "I'm joking, too," he said. The relief that flooded through her was mortifying. "How about you?"

Every time she made eye contact with him it felt he could see straight into her thoughts. She felt a blush start to creep up her neck and willed it away from her cheeks. "What about me?"

"You've grilled Brad. You've practically harassed me. I think it's only fair that I get a turn." There was a mischievous twinkle in his eyes.

She narrowed her eyes. "First of all, *harass* is a strong word. And no. No date tonight for me, either." Despite their playful banter, the admission swung her thoughts sharply back to Boston, to things she'd been trying hard not to think about. An image of Greg getting dressed for a nice dinner downtown, just like they did most Fridays, flashed in her mind. She wondered if he was taking Rebekah out. She wondered if they'd come home and fall into bed after. Leah turned to the window, trying to rid herself of them.

Luke must have sensed it. "Tell you what. Since neither of us has a hot date, there's a spot I'd like to take you."

"Now? Where?" She followed him out to the front of the store.

"No questions," he said, without turning around.

"Wait." Leah halted. "Do I need to change? Maybe I should run home real quick . . . "

But he was already out the door. "I'll wait for you in the truck," he called back.

They stopped at liquor store. "*This* is what you wanted to show me?"

"Nope." Scout was perched on the bench of the front seat of the truck, panting between them. Leah tried to peer around the dog to catch Luke's expression. "Back in a minute."

The next stop was Chatham Pier. It was an especially popular spot for tourists who liked to climb the upper decks to watch the seals diving and surfacing playfully about the fishing boats, before stopping in the small, shingled shed that served as a fresh seafood shop. "You're a Cape girl. Still like lobster rolls?"

Leah nodded. "But you'll never get a parking spot at this hour on a Friday night," she told him. "See? Look how full the lot is. And the pier workers don't let people drive down here anymore . . ."

Luke ignored her warnings, navigating the crowds of people and continuing on to the pier's bottom lot. One of the workers flagged them down and approached.

"He's going to ask us to leave," Leah said.

Instead the guy pointed to a reserved spot. "Hey, Luke. You can park right there."

Leah bit her lip and decided to shut up.

"Buttered or chilled?" Luke asked, not bothering to hide his smile.

"Buttered."

Ten minutes later, they pulled into the far lot on Harding's Beach. "Wait there," Luke said, coming around to the passenger side. When he swung the truck door open Scout leapt over her.

"Are you holding the door for him or me?" she asked.

"Sorry about that. He loves the beach." Luke held out his hand and helped her step down. "For what it's worth, it was for you." He went around the back and lowered the tailgate. "And so is this."

He grabbed the takeout bag from Chatham Pier Fish Market and handed her a lobster roll. Then he slid a cooler in her direction and opened the lid. "I figured you probably outgrew the wine coolers you used to hide under your bed in high school, but I wasn't sure what you liked now."

She gasped. "You used to look under my bed?"

"James did. I just helped him drink the wine coolers."

"Thieves."

"You probably should've thought of a better hiding place."

He swung the cooler around so she could peer inside. Tucked in ice was a six-pack of Corona, White Claws, and a bottle of rosé. She was touched by the selections. "What are you having?"

"Whatever you are," he said.

She grabbed the six-pack. Together they hiked across the beach, past the lifeguard chairs, and up into the dunes. Gulls cried overhead. Up there, nestled in a hollow between strands of dune grass, they settled into a secluded spot.

Luke laid out a beach towel and cracked open a Corona and passed it to her.

"Do you always drive around with a cooler in the truck?"

"No," he said, laughing. "But I like to bring Scout down here to run along the beach at the end of a long day. Sometimes I run with him. Sometimes I bring my dinner up here and take in the view. It's a good place to think."

"I'll say." She did not add that this was the first spot she came to when she returned. Nor that this was the place where she went when her mother died. Instead she stared out at the ocean. The tide was making its way in, the waves lapping gently at the shoreline. To their right the sun had slipped low on the horizon, glazing the sky with streaks of gold. For a while they ate their lobster rolls in silence, watching Scout zip up and down the sand. "So this is your regular Friday night in summer?" she asked.

He swallowed a bite of his lobster roll and turned to look at her. "Summer is my busy season. I don't have much personal time."

"I don't know what I'd be doing if not for the shop. Besides that, all I have is time."

She could feel Luke studying her, as well as the questions that hovered in the air between them. To his credit he let her be, and they sat that way a long time finishing their rolls and beers, and looking out at the sea.

"Are you going to the high school reunion next week?"

"What? I didn't even know there was one." Leah had never been to a reunion. She couldn't imagine she'd want to see anyone who was still in the area.

"They do a general reunion every five years for anyone who wants to come back for it."

"So you've been before?"

"To a couple. It's nice to catch up with people. Hear about what they're up to these days. Meet their spouses, hear about their kids."

"Sounds dreadful. As someone with no spouse or kid to speak of," she added. She did not also say someone whose life has recently blown up and definitely does not want to talk about it to people she hadn't seen in seventeen years.

"It could be fun." He looked at her. "Want to go?"

"With you?"

He shrugged casually. "With or without me," he said. "It might be nice for you to get out of the shop, talk to old friends."

The old friends part was a stretch, as she didn't keep in touch with anyone from home anymore, but he wasn't wrong about taking a break from the shop. She'd done nothing except work herself to the bone that summer. Maybe it was the beer softening the edges of her usual defenses or maybe it was sitting up there in the dunes. Maybe it was Luke Nickerson. "Okay," she said, surprising herself.

"Okay?" He seemed just as stunned. "No argument? No comment on how provincial it will be?"

"I'll go," she said, ignoring his teasing. "With you." She reached for another bottle and handed him one, too. The beer was cold and crisp on her tongue, and she savored it. "Despite Sam Adams and all, I never drink beer when I go out in Boston," she admitted. "I can't remember the last time I had one. Probably here."

"Cocktails more your thing?"

"Dirty martinis. Dry, three olives. That was my fiancé, Greg's thing. Somewhere along the way I guess it became mine, too."

"You know you can get those on the Cape," Luke said.

She laughed. "The thing is, I don't miss them. In fact, I'm not sure I even liked them all that much."

"So the martini *was* Greg's thing?" She knew what he was asking.

"Was," she confirmed. "Just as Greg *was* my fiancé. Not sure if you knew, but we broke off our engagement."

"I did not know. But I did wonder."

So he had thought about her status. "Now that I'm back, I'm beginning to think Greg and I didn't make a whole lot of sense. But it was still a shock how quickly things fell apart."

"I'm sorry to hear that," Luke said. "Endings are always hard."

"You know, you make all these plans. And you just keep going, doing your thing, assuming it will all work out accordingly—until life throws something at you. That's the real test. How you handle the stuff life throws at you." She was rambling, she knew, but she didn't care. The cat was out of the bag. There was no getting it back in.

"I'm not sure, but I think he may be seeing someone already. Someone from his past. So that's a kick in the ass. But other than that, I think I miss the idea of our future more than the future itself."

Leah squeezed the cold bottle hard in her hands. She wished they hadn't strayed into this territory. But then Luke did something she didn't know she needed; he rested a hand on her back. The breadth of his palm was steadying and warm. She could feel the heat of it through the thin cotton of her shirt and instantly she felt herself exhale.

"It's a lot to let go of," Luke said, gently. "Is that why you came home?"

She took a long swig of her beer. "That's just the beginning. I won't bore you with the rest of it."

"You've yet to say anything that I find boring."

And so she told him. About her old job at Morgan Press, and her debut author, Luna, who she was so excited about. About the morning the story broke that someone had done some digging: Luna's story was not true. At least, not truly hers. The news hit the stands before it hit Morgan, and the rush to put out the fires was fast and furious. In the end Leah's job went out with the flames. All the while, Luke listened quietly.

"I think what you're doing is bold," he said when she was done. "It takes guts to come back home and start over."

"Thank you." Tears pressed at the corners of her eyes. It was the nicest thing anyone had said to her since she'd left Boston.

"This is a pretty healing place." He nodded to the beach below. An older couple was walking the shoreline hand in hand. A couple of teens threw a Frisbee. Farther down a few sunset seekers were already setting up their beach chairs facing west. "I wasn't engaged or anything like you, but I did come out of a relationship about a year ago. It's hard starting over."

Leah pulled her knees against her chest, and rested her cheek on them, staring at him. Luke had such a strong profile, she hadn't noticed before. "Have you started over?" she asked. He hadn't mentioned anyone. And he was here up in the dunes, with her, on a Friday night. But suddenly she had doubts. Maybe there was someone waiting for him back at home.

When he turned to her, his blue eyes were flecked with green, not unlike the ocean in the late day sun. "No," he said. "Not yet."

Up in the dunes there was no other sound but the waves below and the call of shorebirds. Leah swallowed hard, her eyes traveling across Luke's face. So familiar, and yet so new to her now.

And just like that Luke leaned in. Without thinking, Leah found herself leaning in, too. A sudden thundering sound erupted and from out of nowhere Scout was upon them. The dog zoomed about, stopping only to shake, spraying them both in sand and salt water.

"Scout, no!" Luke cried. Laughing he held Scout off with one hand, leaning across Leah to shield her from the spray with the other. Together they tumbled back onto the sand as the dog happily raced off. The dunes went still. When Leah opened her eyes, she was looking up into Luke's. There was nothing except the sand beneath her, the sky overhead, and Luke Nickerson in between. When he lowered his mouth to hers, Leah closed her eyes.

Luke kissed her once, his lips like a summer plum, plush against her own.

And then he pulled away. "Leah, is this . . ."

"Yes." She reached for him, pulling him back to her, her mouth searching for his. Luke tasted like cold beer and salt. Like a summer day. And all she wanted was to get lost in him. Luke Nickerson's arms were strong as they encircled her waist, and she rolled over in the sand with him until she lay on top of his chest. Feverishly they kissed, pressed together in the shallow of the dunes where no one could see. Leah did not care if they did. She kissed him until she couldn't breathe, until her head rushed with dizziness.

And then the thoughts came, tumbling like a landslide into her mind. Brad's words: *schoolboy crush*. The shop. Boston. Greg . . .

Leah reeled back. The waves were still rolling, the gulls still crying. She looked around trying to get her bearings.

"Leah?" Luke hoisted himself up on his elbows. "Are you alright?"

"I'm sorry." She brought her hand to her lips, raw from the kissing. "I'm sorry, Luke, but I can't." What was she doing? Now Luke would have the wrong idea. She should never have come.

Hurriedly she began packing up, gathering the beer bottles that clinked alarmingly in her rush.

"Leah, slow down." Luke hopped to his feet, scooping up the empty bottles and the wrappers from their lobster rolls. Their hands brushed against each other as they reached for the six-pack at the same time, and Luke gripped hers in his own. "Please. Look at me."

Heart in her throat, she tried. But she could not. Instead her eyes slid to his and away, so he wouldn't see her embarrassment. "I should go home."

There was no hiding the confusion in his expression, but he didn't press her. "I'll take you."

The whole ride home Leah stared out the window. Scout, still damp from the beach, perched between them, his sandy paws rough against her thigh each time he shifted, but Leah barely noticed. She'd made a huge mistake. Worse, she'd given someone who'd been nothing but good to her the wrong idea. Never before had Leah rushed into things. Since leaving Boston it was all she seemed to do: running home, opening the shop, and now this. Brad was right: Luke still harbored strong feelings for her. Besides Luke she didn't have any real friends here. Her mother had died, her father had moved. Her engagement was off, and her job had been lost. It was one thing to get swept away with a cute guy on a summer night. It was another thing to give the one person whose friendship she relied on so much false hope.

When Luke pulled up outside the shop, she pushed the door open before he had a chance to come to a full stop. "Leah, please wait."

Hand still on the door handle, she stayed in the truck. She owed him this much.

"Is it something I did?" His expression was full of hurt, which only made her feel worse.

"No. You were . . . wonderful." She paused, unsure how to make him understand. "This is not about you."

Luke didn't say anything.

"It's just . . . too much. Too soon."

He turned to her, stricken. "Leah, that's not why I brought you there."

"I know that," she told him. Luke had been nothing but a gentleman. "I'm the one who should be sorry if I gave you the wrong idea. You've been nothing but a good friend."

She could see how the word hit him right in the middle, but it needed to be said. Despite his sweet gestures and good looks and the million little things Luke Nickerson had done right since the day he walked through her shop door, Leah needed to remind them both of the friendship. Because the truth was she'd felt something on the beach tonight that she'd not felt in a really long time. Maybe not ever. And it scared her to death.

Luke was looking at her the same way he had after they'd stopped kissing, like he didn't understand how they got here. How badly she wanted to tell him she didn't, either.

"Good night, Leah."

When his truck pulled away, Leah did not watch him go.

Instead she looked up at the handmade sign hanging over her shop's door. At the steps he'd shorn up. His hands were all over her new start. Luke Nickerson probably didn't understand what happened tonight; she didn't expect him to. She needed his help with the old house. But shoring up her life was on her. And it was something she needed to do on her own.

Lucy

She didn't tell her parents about the gold bracelet she'd found under the seat of Jep Parsons's car. She didn't dare. Instead, she tucked it into the back of her sister's jewelry box, hoping no one would realize Ella had been wearing it the night of the accident. It was bad enough sneaking onto the garage lot and removing the tarp from the Mustang. Her parents were already under so much pressure. Even with Ella making slow progress, things were not improving at home. If anything, they were getting worse. With Ella finally out of the woods, awake and alert, it was like they could shift their anger from fighting for her to fighting who did this to her.

When Lucy got home from the bookstore, there was a strange car in her driveway. She propped her bike up against the garage and walked around the sleek black Mercedes. Inside, her parents were seated on the living room sofa and two people Lucy did not recognize sat across from them in armchairs. The man, dressed in a navy suit, looked up when she came in the door. "Oh, hello. You must be Lucy."

The young woman taking notes on a steno pad beside him glanced up, too.

"Lucy," her mother said, "this is Mr. Jeffries and his partner, Ms. Williams." As if that explained everything. "Would you like a snack?"

She followed her mother into the kitchen, watching as she pulled crackers from the cupboard and a block of sliced cheese from the fridge like it was any other afternoon.

"What's going on in there?" Lucy asked, nodding toward the living room.

Her mother didn't seem to hear. "Oh no. I meant to offer them coffee." She set the box of crackers down and hurried over to the coffee machine. "I should probably do decaf at this hour."

"Mom, who *are* those people?"

Her mother looked at her like she'd forgotten Lucy was there. "Honey, go ahead and make yourself a bite. We won't be much longer, and then I'll start dinner." Then she disappeared into the living room to inquire who wanted coffee.

Lucy took her plate, taking the steps purposefully slow so she could listen in.

The woman was talking about the accident. "So, according to the police report Ella did have a concentration of alcohol that exceeded the legal limit. But that doesn't matter to us in this context, because the defendant was driving."

It mattered to her parents. "Ella should never have been drinking. And she should never have gotten in the car with that fool." Lucy's father threw up his hands, his voice rising with them.

When she reached the top of the stairs and was safely out of view, Lucy lowered herself onto the top step as quietly as possible. From there she could still see the backs of her parents' heads sitting on the couch.

"Unfortunately, these things sometimes happen with teens, Mr. Hart," the man said. "In this case, Ella is the victim. Our job, as her lawyers, is to protect her from further damages." He cleared his throat. "We have two options here. His insurance policy will kick in, of course. But we can also go after the family."

"You mean sue the Parsons family?" her mother asked, sounding alarmed.

"In some cases, yes, people do go after the family."

"Still, it seems cruel, doesn't it? His parents didn't throw the party. They didn't provide the alcohol. It was a bunch of kids drinking at a beach party."

The woman, Ms. Williams, piped up. "I know it's hard not to think of this personally, especially when it involves another family here in town, but it isn't personal, Mrs. Hart. It's a matter of compensation for damages incurred. It's a way to make sure Ella is taken care of."

"Let's also remember, Jep Parsons is eighteen years old. He's no longer a minor."

"What does that have to do with it?" her father asked.

"I'm saying you can file a civil suit without going after his parents."

"He's just a kid. What does he have, besides a totaled car?"

"A whole lot, as it turns out," Williams said.

Jeffries passed her parents a piece of paper. "Jep Parsons has a fifty percent stake in the family business. He has the financial resources."

For a wordless beat her parents turned to each other. "I didn't know he owned part of his father's business," her father said finally.

"Fifty percent. So he does have means."

Lucy sucked in her breath. It was just as Ella had told her. And Jep could lose it all.

"I don't know," her mother said, voice wavering.

"Let me reassure you both, civil suits of this nature are not uncommon in a situation like yours. Ella has suffered severe injuries. There is no way to know for sure how this accident will impact her long term, or what kind of care she may need in the future. You want to be prepared."

"And," Williams went on, "there are the emotional damages to consider. For Ella. For all of you."

"Us? We don't need anything from that family," Lucy's father interjected. "My only interest is for my daughter."

"I understand, but let's examine the emotional suffering already established. Ella was an exceptional student you say."

Even from where she sat on the stairs, Lucy could see her father's posture change. "She was valedictorian."

"Exactly," Williams said. "Ella was supposed to start Tufts University this fall."

Was. The living room went silent as the words hung thick in the air.

"You shared with us that you had to defer her acceptance, correct?"

Lucy's mother sniffed and nodded.

"So we don't know when Ella will go to Tufts. Or even if."

Lucy rested her head against the wall and closed her eyes. They'd not told Ella. Even though Lucy feared she already knew, no one had said the words out loud since the day her father made the difficult call to the school's registrar. They didn't dare.

"None of us knows what the future holds," Williams explained. Her voice was hushed and soft, the way Lucy imagined her own heart beat in its rib cage. "That's why we try to protect our clients by collecting damages. So they may have some alleviation through compensation."

Despite their deferment call to the office of the registrar, each day it seemed some new correspondence arrived from Tufts in the mail. Welcome postcards. Orientation details. All while Ella lay in a hospital bed three towns away. What if Tufts wouldn't hold her place? What if she never recovered enough to attend any college anywhere?

Lucy hadn't realized she was gripping the plate so hard until it slipped from her hands. Down the stairs it tumbled like a rolling disc, the crackers and squares of cheese flying like projectiles. It landed in two distinct pieces on the landing with a clatter. Lucy's parents leapt up from the couch.

"Lucy?" her mother cried, hurrying over. "Are you alright?"

Her father surveyed the mess on the landing and turned back to the attorneys. His resolve was unwavering. "Go after him," he said. "Go after his insurance. His business. Whatever you can get your hands on. I want this kid to pay."

When Lucy arrived at the Sandy Page the next morning, she felt drained. All night her thoughts had returned to the conversation between the attorneys and her parents.

A dull ache already spreading across her forehead, she walked into work thinking of her bed at home, wondering how she would keep it all inside for another day. She was met by the scent of freshly brewed vanilla coffee (Brad's doing). Soft piano music emanated from a few carefully placed speakers (also Brad). At that hour, the morning light coming off the harbor was gauzy. It was an instant balm to her rawness, and Lucy realized she didn't want to be anywhere else.

"Good morning!" Leah chirped from behind the register. Lucy was still trying to figure Leah out; that day she was dressed in white linen pants and sandals with a sleeveless coral top, her hair swept up in a simple clip, managing to look beachy but somehow still elegant. Leah was a type-A boss lady in the flesh, and Lucy thought that was pretty cool. But Lucy could tell that beneath all that Leah had her anxieties. About the shop displays. About the coffee Brad picked. About the customers coming in and the ways they could better serve them. Even with her warm smile and bright demeanor, there was a hint of unsettledness about Leah that others probably didn't see. But Lucy did. Lucy understood anxiety; she wore it to work each day, like a shadow tracing her silhouette. So it was oddly comforting to be around someone who seemed to worry like she did but somehow kept it under wraps. Maybe there was hope for her.

"Luce, c'mere." Leah was also the only person who'd ever called her that, but Lucy didn't mind. "What do you think of the flyers I made for our teddy bear tea party?"

It would be the Sandy Page's first official children's event. Already they'd selected two picture books to be read aloud and discussed setup. The children would arrive dressed for tea, with a stuffed animal of their choice. (All are welcome here!) Lemonade would be served with cookies. Lucy had been shocked when Leah asked her to run the show. It felt like a pretty big deal.

Lucy examined the flyer and her excitement flagged. There were multiple fonts. Garish colors. Weird-looking bears. Had her boss been drunk? "It's . . . cute."

"You hate it."

"It's nice, it's just . . . " Where to begin?

Brad appeared. He had a radar for dramatic tensions. "Ugly," he said decidedly.

"What's wrong with it?" Leah gasped. "I spent all night working on this."

"That was your first mistake," Brad said. "I will never understand why you insist on bringing in sticky children and serving sticky sweets around all your crisp, clean books."

Lucy tried to hide her smile.

"It's part of our community outreach," Leah reminded him. "And it draws business."

"Well, please don't make it my business," he said, before making his escape. "You can make me stock shelves and clean out vermin, but I draw the line at kids."

Lucy took the flyer gently from Leah's grip.

"Maybe it needs to be simpler. And less colorful," she suggested softly. The flyer looked more like a haunted carnival than a kiddie tea party.

"Here." Leah surrendered the rest of the flyers. "I trust you. Can you make a new one by the end of today? I want to hang it in the shop window and outside."

Lucy nodded. She could have it done in fifteen minutes. Leah set her up in the dining room—office at her laptop and left her to it. It felt important to be sitting in her boss's leather chair at her desk, but also a little strange. Each time the chandelier flickered overhead Lucy swung her gaze up. Brad swore it was the captain's daughters. Lucy was pretty sure it was just the old house, but she said a silent prayer just in case. She was printing out the new sample when her boss showed up in the doorway. "Luce, someone is asking for you out front."

"For me?" A short distance behind Leah stood a teenage boy. Right away Lucy recognized the lanky figure of Jep Parsons. He stared back at her from beneath the hood of his sweatshirt.

Lucy froze. There was no way she could tell Leah who he was, because that would mean explaining things. Things she desperately needed to keep separate from the Sandy Page. But she also couldn't escape.

Leah remained in the doorway, looking at her oddly. "Everything okay?"

Lucy swallowed hard. "Yes," she lied. "Here, I just finished this."

Before she could change her mind she handed Leah the new flyer and ducked past her. She strode through the storefront, right past Jep Parsons who followed swiftly after her. Once safely outside, Lucy tugged the shop door closed behind them and spun around to face him on the sidewalk.

"What do you want?" she almost shouted. "Why do you keep coming here?" The boldness in her voice was a surprise even to her.

Jep's brown eyes widened. "Lucy, I'm sorry. But I have to talk to you."

"Well, I can't talk to you!" Warnings flashed in her mind: her father's fist on the kitchen table the night before; the confrontation in the hospital hallway; the lawyers in their dark suits in her living room. And Ella, lying in the hospital bed. All because of Jep Parsons.

"This is my job. You have to stop coming here!"

"But there's something I have to tell you." Despite his obvious distress, Jep Parsons was even better looking up close. His dark hair flopped over his brow in a boyish way that made Lucy almost feel sorry for him. But she couldn't allow that. Not for a second.

"I'm going back to work," she said, spinning away from him. She was done. But Jep wasn't.

"Please. I have to give you something." He reached for hand, and Lucy jerked back. Desperate, he grabbed the hem of her sweatshirt.

"Don't touch me!" she cried, tugging her sweatshirt out of his grasp and breaking into a run. She sprinted around the side of the house and pushed through the side door to Leah's office, slamming it closed behind her.

How dare Jep Parsons try to grab her? What did he think he was going to do? Heart pounding in her throat, Lucy leaned against the door, willing it to slow. She didn't want anyone at work to see her like this. But she had to tell someone.

Ella. When life was recognizable, Ella was the person that Lucy would share something like this with. Only she couldn't. Not anymore

Not her parents, either. Now Reya was the one person who she could turn to. If only she could leave work and tell her.

Should she tell Leah? Her boss seemed so open, so cool; Lucy had witnessed plenty of Leah's own personal moments opening the store. But this was her store, and she wouldn't want any drama going on here. Plus, she was still a grown-up. And grown-ups told other grown-ups when things went down, like Lucy's parents.

At that moment, Leah strode across the store toward her.

Lucy straightened, swiping the hair out of her face and trying to look normal. Had Leah seen what just happened outside?

She held the flyer aloft between them. "This is fantastic!"

"Oh, good," Lucy managed, her whole body flooding with relief.

Leah was beaming at her. "You are so creative, Lucy Hart. I'm going to print these out and hang them up."

Before Lucy could reply, Leah closed the distance between them, pulling her in for a quick tight hug. "Thank you so much. I don't know what I'd do without you."

In Leah's embrace Lucy felt something give. "You're welcome," she managed, choking back a sob. When what she really wanted to say to Leah was, Thank *you.*

She'd arranged to leave work early, telling Leah that she had an appointment. To her relief, Leah did not ask any questions. Except for one.

"Not my business, Luce, but I must say that boy who came in earlier was pretty cute."

"He didn't buy anything," Brad added tersely. "He's been here three times. Clearly not for the books." He leveled Lucy with a teasing expression.

"Three times?" Lucy stammered. She was only aware of two.

Brad leaned across the checkout counter dramatically, resting his chin in his palms. "What Leah is too polite to ask is: Is that your boyfriend?"

"What? No!" Lucy felt herself blanche.

"Brad, someone needs help in the self-help," Leah said in her most businesslike tone, pointing to an older man waving from that section.

"Geesh. Just making small-talk," Brad said.

"Ignore him," Leah told her with a wink. "We'll see you tomorrow."

"I'm sorry," Lucy said quickly. She couldn't leave just yet, not without some understanding from Leah. "That boy, I'm not sure why he's here. I've asked him to stop coming." But instead of reassuring her boss, this seemed to make Leah's suspicions plume.

"Lucy, is he making you feel uncomfortable? Because if he's bothering you in any way, I hope you know you can tell me."

God, she'd made it worse, not better. "No, no, I know him. He's just some kid from school. That my sister knows," she rushed to add.

"Your sister. The one who's away?" Leah wasn't prying. It was just a question. But it was the one Lucy had been dreading.

"Yes," she said, ducking her chin. "I've got to run. See you tomorrow."

An hour later, at Spaulding, Lucy couldn't stop thinking back to how badly she'd fumbled it all. Ella was sleeping, and their parents were down in the cafeteria getting coffee. That's all they did here—sit by Ella or get coffee.

The speech therapist had been working with her when they arrived. "She's going to be tired today," she'd said in hushed tone, "so she may not be up for much more. But I have incredible news: Ella is articulating."

Until now, Ella had only made noises and grunts, largely undiscernible. It was maddening to Lucy at times, but it was a small flame in a dark room—there was some measure of Ella coming back.

For the last few days Lucy had watched her parents sit vigil, settling in like sentinels by her sister's bed. Lucy had taken the seat by her feet. Every now and then she lifted the edges of the blanket and tickled Ella's feet—it was something her sister had always done, swinging her feet across Lucy's lap anytime they sat on the couch or lay in bed to watch a show. It brought Lucy comfort to do it now. Each time she ran her finger across her sister's socked foot, Ella's focus would swing sharply to her. A small sound like a baby's laugh would gurgle from her throat. It was the only time Lucy felt like the four of them returned to their old selves.

Now, with Ella's eyes fluttering to wakefulness and her parents out of the room, Lucy panicked. The therapist said she was articulating. What should she say? Did Ella need her to say something first so she could try to respond?

"How are you feeling today?" she asked.

Ella lifted one shoulder but made no sound.

"The nurse said you're doing really great," Lucy told her. "Really great." But the forced positivity sounded flat, even to her. "I know it sucks being here. We can't wait to bring you home."

In the silence that followed Lucy felt her tongue go dry, her mouth like a corn husk. What was wrong with her? This was Ella. She'd never been shy around Ella.

Unable to think of what to say, she retrieved *Anne of Green Gables* from her backpack. Ella stared out the window as Lucy started to read aloud. She was on her second paragraph when Ella made a sound. Lucy looked up. Hand trembling with effort, she reached across the bed sheets and knocked the book from Lucy's grip.

Lucy laughed. It was the most physicality she'd seen from Ella yet. "No reading today?"

Ella blinked twice, shaking her head ever so slightly.

"Would you like to hear about the shop?" Lucy asked.

Again, the smallest noise came from her throat. Heartened, Lucy went on. "You would love it, Ella. It's not just books—it's seashells in the window and twinkle lights strung from the ceiling. There's a children's corner and a huge YA shelf and gifts and a coffee corner. I can't wait to show you."

Ella was listening, intently.

"My new boss, Leah, she wants me to run a story time tea party for the little kids this week. I made a flyer for it. Want to see it?"

Lucy reached around her back pocket for a copy of the flyer. She'd folded one of the printouts and taken it to show her parents. The bookstore was the only safe subject any of them could agree on these days. But her pocket was empty.

She stood, feeling the other back pocket, which was empty, too. Where had it gone? Lucy patted the front pocket of her sweatshirt, and to her surprise there was a crinkle of paper. She reached inside and withdrew a folded piece of paper. Only it wasn't her flyer.

The paper was lined. And folded tightly into a small rectangle, like a note you'd slip a friend in class. Lucy sucked in her breath, remembering. Jep Parsons had tried to grab her sweatshirt before she ran away. He wasn't trying to grab her arm after all. He was giving her something.

In blue pen a name was scrawled across the note. Only it wasn't hers. It read: *Ella*.

When she looked up Ella was watching her. Lucy closed her hand around the note. "I've got to run to the bathroom."

Safe inside the stall, Lucy stared at the note. It wasn't hers to read. But it was her job to protect Ella. She couldn't share it with her without knowing what it said. There was no other choice. She opened the note.

The handwriting was surprisingly neat. He'd only written two lines.

I love you, Ella.

P.S. Please don't tell

Lucy stared at the writing. *Tell what?*

They already knew he'd been driving drunk. The police toxicology report said so. He'd driven off the road and slammed into a telephone pole. Everyone knew what happened that night. Everyone knew it was Jep's fault.

A plume of fresh rage puffed in her chest. How dare Jep ask any favors of her sister! Especially after what he did. Ella was here in a rehab hospital while Jep was out there living his life. Bothering her family. Showing up at the bookshop. And now—in her condition—he had the nerve to ask Ella to cover for him.

Lucy shoved the note back in her pocket. She would not show the note to Ella. Not now, not ever.

Eudora

It had been a terrible couple of days, especially after she'd been doing so well. Not only had she made it to the bookshop, but she'd gone inside. And talked to Leah. And, miracle of miracles, she had actually felt at peace being there. The first visit was a challenge, but as soon as she was back home tucked into her living room with a glass of iced tea and Alfred and her knitting needles, Eudora's thoughts kept returning to the cheerful space she'd just left. To Leah Powell's nice conversation with her. Even the mention of her guidance counseling days had not set off her anxiety and sent her into a tailspin as it did other times. That night when she talked to her daughter, Caroline, on the phone, she'd told her, "Guess what? I connected with an old student today. And I'm going to see her again."

Caroline had sounded so relieved, it made Eudora realize how much her daughter must worry. The last thing she wanted was to be a burden. Caroline already had her hands full with her kids, Edward and Macy, and her job and her home. Eudora was her mother—not the other way around. That was the problem with her anxiety; it robbed the ones she loved, not just herself.

When she had her next session with Maeve, the following day, Eudora did not request a telehealth appointment. Instead, she left the house early and showed up in person. Sure, she'd had some moments of panic on the drive over, especially as she drew farther and farther from her home. But she employed some of the calming measures Maeve had taught her, and sank into Maeve's comfy armchair right on time, if a bit rattled.

The next day Eudora went back to the shop. And the next day, too. She felt a little silly, all those repeated visits. The staff didn't seem to mind at all though. Brad and Lucy and Leah—they were all so nice. On the fourth day, Leah asked her advice. "I noticed knitting needs sticking out of your bag," she said. "So I'm guessing you knit. I could really use your help with pattern books, if you don't mind."

Eudora had been thrilled to offer her assistance. She'd even been invited into Leah's back office, which was just the coziest little room with a sparkling chandelier and the old damask pattern wallpaper. Eudora's heart caught in her throat. She and Milton had dined in that very room with that very wallpaper at the inn's little restaurant. On a crisp autumn evening when the tourists had gone and the menu bowed to hearty French dishes, they would make a reservation and dress up for dinner, taking a table for two by the window. Right where Leah's desk now sat. Leah had no way of knowing this, of course, so it was Eudora's little secret. How happy she was to scroll through knitting book offerings as succulent memories of beef bourguignon drifted through her mind. The books Leah had in mind were all wrong—too beginner for customers looking for patterns. Eudora helped her pick three appropriate titles.

When she left that day, Leah pressed a bag of the Candy Manor saltwater taffy into her hands. "You really saved me today with your expertise. Thank you!"

Eudora sailed home afloat with a sense she had not entertained in too long: purpose, she realized later.

When she awoke the next day, she figured she'd take Alfred to the bookshop again. This time maybe they'd try to go a little farther from home. Maybe across the street to where people looked out at Chatham Harbor. Those crowds normally made her heart rattle against her rib cage and her palms sweat. But the bookshop was right there—she could turn and look at it—like a life raft in a body of water.

Only Eudora didn't make it out her own door. That morning she had one of her episodes in the kitchen. She could not say what started it. But it was a bad one, and it did not pass. It stayed with her on and off all day, to her great disappointment. Just looking at her walking shoes by the door caused her heart to pound. Poor Alfred did not get a walk and had to go potty in the backyard, something they both disliked. She finally sent Maeve a message, asking for a session. At bedtime she took one of her Valium pills, which filled her with shame, even though she knew it shouldn't.

Two days later, the sense of panic had dissipated. She'd met with Maeve, online this time, and practiced all her breathing and visualization exercises. That day she didn't need a single Valium. But she was afraid now. What if the panic hit her in the middle of the way to the store? What if it was as bad as the most recent one? Feeling defeated, Eudora found herself giving in to the anxiety. She decided to stay in.

Midmorning the phone rang. Eudora's phone almost never rang, except for Caroline, and she never called during the day.

"Hello?" she said warily.

"Hello, Mrs. Shipman?" It was a woman. "This is Leah, from the Sandy Page. How are you?"

"Oh, hello! I'm fine, thank you," Eudora lied. But hearing Leah's voice did have a buoying effect.

"Those knitting books you helped me order just came in. And it got me thinking."

"Oh?" Eudora sensed a question coming. Leah wanted something from her, she could tell. And her curiosity was almost overshadowed by a wave of worry. Almost.

"I have a lot of local customers who are creative, and I have plenty of space here at the shop. So, I was thinking about starting a weekly group." She paused. "People could bring in whatever they're working on, like knitting, and meet in one of my rooms to work together. I love the idea of having a community space for artists." Leah was talking excitedly and so quickly it was hard to keep up. She paused for a breath. "You seem to enjoy my shop, and you know Chatham as well as any local. So I'm wondering what you think?"

Eudora sucked in her own breath. "What I think?" It had been so long since anyone had asked her opinion about anything, let alone asking her assistance in making a decision that sounded rather important. The responsibility of it began to prickle Eudora's nerves. But there was the shop, which she *did* enjoy. And the warmth in Leah's voice. "I think that sounds like a wonderful plan!" Eudora said, ignoring the clanging bells in her head.

"I was hoping you'd say that. Since so many people have already come in asking about knitting books, I think I'll start with that."

"Makes sense. A lot of people enjoy knitting." Eudora wondered which room Leah would use in the house. Maybe the formal sitting room with that beautiful limestone fireplace. Eudora had once danced in that room at a New Year's Eve party. She was so lost in memory that Leah's voice interrupted her thoughts.

"So that's the real reason I'm calling. If I get generate enough interest, might you be willing to lead a weekly knitting group?"

Eudora could not have predicted this. She was a good knitter. And she adored the shop. It had helped to get out of her house each day. But this time she could not ignore the alarm bells. A weekly commitment was out of the question. Being in charge of something was, too. It was simply not possible and sweet Leah Powell had no idea what she was asking of her.

"I'm sorry, dear. But I'm afraid I can't." Eudora could feel her throat tightening with despair. Leah was asking for *her* help. Her daughter, Caroline, and her therapist, Maeve, were in her ear, cheering her to say yes. And her Milton—beloved Milton—she swore she could *feel* him in that house.

But she could not listen to any of the voices who loved her. Nor to Leah, who she could tell was about to say more. Drowning in shame, Eudora cut her off. "It's just not possible." Then she hung up the phone, sat in the chair by the window, and cried.

Leah

It was strange how a change of tone between two people could change the way you felt about other significant things, including yourself. When Luke came into the Sandy Page just before opening the next morning, he appeared friendly as usual. Not even Brad could tell the difference, and that was saying something. But Leah could. From the moment he stepped inside her senses bristled to attention. "I've got the paint sample for the supply units, if you want to take a quick look," he said as he breezed in.

"I can't wait to see it," she said trying to catch his gaze, decipher any hurt feelings or strange new awkwardness. But there was no chance. Luke strode ahead of her to the back.

"Coral Reef, Ben Moore, correct?" He held out the paint can, label up, for her confirmation.

"Correct," she said, glumly. The fresh formality to their exchange stung, but what did she expect? She watched as he pried the lid off the can. Even unmixed, the color was beautiful, the exact coral-red pop she'd wanted for the otherwise white work-space. She watched the paint swirl together with the stirrer in Luke's hand, imagining the rousing of her own mixed emotions.

He painted a section of scrap wood and held it up. "What do you think?" he asked, turning it to and fro in the light.

She had to stand close to him to inspect the color. When he turned to gauge her reaction, there was no evidence of hurt or hard feelings in his expression, but gone was the playful twinkle in his eye.

She forced her gaze to the coral paint. "It's perfect for the cubbies. Thank you."

"Alright then." She stood to the side as he resealed the can and tidied up.

"Luke—"

"I'll get the units painted and let you know when I'll be back to install," he interjected.

So that was it. No mention of the night before. "Did you happen to bring an updated bill?" she asked. All along their working relationship had drawn from their friendship, easy, fluid. To the point she'd had to press him for bills. If he had brought one this morning, would that confirm that it was pure business between them now?

He shook his head. "No, but I can drop one off later."

"Thanks. I'd like to get you another payment, especially since this is a new project."

This time he did not object. "Sure thing." Then, with a quick wave he was out the door again.

"So you've got the poor man working weekends again," Brad mused when she made her way back out to the storefront. "He must really love books." He was reorganizing the front table to make room for new releases. That week everyone was anticipating a new book from a favorite author, creating a fun buzz among the staff: Brad for John Green, Leah for Sarah Addison Allen, and Lucy for Sarah J. Maas. Leah watched him fuss over the display, but her head was elsewhere. "Hello?" Brad waved. "You missed my dig."

"Sorry." Leah went to help herself to a cup of coffee. "Didn't sleep well." When Luke had dropped her off after their beach picnic last night, she'd gone home freshly depressed in a way she hadn't felt since she first came home. After this morning's interaction, she felt even worse. "How did the date with the lobster sweater go?" she asked. She needed a change of subject before Brad began asking questions.

"You mean Ethan." Brad glanced up from the beach reads table looking like he might blush, which was so unlike him. "Thankfully he did not wear the lobster sweater. He did, however, exceed expectations."

The news boosted her spirits. Like hers, Brad's life that summer seemed to revolve around the shop. At least one of them needed a personal life. "I'm happy to hear that! So . . . What's his story?"

He set down the Steven Rowley title he was holding. "Just because we're in a bookshop doesn't mean everything is a *story*."

"Maybe you just don't want to tell it yet." Lucy wandered past. "Has anyone seen my tea party hat? The kids will be here soon. Kids always show up early." Leah realized Lucy was looking about as happy as she felt.

"Check the back closet," she suggested, wondering if Lucy was just nervous. It was hard to tell with her. "And don't worry, we'll hold them off until you're ready." She looked pointedly at Brad. "Back to you. Spill the tea."

"Didn't you store that hat behind the register?" Brad wondered aloud. She followed him to the counter where he crouched down and feigned looking for the hat.

"Stop switching the subject."

Despite the put-upon face he made, she could sense he was secretly dying to dish on his date. "Fine, dinner was elegant. Conversation flowed." He paused. "I swear I saw you put the hat somewhere back here."

"Details?" she pressed. She was not going to let Brad get out of it so easily. He would never do the same for her.

"Ethan's two years older than me and works as an urban designer. Belongs to a cycling club." He looked up from his search to roll his eyes. "I loathe biking. But at least he's fit."

Leah leaned on the counter, listening. "Gainfully employed and socially functional. Where from?"

Brad disappeared behind the counter and the rummaging continued. "As predicted he's a tourist, but it turns out he lives outside Boston. Works for city hall."

"You live in Boston."

"Please, he's here for a week. We aren't even dating."

"I hear potential." She stretched all the way across the counter so she could peer into his face. "And the chemistry?"

Brad looked up. "Don't jinx it."

"So there *was* chemistry."

Brad popped up, holding the tea hat. "Lucy!"

Lucy appeared like a spirit. "You found it!" Then, "Did you kiss?"

The girl was good. And from the look on Brad's face, right on the nail. Leah gasped. "*Did* you?"

"Story time is over." Brad plunked the tea hat on Lucy's head and veered toward the front door to let the kids in.

A gaggle of children with mothers, fathers, and even grandparents in tow paraded into the children's section. There was a rush to grab extra chairs and pillows to sit on, but the overflow happily cemented Leah's plans for a studio space in the old parlor. "Perhaps your knitting lab isn't such a bad idea," Brad muttered.

"Studio," Leah corrected him.

It took all three of them to get everyone gathered, settled, and served. Lemonade was poured (and spilled), cookies were passed, and Lucy got story time going as Brad stood nearby with a mop as soggy as the expression on his face. With the teddy bear tea party successfully underway, Leah took her now-cold coffee back to her office stopping to peek in at the supplies Luke had left in the parlor. Looking at the tidy stacks of materials he'd tucked in a corner made her sad. He was as meticulous as he was talented. And a good kisser, she thought gloomily. There was nothing like a good first kiss. Even though there was little chance of *that* happening again.

When the tea party ended, there was a rush of picture book

sales, and then the store settled into a satisfying lull. "I need a nap," Lucy said.

"You deserve one. Great job today," Leah told her.

Willet Smith came in to drop off more vegetables from his garden. "You're spoiling us," Leah said.

"Heirlooms today," Willet said, thrusting a misshapen yellow tomato across the counter. "Golden Queens. Try them with a little salt and olive oil."

"I'll try one now." Ugly as it was, she could smell that just-off-the-vine sun-filled scent of a summer tomato. Leah sank her teeth into its flesh, groaning with pleasure. Juice running down her chin, Willet was halfway out the door before she could thank him.

Happily, she set the basket of tomatoes on the counter and made a sign out of an index card: *Willet's Queens, $1.00.* Then she selected another and brought it to Brad, who was still hiding out in her office. "You up for our sales meeting?"

Brad, who'd been appalled at the detritus and commotion of the kids, had only somewhat recovered. "Let's get it done," he said. "Then I'm taking lunch break."

"Try this," she said, handing him Willet's heirloom.

"If this isn't the ugliest thing I've ever seen."

"But delicious!"

Brad rolled his eyes. "Let me guess. He still has not bought a book."

"He brings us vegetables."

"Fruit," Brad corrected. "If I may remind you, you're in the book business." He flipped his laptop open. "The man should buy a book. If it kills me, I'm going to sell him one."

The sales figures were decent, if not huge. As a start-up, Leah knew that she would be lucky to come in a little behind the first month. Breaking even would be considered a success. They were just shy of doing that.

"You should be proud," Brad told her, after they'd reviewed his spreadsheets. "These are solid numbers for a brand-new small business."

Her biggest expense, however, was her hires. "As much as it behooves me to say it, I don't really see where you can shave off payroll. As it is, you already stagger Lucy and me with only a little overlap. But I suppose you could rotate us."

Leah couldn't do that to him; she'd promised him full-time work. And especially not after all Brad's help. Lucy was just a kid, and Leah only employed her part-time. It reminded her of Eudora.

"Did I tell you that Mrs. Shipman rejected me?"

"That nice old lady you were so keen on rejected you?"

"First of all, I don't think you should keep referring to her as 'that old lady,' and second, after she rejected me she hung up on me."

To her consternation Brad started to laugh. "Suddenly I like her a lot more. Turns out your Mrs. Shipman's got pluck."

"Well, she's not mine anymore. It makes no sense. I hope she's alright."

It occurred to Leah that the only two people she still knew in town, two of the nicest in fact, had suddenly distanced themselves from her. Was it possible there was more wrong with her life than she'd thought?

It was late in the day when she finally took a lunch break. Her phone had been turned off, and she realized when she turned it back on that she had two missed calls. Leah's stomach flip-flopped when she saw the notifications: Greg had called twice.

It had been a while since she'd thought of him, and she took that as a good sign. His voicemail did not elaborate, just asked her to return his call. She figured she might as well get it over with.

Greg picked up on the first ring. "Hey, Leah. What's up?"

"You asked me to call," she reminded him.

"Right. Yes." Greg sounded off. All their communications had been awkward since the breakup, but today it was more pronounced. "There's something I want to share with you. Before you hear it from someone else."

For better or worse, their Boston friends had remained with him when she left, so Leah wasn't sure who Greg thought she'd hear something from. "Shoot," she said.

"So, I know how this might look since we broke up not that long ago . . ."

"Just spit it out, please."

"Rebekah and I are seeing each other again. In fact, she may be moving in."

Leah inhaled sharply. It was exactly what she'd felt in her bones and feared in her heart leading up to the breakup. To hear it out loud confirmed all her suspicions of the past, giving rise to the ghosts who'd haunted her since. Perhaps it shouldn't have mattered, but it did. A lot.

"I see," she managed to say. She closed the door to her office and sank into her chair. Why was Greg telling her this? He was an idiot, but he wasn't cruel.

"I want you to know that it wasn't something we planned. I had no designs on Rebekah when you and I were still together, I swear. It just sort of happened, afterward."

Leah had heard enough. "Greg, why are you even calling me about this?"

There was a pause. "Because you still have furniture here, and Rebekah wants to bring her own stuff. I wanted to give you a chance to have it, before I donate it to Goodwill."

Leah's mind tumbled back to what furniture he could be referring to. She'd taken everything that was hers.

"The slipcovered sofa," Greg said gently.

"You have got to be kidding me." To be fair, they'd bought it together, but Leah was the one who had convinced him it would look good in their apartment. It had been good to sink into at the end of a long day. She'd almost fought him for it when she left. But Greg reminded her she had no way to lug it back to the Cape nor the space at her dad's cottage, so she'd reluctantly left it behind.

"Rebekah doesn't like the color," he said sheepishly.

"Unbelievable." Leah stood up from her desk chair and paced the narrow office space. "You wanted to hang on to that couch. Now you want me to—what?—come back to Boston to retrieve it, somehow, because your *new old* girlfriend doesn't like that shade of white?" Hearing Greg's voice and learning that he and Rebekah were moving in together—the very thing she'd suspected all this time—was a gut-wrenching blow. But the sofa was welcome absurdity. "Goodbye, Greg." She'd barely ended the call and was still fuming, when Lucy knocked on the door. "You've got a visitor." Leah groaned.

She followed Lucy back out to the storefront, only it wasn't Luke back to work on the cubbies. Mrs. Shipman stood at the register, both hands on the counter like she was holding on for dear life. Her color was pallid, and as Leah rushed up to her, she could see her forehead was a sheen of perspiration.

"Mrs. Shipman! Are you okay?"

Eudora turned, eyes heavy, but smiling. A little color returned to her cheeks. "Yes, don't mind me. It's hot out. And it was a long walk." Her little dog growled softly. "Alfred makes us stop at every mailbox."

From the looks of her it was more than a warm day and a long walk. "I think you should sit." Leah helped her to one of the chairs and sent Lucy for a glass of cold lemonade. Leah knelt beside her, wondering if she should call an ambulance. Trying to remember the steps for CPR. God, she did not want to have to do CPR. "Are you sure you're alright? I'm wondering if you need medical attention."

"No, no." Mrs. Shipman reached for her hand and lowered her voice. "It's just a little panic attack," she admitted quietly. "It's silly, really. Makes my daughter, Caroline, worry, too. I'm sorry."

"There's nothing to apologize for," Leah said, hoping to sound reassuring. It was hard to imagine Mrs. Shipman, who was such a strong and reassuring counsel to so many, suffered panic attacks. "It's not silly at all."

Lucy returned with a glass of lemonade. "We had a tea party today," she told Mrs. Shipman. "So there's tons of left-over lemonade. Don't worry, the weird red floaty things are strawberries."

At this Eudora brightened. "A tea party?"

"For story time," Lucy went on. "It was Leah's idea, but I ran it." She sat across from Mrs. Shipman in the opposite leather chair. "Decent crowd. Though I think there were more stuffed bears than kids." She glanced over her shoulder and then turned back to Mrs. Shipman. "Brad had a rough morning. He's not exactly *kid-friendly*."

Leah was watching in disbelief. Aside from the children who came in, this was the most she'd heard Lucy talk since the day she hired her.

"Well, isn't that wonderful?" Eudora took a deep sip of lemonade. "And I like the strawberries. Nice touch."

Lucy grinned.

Leah was relieved to see that she was looking better, and her breathing seemed to have calmed. Whether it was Lucy or the lemonade, who knew, but at least it didn't appear she'd be calling 911 that morning. "Feeling better?"

"Much, thank you. And you, too, Lucy." She looked up at Leah. "I had to come in today, for two reasons."

"Lucy, why don't you check on the register?" Whatever it was she was going to say, Leah had a feeling it was of a private nature. When Lucy was gone, Mrs. Shipman went on.

"I'm sorry for hanging up the phone like that. It was deplorable."

"Oh, it's alright," Leah told her. "It goes with the week I'm having."

"No, it was rude and uncalled for. I think it's because I was scared."

"Scared?"

Mrs. Shipman nodded. "I'll tell you why, but only because of the second thing I'm about to say." She swallowed hard. "I would like to take you up on your offer. About the knitting club. I think it's a wonderful idea."

"Oh! That's great." Leah was thrilled to hear this. Suddenly the store felt a little brighter, her plans for the studio a bit more hopeful. "We would love to have you."

"The reason I was scared was because this club is something I would really like to do. But then I remembered my panic attacks. You see, I've had a little trouble with anxiety since I retired and my husband died." She stared at her shoes. "I've missed out on a lot of things."

"I'm very sorry to hear that," Leah said, feeling every ounce of it.

Mrs. Shipman looked up at her. "I don't want to miss out on this."

On the slow drive home, Leah took the scenic route. She coasted past Chatham Lighthouse and the crowd at the beach parking lot. Past Chatham Beach and Tennis Club. Over the wooden drawbridge at Mitchell River, where her tires thunked happily along the planks and up Stage Harbor. The evening was balmy and beautiful; she rolled down her window and turned on the radio. As she'd feared, Greg had moved in with Rebekah. The bookshop was in flux. So far, she had two hired staff, one largely unpaid carpenter who was barely speaking to her, and, as of this afternoon, a much-needed volunteer with a crippling anxiety disorder. Taylor Swift's "You're on Your Own, Kid" came on. Leah smiled sadly and turned up the volume.

Luke

He respected what she'd asked for, and so he tried to give it to her. But damned if it wasn't hard.

Luke was a loner. It was something he'd grown accustomed to in recent years, despite it not being something he yearned for, as some people did. Like Mrs. Shipman, who seemed to prefer her own company after a lifetime of serving and offering guidance to others. What worried Luke was that he'd not lived that lifetime yet. He wasn't necessarily on board with retiring socially, as she had. Or as his father had, having left Chatham and moved to Florida where he spent long afternoons solo on his boat, fishing. Unlike them, Luke had not lived a life with a partner. With a house full of children and noise and the bustle of family. That was how he'd always pictured his future. It was what he'd thought he wanted. It was what he'd almost signed up for in his last relationship, until he realized she wasn't the one. But after a long winter on the Cape where one gray day tumbled slowly into the next, and the town was as empty as his house, Luke had come to the realization that at his age if he hadn't settled down yet, he might not ever. And though the thought did not sit well with him, he tried to make peace with it.

Sure, he'd had opportunities for relationships, but he knew planning a future meant sacrifice. Luke was willing to sacrifice, but he was not willing to settle. Winters were slow and quiet, left to the locals, most of whom were either retired or married. Come summer, the town was brimming with women, many of them attractive and interesting—but with husbands and partners and families in tow. As unparalleled as a Cape Cod summer was, it was hardly conducive to meaningful matchmaking. Vacationers came and went. Among them were a handful of single women his age, many of whom approached him in the Squire pub or the Red Nun, emboldened by their transient status. But Luke wasn't a twenty-one-year-old kid looking for a good time and a swift exit. As the summer crowds clogged the local pubs, these days he took his kayak out on Oyster Pond or stayed home with Scout. It was easier that way.

He'd run into a former classmate, Todd, at the pier the night he'd taken Leah for lobster rolls. She didn't see him as she'd stayed in the truck with Scout. But he'd certainly noticed her. "Got yourself a pretty girl, huh, Nickerson?"

Luke had glanced back at the truck. "She's just an old friend."

"That's what they all say," Todd said, laughing gruffly. Luke couldn't help but notice Todd looked like life had worn him down, dulled his patina. "Me? I'm a free man. Can come and go as I want. Got only my job and my dog to worry about."

Luke hadn't known exactly what to say. He wondered if that described him.

Todd apparently had the same notion. "It's alright, Nickerson," he said, clapping Luke on the back. "Some of us are just meant to be alone."

All of that began to change when Leah Powell came home. Working so closely alongside her had been infuriating and exhausting and altogether consuming: she wanted things from him that were nearly impossible to deliver. Yet he did. And he found himself emotionally buoyed despite the physical exhaustion. Staying up all night to paint her sign or frame her shelves was not just something he was willing to do, it was something he needed to do. In their weeks together, there was no denying the connection they shared; history was one thing, but chemistry was another entirely. And damned if they didn't have both. Still, he did not let his thoughts get ahead of him. She was a woman deep in transition, still reeling from her old life while trying to start anew. Luke was not stupid. Nor was he about to saddle himself with any of it. He had too much respect for both of them. And so he did as he was asked, as a friend and an employee, and tried to keep thoughts of anything more at bay.

And then the night at Harding's Beach flipped everything on its head. It had been a long week, and that night she'd seemed so down on her luck. After opening up to him about her fiancé and her job and all the things she'd walked away from, Luke couldn't very well leave her alone in the empty shop. When he asked her to go to the beach it was for a change of scenery and subject. That was all.

But the night turned into so much more. In the span of a few minutes it started and ended something he hadn't even known he wanted. Before he even had time to grasp what was beginning, it was over.

Now, he had to finish the damn job and get out of there. There were six wooden storage units to be framed, painted, and installed. Then he would really be done. He pulled the final piece of white oak off the table saw. The wood was far too nice to be painted, but he had excess from a previous project and was trying to help her keep costs down. Plus, the density would prevent it from sagging or warping; he wanted it to last for her. It would be so easy to just slap it together and throw on a coat of that red paint she favored. But he didn't cut corners. Luke set the board atop his workbench, grabbed a section of medium grade sandpaper, and got to work sanding down the edges.

When he played baseball as a kid, his father used to tell him, "Keep your eye on the ball and your head in the game." It was the same advice he gave when Luke took over his carpentry outfit and turned it into his own custom woodworking business. It was how he'd tried to conduct himself his whole life.

This summer Luke had fumbled. He'd let his eye get pulled away. He'd allowed his head to get tangled with someone else's problems, and his heart with the past. Despite the mixed signals, Leah had set firm boundaries. Even if it meant going against everything he felt, he'd respect them. Maybe, like his old friend at the pier said, he just was meant to be alone.

Lucy

W hat do you think it means?" Reya and Lucy sat at opposite ends of her bed, cross-legged and facing each other.
It was the communication position they'd adopted since they
were little, whenever one had news that required a huddle. *Meeting of the minds,* Reya called it.

Lucy stared at the note resting on her bedspread between
them. They'd gone over it again and again. "I don't know. If Jep
really loved her, why would he be asking her not to tell?"

"And what is the secret he doesn't want told?" Reya wondered
aloud.

Lucy had recoiled when Reya suggested maybe Ella was pregnant. "How can you even say that?" she'd cried.

"I don't know. It's probably the biggest reason for a guy to ask
a girl not to tell."

"She's not pregnant. The hospital would've picked up on that
with all the tests they did. My parents would know, and believe
me, I would, too."

"Maybe he did something to her," Reya said. "Something bad." At which they exchanged looks. The sad truth was, he had.

"It has to be something from that night," Lucy concluded. "Because he hasn't been able to see her or talk to her since the accident. And he's getting desperate."

Reya agreed. "But what?"

The only conclusion they could draw was not to tell Lucy's parents about the note. They wouldn't know what it meant, either, and it would only serve to incite them.

"I can't believe your parents are suing him," Reya whispered, glancing nervously at Lucy's closed bedroom door.

"Why not?" Lucy prickled. She'd had the same feeling herself, but hearing it come from her best friend's lips put her on the defense. "It's for all the medical bills. Everyone does it. Our lawyers said so."

"I get it. It just seems so personal." Reya shrugged. "He's not going to college or anything, like the rest of us. That business is all he's got."

"Ella's not going to college now, either," Lucy reminded her.

Reya grabbed her hand and squeezed it. "Shit. You're right. I'm sorry."

Lucy went to her door and peered up and down the hall. "I'll be right back," she whispered. In Ella's room she found the bracelet right where she'd left it, tucked in the back of her jewelry box. She ran back across the hall with it and closed her door again.

"Look." She set it on the bed. "I found this when I went back to the garage. It was on the floor of the car."

Reya held it up between them, the tiny emeralds glittering in the windowlight. "I still can't believe you did that," she said, but she looked impressed. "Next time wait for me?"

"It wasn't like I planned it." But suddenly Lucy had an idea. "Wait. I know how we can find out more. If you're not too chicken."

She watched her friend puff up in offense. "I'm no chicken."

Lucy laughed. "Good. Then let's meet up with him."

"Jep?" Reya's big brown eyes got even bigger. "No way."

"Why not? It's the only way we can find out what all this means. And there's a chance it can help Ella." She thought back to the hospital visit when Jep showed up. "You didn't see her, the way she fought when she heard his voice that day."

"Maybe it was PTSD."

"No." Lucy knew her sister. "She wanted to see him. I'm sure of it."

"I don't know, Lucy. Your parents will kill you." Reya was a rule follower, even if she was tough. But Lucy didn't want to do it alone. "How would we even meet up with him? Go back to the garage? Then his father might see us."

"No. We'd have to meet somewhere public, but away from our families. Like the beach. What do you say?"

Reya threw her the same exasperated look she always did when she thought something was a really bad idea, but she would still do it. "Fine. But you set it up. And I'm only going for emotional support."

Lucy tousled her hair. "Look at you! My very own therapy dog."

The next day at work, Lucy tried to decide how to reach out

to Jep. The most obvious way was to look him up on Snapchat or get his number from someone. But she was too afraid of the lawsuit to do that: her father had made it very clear they could have zero contact. It would have to be through someone else. Or a chance meeting.

She was so distracted by her scheming that she accidentally rang up a thirty-two-dollar book as thirty-two hundred dollars. Brad had to redo the whole transaction on the register. Luckily, he was in an unusually good mood. Lucy wondered if it was the new boyfriend. Brad would never say. For someone who loved to dissect everyone else's business, he sure was mum about his own. It didn't matter. Ethan came in almost as much as Mrs. Shipman did lately. Each day Ethan showed up just before lunch, always dressed to impress, and the two went out together. Leah thought it was cute the way they were so shy with each other in front of the rest of them, even though they held hands the second they hit the sidewalk. Mrs. Shipman called it young love. For an old woman, she sure got things.

Mrs. Shipman was back to her daily visits. Lucy was glad she felt better; that one day she came in so breathless and pale was worrying. The energy in the store felt different with her around. Brad could be so fussy and proper in one breath and then teasing and snarky the next. Leah was all over the place, fretting over spreadsheets and paint colors. Mrs. Shipman was kind of like the mother bird they all hadn't known they needed. If the bookstore was a nest in a tall tree on a windy day, when she was around their perch felt steadier.

Lucy liked that Luke was back, too. Just that morning he

showed up to install the red cubbies in the studio space. But then Leah was acting all strange. She was probably nervous because they had their first knitting night that evening and the room wasn't ready yet. That was the story with everything at the Sandy Page, but at least it kept things interesting.

"Lucy, dear, would you give me a hand?" Mrs. Shipman was struggling to carry a basket of yarn, a bag of knitting supplies slung over each shoulder like a pack mule.

"Let me take that," Lucy said, relieving her of the big basket. It teemed with balls of yarn, in all kinds of interesting colors. When she set it down in the studio, she couldn't help but run her hands across the fibers.

"They just beg to be touched, don't they?"

Mrs. Shipman was blinking at her through her glasses, which Lucy realized in that moment were the same coral red as the new cubbies Luke was drilling noisily into the wall.

"Sorry, ladies. This is the last one," Luke promised.

Dust rose around them, but Mrs. Shipman didn't even seem to notice. "Here, honey," she shouted over the drill. "Feel this one. It's alpaca wool. Isn't it lovely?"

She held out a ball of yarn the color of amethyst. When Lucy held it against her skin, it was soft as a kitten.

"I don't suppose you knit, do you?" she asked.

Lucy shook her head. "No, but my mom used to. She made us sweaters as kids."

"You and your sister?"

At the mention of Ella, Lucy decided she should probably get back to the storefront to man the register. But something about

Mrs. Shipman made talking about her sister less dangerous. "Yes. My mom knit us matching green ponchos one year. And a lot of sweaters and hats."

Mrs. Shipman's eyes twinkled behind her glasses. "Weren't you both lucky, wrapped up in your mother's love." The way she said it made a warm feeling come over Lucy. Her mind drifted back to her second grade classroom, to the cotton candy–pink sweater she liked to wear to school. A brown rail fence ran across the front and a tiny white lamb sat in the corner. Just thinking of her pink lamb sweater Lucy could almost feel the wool collar brush against her chin.

"Are you going to teach people to knit sweaters?" Lucy asked. She was suddenly in less of a rush to get back to the register.

"Goodness, no. That's advanced work. Tonight I'll start with a basic knit stitch." She sized up Lucy, as if guessing her height and weight. "Would you like to learn?"

"Oh, I'm not so good at crafts."

"Nonsense." Mrs. Shipman waved a hand. "Knitting is an art, and art is for all."

"Art is for all," Luke boomed, coming to stand behind them. He gestured to the cubbies, which were firmly installed against the far wall. Leah had painted the room in Dove White and the coral cubbies looked like a little sea reef set in the corner. "Finished and ready for your knitting supplies, Mrs. S," he said.

"My word!" Mrs. Shipman turned to admire his work. Lucy had to admit with the high ceilings and natural light, the bright cubbies just worked. "Where is Leah? *Leah*," she called, hurrying to the French doors that led into her office. "Hurry!"

Lucy had never heard anyone tell Leah to hurry anywhere in her own store, but Mrs. Shipman had such a nice way about it, hurry she did. As did Brad. Even Ethan, who must have just returned from lunch with him, popped his head in the doorway.

"Well, well, well. The knitting lab is finis," Brad said. "Let the games begin!"

They all looked at Leah who stood in the doorway, arms crossed uncertainly against her chest. Especially Luke, who seemed to be holding his breath. Was she upset with the outcome?

Leah swiped at a corner of her eye and then Lucy understood. "They're beautiful," she said. "Just beautiful."

Lucy half expected Leah to hug Luke, like she always did when he solved a problem or fixed something broken. Which was pretty much all the time. But this time she went to the cubbies instead and bent down beside them like one would a small child, running her hands lovingly across their tops. This seemed to be enough for Luke, whose entire posture relaxed at the sight of it. "Are they to your liking then?" he asked.

"Better," she said. "Thank you."

And then it was all hands on deck. The big table Leah had brought from her own house was moved from its storage spot in the old kitchen to the middle of the gleaming floors in the new studio. Brad and Lucy collected various chairs from around the house to sit around it. Even Ethan rolled up his sleeves, helping Luke haul in a rocking chair (you can never have too many reading seats in a bookstore! Leah insisted) that Lucy had never seen before.

"That's a gift, from my house," Mrs. Shipman explained, proudly. All faces turned in her direction. "I asked Luke to help me deliver it. I figure if I have a comfy chair here I'll feel more at home when I teach my classes."

Classes, Lucy noted. As in the plural. Mrs. Shipman wasn't going anywhere.

Together, Lucy and Leah worked to fill the cubbies with artful collections of supplies: stacks of canvases for the Paint and Sip scheduled later that weekend, tubes of acrylics that went into trays, brushes that went into coffee cans. There were sponges and palettes, pencils and scissors, yarns and needles, and baskets for all of it. By the end, with some aesthetic rearranging by Brad and once more by Leah, the studio looked like a cross between someone's family room and a middle-school art class. "Perfection," Mrs. Shipman said, and Lucy couldn't disagree.

The buzz of activity at work was enough to take her mind off of Jep's note and the lawsuit and Ella who could now use a spoon but still wasn't talking. But each day when Lucy grabbed her bike from the side of the shop where she'd left it, the worries found her there. They rose up on the sidewalk in front of her, like invisible ghosts, and trailed her the whole way home.

"Are you staying for the knitting class?" Mrs. Shipman asked her at closing time.

Lucy hadn't planned to, but suddenly she wanted to do nothing more. "Yes," she said "I am." Her father would be at the motel all night. Her mother would be worrying over hospital bills. Anything was better than going home to the still house on Bay Street.

The knitting class turned out to be a tea party, not unlike Lucy's teddy bear story time. Only the stuffed animals were little old ladies, and one little old man who'd thought it was a book club but stayed anyway, and a middle-school girl with her mom. And there was real tea, this time. Leah tiptoed about the group with steaming mugs as Eudora led an introductory lesson in simple stitches. Lucy learned the knit stitch as well as the garter. At first the yarn kept slipping on her needle. It was hard to keep the right tension in the fiber. Too many times Lucy's stitches appeared on her needle by accident. But she eventually got the hang of it, and soon she had two rows of sort-of-crooked V's with only a few glaring holes. "You're a natural!" Mrs. Shipman beamed, coming around to inspect her pupil's work. Most of the knitters were not total beginners. Lucy suspected they came to chat and sip. One woman asked if there were any donuts to dunk. Lucy thought that was pushing it, but Leah made a note. At the end, when Leah called time, everyone milled about the store before Leah slowly herded them for the door. No one wanted to leave.

The sky was almost pitch-dark, not great for riding a bike across town. Lucy had promised her parents she'd get a ride, but Leah seemed worn out and her house was on the opposite side of town. Brad had left before the class started. There was no one to ask. She went around the side of the house and grabbed her bike. She was just wheeling it down to the sidewalk when Mrs. Shipman came out the front door with her bag of knitting. "Oh! You scared me." She laughed, then took one hard look at Lucy and her bike. "You can't ride home in the dark."

"It's okay," Lucy lied. "I don't live far."

"With all the tourist traffic? You're likely to get mowed down by some New Yorker in an SUV." She patted the handles of Lucy's bike. "Put this back around the side of the house. I'll take you home."

"But you walk," Lucy said. She'd seen Mrs. Shipman come in breathless and hot enough times to know.

She watched as Mrs. Shipman rummaged around in her knitting bag and pulled out a set of keys, which she dangled in the air between them. "Because of all my supplies, tonight I drove."

Lucy was relieved for the ride. But as soon as they got in the little sedan and started down Main Street, she had her doubts. Mrs. Shipman was a wreck. She gripped the wheel, pumped the brakes, and one time shot around a rotary faster than Lucy knew she meant to. Thankfully they pulled up to Lucy's house in one piece. "You can drop me here at the mailbox," Lucy offered. She didn't like Mrs. Shipman's chances of backing out of her narrow driveway.

"My pleasure." Mrs. Shipman squinted at the mailbox illuminated by her headlights. "Hart. What a lovely name." She paused, thinking. "Now, why does that name sound so familiar?"

Lucy froze. She knew why, but she wasn't about to say so. "Thanks for the ride!" she said, hopping out of the car. Before Mrs. Shipman could say another word Lucy was jogging across her yard, praying she didn't put two and two together.

Eudora

All the time, Eudora overheard her grandkids talking about their Snapchat streaks like bragging rights. Well, she had a streak of her own going: for five days in a row she'd made it to the bookstore. And on the fifth, she'd driven her car and taught a class! *Taught* was a bit of a stretch, but she'd introduced herself and demonstrated the stitch for the evening. That was something.

As expected, the group of attending knitters had been eclectic. Creative people always were. Among them was one strange attendee, a Mr. Willet Smith. He showed up with a bag of what did not turn out to be knitting materials but vegetables. At the end, he thanked her for an enjoyable evening, handed a tomato to each guest, and left. Still, Eudora had survived all of it.

The class, if she could call it that, did not give her a panic attack. Nor did it make her feel sweaty and nauseous. The driving Lucy home part had been nerve-wracking, but even that she managed. What had commandeered her thoughts since that night was the sweet girl whose last name she now knew: Lucy Hart.

When Eudora saw the last name on the mailbox she was struck instantly with sadness. Though, at first, she could not say why. Lucy was a delightful girl, the house was quaint and cute. There was no reason for the dark feeling that came over her driving home from Lucy's. But the mood stayed with her, distracting her to the point she forgot her fear on the rotary and that ugly intersection off of Main and Stage Harbor. It stayed with her right to her own front door when she turned the key in her lock and greeted Alfred in the living room. And then she remembered why the name was so familiar.

"Hart!" she said to Alfred. "That's the family from the news."

The Hart family had been all over the local news at the start of summer. There was no way to live in a small community like Chatham and not know what had happened. Even for someone like Eudora who kept to herself. The accident was a terrible one, featured for a few days on the local TV stations. The story filled the front page of the newspaper, first as a breaking item, and later as announcements for fundraisers by the Congregational Church and the Chatham Fire & Rescue to help the family address growing medical bills. Eudora could not begin to imagine the costs amassed, or the personal suffering, but what haunted her most were the details given about Ella Hart: eighteen years old, valedictorian, Tufts University admitted. As a former guidance counselor these pieces of information painted a picture of a young woman poised to embark on a big, bright future. All of it was simply heartbreaking.

It brought into sharp focus Lucy's reserved nature. No wonder she didn't want to talk about her sister. The Sandy Page was probably the only reprieve she had from her family's tragedy. Eudora was quite certain neither Leah nor Brad was aware of any of it. Which begged the question: Would it be in Lucy's best interest to tell them, or not? Even in retirement, Eudora could never quite turn off the counseling drive. And given all she'd just learned, Lucy Hart was probably in need of some counsel.

Eudora was exhausted. From the knitting club's inaugural meeting that night. From driving her car not just to the store as planned, but adjusting her plans to drive several miles across town to ferry Lucy safely home in the dark. From all the thoughts racing around her head about the people in that shop: Leah and her entrepreneurial ideas, that now involved her. Lucy and her sad family situation. Even Brad, who showed all the signs of young love with his new beau. How was it possible that one little bookshop in one little old house could contain all that hubbub?

"Come on, Alfred," Eudora said, getting the dog's leash from the hook on the wall. The little dog spun in circles of joy, elated that they were going out at this late hour on an actual walk! It didn't even occur to her to let him out in the backyard, the easy thing to do. After all the excitement she'd endured, what was a moonlit walk through the neighborhood?

Leah

It was mid-July and as much as she was afraid to say it out loud, things were going better than she'd dreamed possible at the Sandy Page. The same could not be said for her personal life.

Despite her suspicion and fear that Greg and Rebekah would get together in her absence, the confirmation of it had been an ugly blow. It left her feeling played for a fool. Worse, it left her angry at herself for ever doubting her intuition. Fortunately the shop demanded all her time and energy, leaving her little time to dwell.

As she'd known he would, Luke went above and beyond to help her unveil her studio space for their first knitting night. Leah was tickled by the crowd that gathered: a far cry from a Taylor Swift–size audience, but she'd take it. And Eudora had surprised her—not only had she shown up and led the group as smartly and surely as only an educator can, but there had been little sign of her nerves. A bonus was Eudora's art-teacher friend, Marcia, who joined them, also agreed to lead the paint and sip that was next on Leah's radar. Of course it all came with a cost, which she kept reminding herself was part of a small business: you had to invest in yourself. It was easy to say and getting harder to do.

"You have to charge if you're going to run events that cost you," Brad advised, the next morning. They were rearranging the armchairs by the windows and setting up a small table of local authors between them.

"I did some research. I think twenty dollars a head for the Paint and Sip is fair," Leah said.

"No, you forgot to include the wine."

"That is including wine," Leah said exasperated.

Brad made a face like he'd tasted poison. "*What* are you serving these poor people?"

"Don't be a snob."

"Twenty dollars wouldn't even cover the bottle of wine I brought to Ethan's last night."

Leah ignored the comment but seized upon the topic. "Speaking of, how are things going?"

"Too well. He leaves on Saturday." Brad flopped into one of the chairs.

"You're spending a lot of time together. Have you met his family?"

"I kind of had to, since they're all staying in the same rental. And it's not like I can bring him to my place." He glanced out the window at a little girl and her mother walking their Doodle by. "It was weird meeting his parents and sister so soon, but they're really nice. They asked me to stay for dinner."

"Brad! Things are cruising along." She was happy for him. Ethan seemed like a stand-up guy, and the fact he'd introduced Brad to his family, despite the rental, was a big deal. "That's great!"

"It would be, but there's the matter of my vovó." His whole expression changed at the mention of his grandmother. Leah liked Maria; she was so generous and supportive of the shop. And her pastries were to die for. But even in their limited interactions Leah could sense a strict traditionalism about her. In the handful of visits she'd made to the shop she was quick to rein Brad in if he made a joke, scowled at the teenage girls in their crop tops who sashayed through the shop, and made a poo-pooing noise in her throat when she read the back jacket of one of their bestselling romance novels.

"Where does she think you are when you're with Ethan?" Leah asked.

"I have no choice but to lie. I tell her I'm working late, or that I'm having dinner with you."

"Me? Give me a heads-up before you do that next time. She's in here sometimes, and I might screw up."

"That's the least of my problems." He sank into the depths of the armchair looking suddenly like a small child. "I'm living a lie. Going back and forth, hiding things from her. I'm finally having fun and have met someone like she wants me to do, but I can't tell her about any of it."

"It must be exhausting." Leah sat down on the arm of the chair. "Use me as an excuse anytime. If she asks, I'll tell her I need you to work overtime." A thought came to her. "And if you and Ethan want a place to hang out or cook a nice dinner together, use my place."

Brad brightened. "Really? He's done so much for me, I would like that."

"Anytime." It was nothing for her to hang out at the shop for a few hours if Brad wanted to make a romantic meal for Ethan. At least someone had a personal life that summer.

Her thoughts turned to Luke. They'd not talked at all since last Friday night at Harding's Beach, except briefly about work. He'd finally dropped a bill off; it was not lost on her that he handed it to Lucy and left before Leah even realized he was in the shop. She couldn't blame him—he was giving her the space she'd said she needed. What she was not prepared for was just how much she missed the camaraderie and the company. It would have been easy to drop a check in the mail, but she had another idea.

Luke lived out by Oyster Pond, a saltwater tidal pond connected to the sound by a river. Homes in that part of town were known for their water frontage and private docks, coveted for their deep water access to Stage Harbor and Nantucket Sound. Growing up, it was an area shared by both summer people and locals whose homes had been in their families for generations. These days, gone were the modest cottages as well as the locals; Oyster Pond was primarily inhabited by wealthy summer families and their powerboats. As she turned off Route 28 and up Barn Hill Road, Leah had to wonder how Luke had managed to snag a place up there.

She slowed, admiring the grand summer houses with their

seashell driveways and stately facades. Tucked among them was an unremarkable driveway that sloped down toward the river and a stand of trees. Leah read the number on the mailbox and turned down it.

At the bottom, flanked by cedar trees and hydrangea bushes, sat a tidy two-story cedar shingled house. Already she could see the flicker of light reflecting off the water through the front windows. It was not nearly the biggest house along the bluff nor the showiest, but it was Cape Cod perfection perched along a grassy knoll with a view of Nantucket Sound. Luke's pickup was parked in the driveway.

Leah was halfway to the front door when the loud hum of a table saw came from the back, so she followed a stone path along the side of the house. As soon as she rounded the corner the lawn opened up to a sparkling vista. Leah drew a breath. Here the yard was wide and lush with a hint of wildness about it, bordered on one side by a pair of Adirondack chairs and on the other by an old gray boathouse. Below the swath of carefully shorn yard the property spilled down to the river, the lush greens giving way to the wheat-gold of estuary grasses. A long narrow bridge stretched from the base of the yard to a tiny dock where a Sunfish was tied off. Summer cottages towered on the bluff across the way. Shielding her eyes from the sun, Leah followed the sightline of the river to the sound and beyond. "God, Luke," she whispered to herself. "You've landed yourself a slice of heaven."

The sound of barking filled the air and Leah spun around to see Scout romping toward her from the boathouse. As she bent to rub Scout's ears, she got a better look at the building. The cedar shakes were weathered to a silver patina by time and the salt air. A set of double doors hung open at the front. The sound of the saw stopped, and a moment later Luke appeared in the doorway.

He squinted in her direction, then lifted a hand in greeting. "I guess you found me."

"Luke!" Leah held out her arm to the view. "This place. It's unbelievable."

"Sorry I didn't hear you." He nodded to the boathouse. "I was working. What brings you by?"

"I brought you something." Leah walked over, the golden light of late day spilling across the grass at such an angle everything seemed to shimmer. She handed him the envelope with the check.

"You didn't have to come all the way out here for this."

"It wasn't that far." Leah shifted uncomfortably. Was that code for he didn't want her here? "You more than earned it."

He tucked the envelope in his back pocket without opening it. "How'd the studio night go?" he asked.

"Really well. I couldn't have pulled it off without your help. Thank you, again, Luke."

"I'm glad it worked out." Luke's jeans and shirt were sprinkled in a film of sawdust that took on a golden hue in the sun. Leah noticed a fleck of dust on his cheek and without thinking she reached out to brush it away.

"Sorry," she said, laughing shyly. "You had a speck of sawdust on your cheek."

"Kind of comes with the territory." At least he was smiling.

"So, can I see what you're working on? Since I came *all the way out here.*"

Luke hesitated, as if he were weighing options, but gave in. "Alright. Follow me."

A sign hung over the door, not unlike the one he'd made for her shop: *Saltwater Woodworks.* "So you operate your business out of this old boathouse?" she asked. It was large enough to house two midsize Boston Whalers, she guessed.

"I have everything I need here." The boathouse interior was an open-space workshop smelling pleasantly of freshly cut wood. The floor was a basic concrete slab and the walls were rough-hewn wood, not unlike an old New England barn. Heavy work-benches ran along the walls. In the corner sat a squat cast-iron stove, which she imagined heated the place in winter. There were table saws and sanders as well as all kinds of industrial wood-working machinery Leah did not recognize.

"Wow, Santa's workshop has got nothing on this place." She stopped by a large machine holding a delicate piece of turned wood. "What's this?"

"That's a lathe," Luke said. "I use it to create custom archi-tectural pieces like pedestals, columns, drawer pulls, that kind of thing." He adjusted the mechanism and removed the sculpted piece of wood, handing it to her.

"You made this with that machine?" The symmetry and or-namentation were intricate.

"That's a column. I'm installing it at the base of a cupboard in a kitchen, so it looks like a built-in piece of furniture."

Leah rolled the smooth wood piece in her hands, appreciating the weight and design. She lifted it to her nose. "I love the smell of fresh-cut wood. It makes me think of new beginnings."

Luke said nothing, but for the first time since the night at the beach his eyes twinkled appreciatively.

Luke explained things as Leah took her time moving through the workshop, running her hand across a plank of dark wood: "That's cherry." Squinting at a set of drawings tacked to a wall: "Design layout for a kitchen." Tracing the swirling pattern of a honey-colored tabletop: "That's bird's-eye maple."

"It's so beautiful," she said, leaning in. "It reminds me of the pattern at the edge of the shoreline. You know the way the waves swirl the sand around?"

Luke nodded reverently. She was speaking his language. "Like ripples."

"This is a pretty special place," she told him, when she finished her little self-guided tour. It was an immersion in color, texture, and pattern. Standing in the boathouse with the doors thrown open to the elements, Leah could feel the connection to Luke and his work, and talking about it with him made her feel a glimmer of connection between them once more.

"Luke, about last Friday night," she began, gently, "I hope I didn't hurt your feelings."

His eyes swung to hers. "Leah. There's no need to revisit it."

It was obvious he did not want to discuss it, but she was keen to explain herself because the strange formality between them wasn't what she'd intended.

"I know I asked for space, but suddenly there's so much of

it." When he didn't say anything, she went on, "You used to be around all the time at the shop, and now you're not. I guess I miss the friendship."

"Jobs like that require people to work closely. There's a beginning and an end." He paused. "Kind of like one of your books."

Leah appreciated the analogy, even though it made her feel a little sad.

"The job is done now," he added. She understood his meaning. Luke was setting boundaries of his own, just as she had. Fair enough. She should go and leave him to his work.

When she got to the doorway, she turned and looked back. "So we're still friends, even after what happened Friday?"

Luke shook his head, a small laugh playing at the corners of his mouth. "We are still friends. Come on, it was just a kiss."

Just? She looked out at the water, freshly stung.

"Hey," he said. She sensed an olive branch being extended. "You still planning to go to the reunion?"

She wasn't, at least not anymore. "Not sure," she said, leaving the door open.

"I think it'll be fun. You should go." *You should go.* Not, *You should come with me.* Still, it was something.

"It's this Friday?" she asked. She really did not want to go. But maybe it would give them a chance to find their footing.

"Friday night at the Wequassett Golf Club. Do you have the details?" he asked.

"Text them to me, and I'll think about it." Smiling, she bent to say goodbye to Scout and started back across the yard. The late-day sunlight was bouncing off the water, a million little refractions of hope on a midsummer evening. Leah could feel Luke's eyes on her back as she walked. She'd come to deliver a check she could barely afford to write, but at least she was leaving with more than she'd come with.

Lucy

Best friends can be unicorns. It was the first thought Lucy had when she got Reya's text the next morning. *I got his number. Want me to text him for you?*

Lucy was getting ready for work. She'd asked Leah for a half day so she could visit Ella at rehab in the afternoon. It had been only a few days, but it felt like ages since she'd seen her. Now Reya had Jep Parsons's number.

She texted Reya back, thanking her and telling her exactly what to say to Jep. *Got it. BRB when he answers,* Reya replied.

Lucy was so nervous she could barely choke down her cereal at the kitchen table. She stole a look at her parents seated across from her. They'd been dead serious about staying away from Jep Parsons. The lawsuit had been filed. There could be no mistakes. But she had to know about that note. It was a clue about that night, and it might be a clue for helping Ella.

"Your sister will be happy to see you," her mother said, as she sipped her coffee. "She's making so many gains."

"That's great." Lucy glanced surreptitiously at her phone to see if Reya had replied yet.

"The physiatrist took her to the pool yesterday and helped her walk back and forth in the shallow end," her mother went on.

"You should see her! Walking almost all by herself," her father said. Lucy couldn't help but note it was the same pride he'd shown when Ella had been awarded her scholarship, only now it was over her ability to walk.

"Has she talked yet?" Lucy asked. Until the two of them could speak, it was like part of her sister was still gone.

"She's trying," her mother said, staring into her mug. So far Ella's communications had been guttural, unintelligible to the family and frustrating for her. It was heartbreaking for Lucy to sit there and watch her struggle, never knowing what to say. "The good news is, she's not giving up after a word or two, like before. I can tell there's something she's trying to say."

Her phone vibrated in her lap. It was Reya. She snuck a peek under the table.

He replied. He wants to meet you.

Lucy glanced at the clock and excused herself from the table. *Ask if he can meet this morning. At Lighthouse Beach.*

I'm coming too.

Fine. Tell me what he says.

There was a long pause while Lucy waited, heart pitter-pattering. Then dots on her screen. *He said yes! What time?*

If she left now, she could be at Lighthouse Beach parking lot, just across the street from the Sandy Page, in twenty minutes.

20 minutes? She waited, thinking. It was probably too soon. Jep wouldn't have time to get there. Was she willing to be late to work for this?

A minute later, Reya replied: *He said ok. I'm leaving now. WAIT FOR ME!!!!!*

Lucy laughed aloud, but her heart was now pounding.

Tell him the bottom of the steps. The overlook at Lighthouse Beach parking lot was set high above the beach. The steps down to the sand were steep and many, but she didn't want to risk anyone she knew driving by and seeing them together.

Lucy ran back into the kitchen and grabbed the lunch bag her mother had left on the counter. "Leaving already?" her mom asked.

"I'm going to work early," she lied. "Since I'm leaving to see Ella this afternoon."

"Alright. Remember, I'm picking you up at twelve-thirty."

"I know." She kissed her mom's cheek and ran out the door for her bike. Jep Parsons had agreed to meet. It was time to ask him about the note.

She pedaled so fast she made it to the lot five minutes early. Lucy left her bike against the guardrail at the edge of the lot and looked around. Neither Jep nor Reya was there yet. Across the way the Sandy Page Bookshop stood empty and still dark; there was no sign of Leah's car parked along the curb yet. Chatham Harbor glittered cerulean blue beneath a matching sky, the narrow strip of North Beach Island casting its golden glow between the two. A few cars pulled in and Lucy squinted in the morning sun trying to recognize drivers. What was Jep driving these days since the accident? She recognized none of them. Resigned, she started down the steps to the beach below.

"Lucy!" It was Reya, coasting across the parking lot. She ditched her bike by Lucy's and joined her, breathless. "He's not here yet?" They scanned the lot together.

"What if he doesn't come?" Lucy worried aloud.

"Oh, he's coming," Reya assured her.

A minivan full of kids parked nearby. Then a Jeep with kayaks strapped on top. Finally, a gray pickup pulled into the lot. *Parsons's Garage* the lettering on the driver's door read. "Great. Nothing like meeting in secret."

"Relax," Reya told her. "Go down to the beach. I'll tell him you're there."

As Lucy descended the stairs, nervousness overtook her. What exactly did she expect to get out of this meeting? She'd already told Jep to leave her alone. What made her think he'd tell her anything about that night? She only had one thing for leverage: Ella. Jep seemed like he'd do about anything for access to Ella.

She kicked off her sneakers in the sand and waited at the bottom of the steps. That section of the beach was still in shadows, protected from the bluff above; the sand still cold from the night before. A middle-aged couple made their way down the stairs. Then a bunch of kids. Finally, Reya appeared with Jep Parsons right behind her.

Lucy crossed her arms, readying herself as if for battle.

Reya and Jep joined her and for a moment they stood together in an uncomfortable huddle, silent. Jep, in blue coveralls, looked like he was dressed for work at the garage. His eyes were clear and bright as he addressed her.

"Did you give her the note?"

"What did you mean by '*Please don't tell*'?"

He ran his hands through his beautiful hair and walked a few yards off, exasperated. Just as quickly he walked back. "You read it?" he scoffed. "Of course you did. I don't even care."

Jep was angry at *her*? Well, Lucy had plenty of anger stored up, too. "You shove a note in my pocket for my poor sister that says '*Please don't tell*' and you really expect me to just hand it over to her?"

Jep was not budging. "Just give it to her. She needs to know."

"Know what?" Lucy demanded.

Jep shut his mouth, staring at her as if trying to decide something.

"Do you even know how bad off she is?" Lucy asked. Jep had no idea what he was asking of her. It was her turn to make demands.

"I don't know anything," he said. "Because your family won't let me near her!"

"Why would they? She could have died."

"I tried to protect her," he cried. "I'm still trying. You have to give her that note. She'll know what it means." Jep took in a raggedy breath. "It will help."

He needed a reality check. "She can't talk, Jep."

"What?"

"I don't think she can read, either. So forget about your stupid note."

"What do you mean?" The shock on his face seemed genuine.

"She can't walk, she can't stand up on her own. She can't even tell us what hurts." Lucy's voice cracked. It was the last thing she wanted, but standing on the sand between her best friend and her worst enemy she felt all the pieces she'd tried so hard to hold together crackle.

"I didn't know!" Jep insisted.

"Ella isn't going to Tufts, Jep. Ella can't even say her own name."

"Fuck." Jep held his head in his hands, bending over like he might be sick. "My parents said she was getting better. That she left the hospital and was in rehab." He straightened, looking at Lucy pleadingly. "They said she was better."

"Ella may never get better." And then without warning, Lucy's eyes filled and she tasted salt. A sob erupted from her throat. Reya was on her, pulling her in tight.

"Just go!" Reya shouted at Jep. "Just leave her alone."

Jep didn't budge. "Please, Lucy. Let me see her. I need to see Ella."

Lucy let go of Reya and turned to face him. "I can't do that," she said. "But if you tell me what it means, maybe I'll read her the note."

Jep shook his head adamantly. "Lucy, there are some things you can't know. Believe me, it's for her sake."

There was something he was hiding for reasons he thought noble, but she had a right to know. Ella was hers, too.

"What are you asking Ella not to tell us?" she repeated. "If you really want to help her, tell me."

"Just give her the note," Jep said. He broke away, heading for the beach steps at a jog. She watched him take them two at a time until he disappeared at the top of the parking lot.

"That was intense. What are you going to do?" Reya asked, breathless.

Lucy felt all the wind of indignation leave her sails. Something about Jep's desperation had hit a nerve. "I have no idea."

When she arrived at Spaulding, Lucy found her sister's bed empty. Trish, one of Ella's nurses, sailed into the room and began stripping the bed.

"Oh hi, honey! Love the sneakers."

Lucy glanced down at her pink Converse's then at the empty bed. "Where's Ella? Is she okay?"

"Better than okay!"

As much as she needed her escape at the Sandy Page, Lucy missed Ella. It was why she'd decided to ask Leah for the afternoon off. "Spend time with your sister," her mother had urged when she dropped Lucy off that afternoon at Spaulding. "She needs you."

Lucy knew her mom didn't mean to make her feel bad, but the words did. That summer the whole focus had been on Ella—as well it should have been—but sometimes Lucy grew weary of the intense vigil. From the medical stuff and the legal stuff and all of the unknown fear that they went to sleep with

night after night. Was it wrong of her to seek refuge in the
pages of the books at the store? To pedal away from home each
morning on her bike like her life depended on it? Everyone
deserved a break. But as she watched her mother drive away,
a fresh lump of guilt settled inside her. When did her mother
ever get one?

"Where's Ella now?" Lucy asked Trish. Today she would
make up for her absence. She'd spend as much time as her sister
wanted.

"She's just finishing up at PT. You can go down to the gym
and say hi. Danny won't mind."

Danny was the physical therapist, and almost as upbeat as
Trish but a little firmer, like an athletic coach. The more time
Ella spent at Spaulding the more Lucy began to feel like the staff
there were becoming part of their family. Lucy had to wonder at
the kind of people who worked there; they saw perfectly healthy
teens and children come in with traumatic injuries. Devastated
parents. Lives upended by a single senseless accident. And yet
every member of the staff there seemed happy. Always smiling.
Encouraging. Seizing upon the smallest sign of progress and feed-
ing it back to their patients like nourishment. Lucy wondered if
the staff there realized they were helping the family members as
much as they were the patients.

She found Ella and Danny on the first floor, in what they
called the gym. Lucy hovered in the doorway, watching. Danny
had Ella standing between a set of parallel bars lowered to hip
level. Lucy watched her sister, arms braced, hands on the bars as

she moved slowly along. The look on her face was pure determination, all just to walk with balance.

"That's it, nice and easy," Danny said. "Let's try to rely less on the bars. Can you straighten, just a little?"

Ella lifted one hand from the bar too quickly and her lower body swung hard out from under her. Lucy found herself leaping forward arms outstretched, though she was too far away to make any difference. Neither Danny nor Ella saw her: like a reflex, Danny tucked one arm around Ella's waist to steady her, and then, to Lucy's exasperation, let go again.

"Alright, let's try once more."

Lucy watched nervously as Danny positioned himself alongside Ella. Why didn't he stand closer? What if she fell? What if she hit her head again?

Ella didn't seem afraid, however. Her long dark hair was pulled back in a ponytail, her brow knit with focus. Lucy knew that look. She stepped closer, not wanting to interrupt, but drawn in nonetheless. As she did, she could hear Ella's deep intakes of breath between steps. See the tremor in her thigh muscles. A stray strand of hair stuck to the side of her forehead. It was then Lucy realized Ella's face was drenched in a sheen of sweat. A chorus of silent cheering swelled in her throat. *You can do this, Ella. Keep going.*

Ella made it to the end of the parallel bars and slumped against them. But her expression was all smiles as Danny cheered her on.

"Atta girl! That's the grit I want to see."

"You did it!" Lucy cried. She hadn't meant to say it out loud, but she realized she had when both heads swiveled in her direction. As soon as Ella saw her, her expression shifted. Her knees sank beneath her and Danny reached around her to draw her upright.

"I think we've done enough today," Danny said. "Let's get you back to your room so you can visit with your sister." He helped Ella back to her wheelchair. "Hey there, Lucy. What do you think of our superstar?"

"Hey, Danny," Lucy said, but her eyes were on Ella. "I think she's amazing." She reached for Ella's hand, but Ella slid it out of reach. Her expression of triumph had given way to embarrassment.

"Now, Ella, don't think you're getting out of tomorrow's session just because you nailed it today," Danny said, wheeling Ella to the door. "I think you're ready for some steps."

Lucy followed them back upstairs. When the elevator doors opened to the second floor, a little girl with a bandaged head was waiting outside them with her mother. "Hello, Princess Madeline!" Danny greeted her, as he wheeled Ella by. "I'll be down to see you in just a minute."

As she passed them Lucy smiled at the little girl, but kept her eyes averted from the mother's. She felt bad, but she already knew what she'd see; she'd spent all summer feeling it herself.

She waited as Danny helped Ella rise from her chair, and position herself by the bed. "Sit first, then scoot," he directed. Lucy tried not to stare as Ella strained to tuck her knees up and swing them over, her face puckered with effort. "Use those stomach

muscles," Danny encouraged, but he did not step in. It was ago-
nizing to watch. Why couldn't Danny just help her? Clearly she
was exhausted. But when she eventually settled herself against
the pillows, Lucy could see the reason why all over Ella's face.
"See? You're going to put me out of work," Danny joked. Ella
was so tired she could only offer a weak smile.

Lucy excused herself and went to the bathroom. Only a few
days ago she'd hid in there with the note from Jep. And here she
was with it, again. It wasn't clear to her why she'd brought it with
her until she saw Ella in the PT room. Now she knew what she
had to do.

Jep's note was frayed from being carried around and read so
many times. She still did not know what he'd meant. It didn't
matter. Jep had written only two lines on the page of notebook
paper, with several spaces between.

I love you, Ella.

P.S. Please don't tell.

Ever so carefully Lucy tore the page in half, splitting the message. She refolded the two pieces and shoved the one she wanted
in her front pocket.

Back in Ella's room, Lucy pulled up a chair. "You were amazing today," she said. "You're getting stronger and stronger."
Again, Ella looked pained by the praise. She didn't want Lucy to
see her struggle.

There would be no reading of *Anne of Green Gables* today.

Instead, Lucy pulled the note out of her pocket and set it on the blanket across Ella's lap.

At first Ella stared at the folded paper. Lucy watched her pick it up, her fingers shaky still. But the light that registered in her eyes when she saw the handwriting was instant.

"You know who that's from?" Lucy asked.

Ella couldn't tear her eyes from the note, still folded. She nodded.

"Would you like me to read it to you?"

With trembling fingers Ella opened it. When it lay open, Lucy watched Ella's eyes travel across the message once, then twice. Then up at her.

Ella made a noise in her throat, her lips moving. Lucy couldn't understand what she was saying. She tried to guess. "Jep came to see me. He wanted you to have it."

Ella made another noise, still unintelligible.

"I was afraid to give it to you," Lucy went on. "I didn't want it to upset you. Is it okay that I did?"

Ella nodded her head. Without warning, her face crumpled, tears streaming down her cheeks.

"Shit." Lucy grabbed her sister's hand and the note dropped on the bed between them. "It did upset you." She never should've let Jep get to her; she should've listened to her gut. Lucy began to well up, too. "I'm sorry," she cried, laying her head on Ella's lap.

Ella's hand went to Lucy's hair, stroking it. It was what she'd done when they were little girls and Lucy would bring her hurt feelings to her big sister. When Lucy looked up, Ella was shaking her head back and forth, a smile so full and so beautiful spreading across her face. "You're not upset?" Lucy managed.

Ella shook her head again, bringing the note to her chest. She pressed it there, tight against her heart, and finally Lucy understood.

When Ella opened her arms, Lucy surrendered. In one mercurial motion she slipped from her chair and onto the bed, spilling into Ella like water, all the punctures and hollows between them filling once more. Heads pressed together, the sisters wept, Jep Parsons's note collecting their tears like raindrops.

Leah

High school reunions were like a small-town carnival: subpar food; clowns from your past; roller-coaster emotions. And, from the look of the former football players already saddled up at the bar, maybe some throwing up after. She was not exactly dying to be there, but she'd told Luke she would come. If she were honest, she was looking forward to seeing him. If she were brutally honest, a part of her was curious to see what everyone looked like seventeen years out of the high school cafeteria.

The tony venue did not hurt. The Wequassett Resort and Golf Club was probably the most sophisticated thing to happen to the Chatham High class. If nothing else was gained that evening, Leah would be happy to sit on the terrace overlooking Cape Cod Bay with a crisp gin and tonic. For the occasion, she'd donned a buttercream linen sheath dress that both showed off her legs and sent her somersaulting back to Greg for an ugly minute: it was the same dress she'd worn to his sister's wedding three summers earlier, the very event that initiated a conversation about their own future. At first it made her wonder what Greg was doing. Then it made her determined to try to have some fun that night. She'd done her makeup and blown out her hair. Despite the fact there was no one here she really wanted to see, she needed to look good when she did.

The first familiar face she reunited with was Jennifer Flint, class president and yearbook editor, who was apparently still at it manning the registration table out front. "Leah Powell! You haven't changed a bit."

"Neither have you," Leah said. Jenn sported the same nondescript attire and no-nonsense bob. She riffled through the pages on her clipboard and scanned the table. "I'm afraid I don't see your name on the list. Did you register?"

"Shoot. I was hoping to do that tonight."

"Tonight?" The look on Jenn's face was more akin to an employee behind the DMV desk when you showed up with the wrong paperwork than an old pal you once changed alongside for gym class in the girls' locker room. "You *really* should have preregistered."

Leah shifted uncomfortably in her slingback shoes. "I'm *really* sorry."

After an irked shuffling of name tags and Sharpies, Leah was granted admittance to the dining room. Now she definitely needed a drink. She glanced around the room for Luke.

Chip Tanner, legendary track star and stoner, was at the bar along with some of the guys from the football team. His face was weathered by sun and likely a continuation of his partying ways, but he still had a thick head of wavy blond hair. He gave Leah a favorable once-over and spun her way on his stool. "James's sister, right?"

"Right. Leah," she reminded him.

"Leah! You were the women's soccer goalie."

"No."

"Field hockey?"

She shook her head.

Chip was lost. "So how's James?"

After a few more awkward reintroductions at the bar, Leah escaped with her G&T to the open-air terrace. The resort, set atop a rocky bluff overlooking the bay, boasted a view that conjured the southern coast of Italy as much as it did New England. At that magical hour the water mirrored the dazzling sunset streaking the sky. Leah leaned over the railing and inhaled. There was still no sign of Luke. She wondered if she'd make it through dinner or cut out early.

From inside came a series of shrieks and laughter. A small knot of women had gathered in the dining room entrance, embracing and emoting as if they were winners on a game show.

"The it-girls," someone said flatly. Leah turned. She recognized the dark-haired woman a few feet down the railing but couldn't recall her name. "Marcy Brooks," the woman said, jutting out her hand.

"Marcy! Oh my gosh. It's good to see you." She and Marcy had not been close, but they'd shared classes and been paired up in chemistry lab. Leah had always admired Marcy's sardonic wit.

"It's okay you didn't recognize me," Marcy said, running a hand matter-of-factly across her midsection. "This is what three kids do to you. And an ex-husband." She paused. "And his latest bimbo."

"Wow. You have not wasted any time," Leah said. "Are you here stag, too?"

"I'm home for my parents' fiftieth. Figured I'd show my face." Another whoop erupted inside from the it-girls group who'd joined forces with the guys at the bar. "Had to confirm that the social hierarchy remained intact."

Leah laughed and shook her head. "I guess some things don't change."

"So did you end up becoming a chemist? Mr. Appell was so inspiring." It was a sarcastic nod to their old lab teacher.

"You saved me from that man," Leah told her, moving closer. "He was so mean."

Marcy lifted a shoulder like it was no big deal. "He was a misogynistic ass. We girls have to stick together."

"I will never forget the time you stood up and told him to shut up. He was chewing me out in front of the whole class for a wrong answer." It was probably the bravest thing Leah had ever seen someone her age do at the time. "What're you up to these days?"

"I'm a civil attorney for the Southern District of New York's DOJ. The damn kids suck up the rest of my time."

"That's incredible, Marcy. And totally unsurprising."

"How about you? Didn't you go into publishing or something like that?"

Leah let out a low whistle. "Something like that."

"Hmm." Marcy appraised her. "I sense another drink is in order. Shall we?"

For the next half hour, Leah surprised herself by how much fun she had. Together she and Marcy navigated the homecoming queen and the it-girls, who proved slightly less annoying than Leah remembered, and grabbed another drink at the bar. The small crowd had rounded out. Many of Leah's former classmates turned out to be married with little ones, and most lived out of the area. A handful of the locals had heard about her store. It was fascinating to see whose careers had blossomed and whose hairlines had waned. As drinks were poured and nineties music pumped through the speakers, a few took to dancing. Leah enjoyed the sensation of the gin loosening her limbs, along with her nerves. Some in attendance were well ahead of her.

Marcy nodded to the bar where the former athletes kept adjusting their comfort waistbands and throwing back beers. "I may be swinging single tonight, but looking at these guys doesn't inspire any high school crush." Her gaze traveled across the room and stopped. "Although . . . there's one I'd make an exception for."

Leah turned to look. In the doorway stood Luke, looking crisp and cool in a blue button-down and khaki linen pants that highlighted his summer tan. Marcy sucked in her breath.

"Wasn't he friends with your brother?"

"Still is. Actually, I've seen a decent amount of him since I moved back."

Marcy raised her eyebrows. "Decent or indecent?"

"Oh, please." Leah slapped her arm playfully and looked up in time to see Luke heading their way.

"You made it!" he said, leaning in to peck her cheek. Was he wearing cologne?

"I wasn't sure *you* would," Leah joked. "You remember Marcy Brooks?"

"Of course I do. Good to see you." Luke pecked her cheek, too, and as he did Marcy made a swooning face at Leah.

"I'm going to grab a beer," he said, glancing around the party. "May I get you ladies anything?"

Leah agreed to another gin and tonic, though what she needed was some food. Marcy said she'd love a club soda. "Let's hit the buffet while we wait," she wisely suggested.

The resort had set out an artful array of coastal appetizers along with summer salads, and platters of grilled fish and steak. They filled their plates and took seats at an empty table. "Looks like we may have to rescue our drinks," Marcy mused. Over at the bar, Luke was stuck talking to a group of guys he used to play soccer with, holding their drinks.

"I'll relieve him." Leah was halfway through the dense crowd around the bar, thinking what a great evening it was turning out to be and how much greater it felt now that Luke had arrived, when a woman cut her off. She was petite and blond, in a snug little red dress, and to Leah's consternation she stayed in her way, right up to where Luke was standing.

Before Leah could call his name, the woman in red threw her arms up. "Luke Nickerson?"

Luke's head snapped in her direction. "Holly?" He did not see Leah right behind her. What he did do was set both drinks down on the bar just in time for Holly to throw her arms around his neck and shriek. Only then did he look up and notice Leah.

Who the hell is Holly? Leah wondered.

"Holly, do you remember Leah Powell?" Luke interjected, when she finally let go.

Holly threw her a cursory look. "No." She turned back to Luke and launched into conversation.

"Uh, excuse me," Leah said, pivoting around her as politely as she could. What she really wanted to do was shove her. "Luke has my drinks."

There was the briefest pause as Luke passed them to Leah, and then he, too, became lost in whatever Holly was saying.

"Who is that?" Leah hissed, returning to her seat. Marcy had witnessed the whole thing.

"Holly Houston. You don't remember her?"

Staring at Holly's tiny backside, Leah could not.

"Chirpy cheerleader, maybe three years below us?" Marcy went on. "I only remember her because of her pole-dancing name. And how flirty she was with the upperclassmen. She's vapid but harmless."

Watching Luke look at Holly, she suddenly didn't seem so harmless. Unsurprisingly, he did not find his way back to them.

As the night went on, Leah caught up with people she remembered and connected with a few she didn't. Small talk had never come easily to her, but the libations and ocean air coming in off the terrace lent a pleasant gauzy feeling to her interactions and a particular lightness she had not felt in ages. All the while, she tried not to sneak glances at Luke, who made the rounds. It was a reunion, after all. The confounding new constant was Holly, who seemed to join him at every turn, despite the fact she was there with a sizable group of her own friends. It was none of her business, so

Leah danced. She listened to Jenn Flint's class speech and tried not to laugh at Marcy's running commentary. She took breaks outside catching her breath and enjoying the ocean view, and then returned to the action on the dance floor. When Marcy bid a good night, Leah was surprised at how late the hour was. "How'd it get to be eleven-thirty?" Leah gasped, walking her out. "I didn't think I'd last here for an hour. Thanks to you, I made it through the night."

Marcy hugged her goodbye hard. "I am not leaving town before stopping in your bookshop, I promise. Such fun with you tonight!"

When Leah wandered back inside Luke was on the dance floor. And right there with him was Holly Houston. Holly's tight red dress hugged every bit of her physique as she swayed. Every now and then she leaned in to say something to Luke, and Leah couldn't help but notice the way she touched him each time: her hand on his arm, her palm against his chest. The whole picture sucked the joy she'd felt all night right out of her. She steered past the dance floor for the terrace.

Outside, the bay was steeped in shadow. Lights from distant boats blinked lazily against the night sky.

"Having fun?" Luke swept up alongside her on the railing. His hair was tousled from dancing, his cheeks flushed.

"*You* seem to be," she said.

"Yeah. It's a good turnout tonight. Nice to see so many familiar faces."

Leah kept her eyes trained on the water. "Like Holly's?" She heard how it sounded, and she hated herself for saying it aloud. "I don't remember her," she added quickly.

Luke laughed softly, as if reminiscing. "We went to the prom together. She was a year below my class. I haven't seen Holly Houston in ages."

Leah smirked.

"What?" he asked. She could feel his eyes on her.

"Nothing. Kind of a stripper name, isn't it?"

Luke didn't say anything at first. Then, "Mean doesn't look good on you, Leah."

"Relax. I'm just kidding," she protested. But the truth in Luke's comment stung. More than the fact she didn't like his scolding, Leah disliked how petty it sounded. Still, she couldn't shake it.

"Holly just moved back to town," Luke went on. "Sounds like she's going through a tough time."

"Sounds like she's really brought you up to speed." So, Holly was here to stay. And apparently so was mean Leah.

Luke let out a long, conflicted breath. "I wanted to say hi since I haven't crossed paths with you much tonight, but it sounds like you'd rather be alone."

She wanted to ask him why they hadn't crossed paths, but this time kept her mouth shut.

"It looked like you were having fun on the dance floor earlier. Good night, Leah."

"Good night," she managed. Feeling childish and small, she waited until the sound of his footsteps disappeared.

It was time to go home. Back inside the crowd had thinned. Leah skipped the lingering good nights and headed for the exit. Outside the sky was dotted with stars, the air brisk. She rubbed her bare shoulders. It had all seemed so perfect a few hours earlier.

As she headed toward her car, she heard laughter close behind. The clatter of heels on pavement. Leah turned as Holly stepped out of the shadows and into the light of a streetlamp. Holly stopped and looked over her shoulder. A second later, Luke followed. Leah stepped back between two cars, out of sight, as the two walked across the lot together. As Luke opened the door to his truck, and as Holly climbed inside. The truck rumbled to a start and reversed out. They drove right past her, down the resort driveway, two silhouettes in the cab of the truck. Heart in her throat, Leah stood there until the taillights disappeared.

Eudora

What was it about a group of women gathering together, with nothing between them but a few balls of wool and knitting needles? As she and Alfred walked to the Sandy Page Monday morning, Eudora couldn't help but wonder at the magic of it.

The first lesson she'd taught had turned into a second, and then a third. Admittedly, the group had whittled, but there were now six solid regulars. Most of the women present already knew as much, if not more (looking at you, Carol!) than Eudora, but that was beside the point. The two beginners, a young mother looking for a small haven from her newborn's nursing schedule, and Lucy, who joined when she could, gave Eudora conviction to continue teaching. In truth, it was a social clutch where Eudora suddenly found herself thrust into making conversations, airing grievances, exchanging recipes, and for a few brave if ill-advised moments, talking politics. Really, Eudora was not teaching anyone anything. She was learning to connect, to feel alive. It felt good to feel alive, again.

It was also nice to have Alfred in attendance. That said, he was not as compelled to engage. Alfred, in all his wisdom and disinterestedness, staked out a hiding spot near Eudora's feet beneath the little red table where Leah left a pitcher of iced tea for the group. Whenever someone served themselves the table vibrated softly with growling noises. Still, all were welcome.

As invigorating as Eudora found the Sandy Page studio, there was trouble afoot in the storefront. She felt it in her guidance counseling bones the moment she walked through the door that morning, a vibrato emanating from Leah's office and extending to Brad at the register. Lucy had not yet arrived, which was a good thing. Eudora wanted to speak to Leah about the Hart family's tragedy. Poor Lucy was going through a lot and somehow holding it all together. One thing Eudora knew from her career: no one could hold it in forever. First, though, she'd deal with Brad. The read she was getting on him that morning was troubling.

"How did the Paint and Sip go?" she asked. Eudora had hoped to attend, but she was still pacing herself. Despite the joy of the knitting group, she needed a recovery day in between.

"Fine," Brad said, dully. Was he being sarcastic? When he did not elaborate, Eudora pulled up a chair. The store was quiet, and she had an hour until her group arrived.

"I wish I had been able to come. What kind of turnout did you get?"

Brad looked at Eudora over the screen of his laptop. When he realized she wasn't going anywhere, he closed it. "I don't know. Maybe twenty-five people?" Brad was a numbers guy; he was also a stickler for accuracy. She waited while he checked the sign-up slip on the clipboard by the register. "I stand corrected. Twenty-eight."

"That's a robust group! Did your grandmother join, too?" Brad's grandmother, Maria, came in twice weekly with her pastries. He'd mentioned bringing her along.

"She came," Brad said, his face clouding. Brad glanced back at Leah's half-open office door and lowered his voice. "And then Ethan did, too."

"I see." Eudora knew Brad was gay. Through various conversations, she'd surmised that his grandmother did not. "Did they meet?"

"God, no. Thankfully it was a big group. But she saw us talking throughout the evening, and she recognized him from one of her pastry drop-offs. On the ride home she had a lot of questions."

Eudora's heart heaved. She wanted to reach across the counter and give Brad a hug.

"That must weigh heavily on you, having someone new in your life that feels so special, and not being able to share it."

"I've thought about telling her, but each time I come back to what my parents say: Why cause division in the family?"

Eudora wanted to say that it sounded like it already had; here was poor Brad suffering silently, keeping an important part of himself in the dark. Instead she got him a cup of coffee and added a little extra sugar. "Families are complicated. I don't have answers, but I'm always here to listen."

"I'm sure it will be fine," Brad said, already brushing his feelings aside and opening the laptop. "As it is, Ethan's vacation is over. He's leaving tonight, so it won't be an issue anymore."

"Ethan leaves tonight?" Leah joined them, holding a thick binder that she dropped on the register counter with a loud *thunk*. "You guys are still going to see each other though, right?"

"Yes, yes," Brad said, rolling his eyes. "He'll be back or I'll go there; we're still figuring it out." That part made him smile, Eudora was heartened to see. "What is all this?" he asked warily, eyeing her overstuffed binder.

"Ideas." Was Eudora imagining it, or did Leah also look about as wrung out as Brad? There were deep circles under her eyes. "I haven't been sleeping much, so I've been going over ideas for the shop space." She opened the binder and spun it around for them to see.

"Here we go," Brad said, meeting Eudora's eyes.

"Why aren't you sleeping?" Eudora asked. She was perhaps overstepping, but Leah had offered it up.

"Business stuff," Leah said, without elaborating.

Eudora didn't believe her. When she'd seen Leah on Friday, she was leaving to get ready for her high school reunion and sounding half-hearted about attending. Maybe it had been a bigger event than she'd been prepared for. "How was your reunion at the Wequassett?"

Leah made a face. "It was fine."

Her second *fine* of the day. Clearly it had not been, but luckily Brad swooped in. "What did you wear? Did Luke go? Any cute high school crushes show up?" Like Eudora, Brad sensed something there. Unlike Eudora, he was not afraid to pry.

Leah was having none of it. "A boring sheath dress, yes, and no."

"That's it?" Brad had hoped for more.

"I reconnected with my friend Marcy."

"Marcy?" Brad's nose wrinkled. "You've never mentioned a Marcy. I want to hear more about Luke."

"Actually," Leah said, redirecting their attention to the binder, "my latest idea involves him. Eudora, I could use your help, too. What do you both think of carving out a café area here in the shop?"

By the time Leah had finished explaining her vision, Eudora felt she might need a nap. The girl had so many ideas. This time she got *herself* a cup of coffee. "I think it all sounds very interesting," she said.

Brad was more skeptical. "You want to open a café and serve food in a bookstore? Why don't we just invite that crazy old man to come back with his tomatoes?"

"That's exactly what I'm going to do. Willet is the one who gave me the idea."

"I don't cook," Brad said, holding up a hand like a stop sign. "I drew the line at kids, but I need to add cooking to the no list."

"Relax. We could sell coffee, like we already do, but on a larger scale: I'm thinking lattes, iced drinks, that kind of thing. And a few pastries, like your grandmother makes. If that goes well, we could add a simple sandwich or soup of the day. Imagine Willet's heirloom tomatoes for a specialty grilled paninis!" Leah looked between them. "I know you think I'm crazy, but I'd keep it small and only sell things locally sourced. And let's not forget, this place used to be a general store. We'd be bringing back that chapter of the house's history."

Eudora was getting hungry just listening. And nostalgic. How many times had Milton told her about the penny candy and ice cream he used to buy here? She loved that Leah was honoring all of the captain's house history and its many lives. A café was a lot to take on, but Leah had a point. Look at the big chain bookstores: they had cafés that drew in business. If she kept it small with a local flair, it could be brilliant. She voted yes.

By then Lucy had arrived. She, too, voted yes. "People like to eat," she said matter-of-factly. Brad was the lone holdout.

"We've talked about this, Leah." Eudora could see him putting on his financial advising cap. She couldn't blame him. "Grow the business slowly and organically, like a garden. You're basically dumping in genetically modified fertilizer and lighting it on fire."

"That would smell pretty bad," Lucy said.

As predicted, Leah remained stalwart. "We've got a big empty kitchen with a window that opens into the studio space. The house is practically crying out for it. I'm just listening."

"You do realize how that sounds, I hope." With all three women staring him down, Brad threw up his hands. "Fine. You're going to do what you want."

Which made Leah smile. "And you're going to help me." She paused, her expression growing serious. "And hopefully Luke, too. With the kitchen."

"Why wouldn't he help?" Brad mused, already returning to his laptop. Lucy drifted off to the children's section and Leah to her office, leaving Eudora standing in the swirl of their wakes.

There was that vibrato again, coming through the walls of the old house. Eudora felt it in her chest. Something must have happened with Luke and Leah at that reunion. Eudora would have to find out what. For now, she'd fill her in on Lucy's situation at home. And she'd follow up later with Brad, to wish him a nice evening with Ethan.

When Eudora's knitting group arrived and settled in, her nerves were twitching. Only this time it was not an incoming panic advisory. There was no anxiety; this time it was something else. Something uncertain and not entirely comfortable, but definitely not panic. As Leah arrived with iced tea and Alfred scooted under his table with minimal growling, suddenly Eudora knew what it was: anticipation. Her head and her heart were buzzing back to life, out of retirement and back to work once more. Unpaid as it was, she'd not felt so rich in a long time.

Lucy

Her secret was out at work, and Lucy knew just who to blame. Shortly after she arrived, Leah called her into her office.

"Why don't you shut the door, honey." As soon as she saw the look on Leah's face, Lucy understood. It was the look people had given her all summer: in the market, on her neighborhood street, whenever some well-meaning person who knew about Ella bumped into her. She hated that look.

"Lucy, some information just came to my attention. I feel terrible that I didn't say this to you sooner, but I'm really sorry to hear what happened to your sister." Leah gestured to the green velvet couch, but Lucy shook her head, no. No, she did not want to sit. She did not want to be here listening to whatever incoming tide of sympathy she was about to drown in.

She beat Leah to the punch. At this point in the summer, Lucy had it down like lines memorized for a school theater production: "Thank you. That's kind of you to say." She waited, as she always had to, to see if this was satisfactory enough to shut the person up. The way Leah was looking at her, it was not. So she went on with the next set of lines. "My family appreciates the support, but we're doing fine. Ella is getting better each day."

"Well, I'm very glad to hear that," Leah said, leaning back in her chair. "I can't imagine what you've all gone through." She leaned forward, hands clasped solemnly on the desk. "But it's you I'm wondering about."

Here it comes, Lucy thought.

"Is there anything you need? Time off? Shorter shifts? Because I'm happy to give it to you." Her expression was so sincere, her words so kind, and yet all Lucy could think of was punching her boss. Right after she punched Eudora. "Whatever you need, you've got my support."

Lucy felt the muscles in her jaw trigger, felt the familiar grind of molar on molar. This shop was her one safe place. Now everyone knew and it was over. "Is it okay if I get back to work, now?"

For a moment Leah didn't say anything. "Sure, of course." Lucy was halfway out the door as Leah went on. "I appreciate what a great job you're doing . . ."

Eudora was setting up for her knitting group in the studio as Lucy blazed through.

"Oh, hi, Lucy! I brought you something." She reached into her bag and pulled out a brand-new ball of yarn. As she stormed by, Lucy caught the exquisite amethyst color out of the corner of her eye. "It's that special yarn you liked so much."

She left Eudora standing with her hand out, the stupid lovely yarn just sitting there like a bird in her palm. It hurt Lucy's heart. And that made her even madder.

"Are you able to join us today?" Eudora called after her.

"No thanks," Lucy said, over her shoulder. She hated herself for doing it. Eudora was one of the nicest people she'd ever met. This never would have happened if Eudora had kept her big mouth shut.

All morning she avoided the studio. When the knitters, and the old man with the vegetables who kept showing up to join them, wrapped up their gabfest, Lucy kept her head down, organizing books in the children's section. When Eudora emerged, later, with her little dog and looked in her direction, Lucy ignored her and made haste to the nearest customer. She could tell Eudora was waiting; she probably wanted to show her that yarn again. She would ask how the knitting was going.

That was another thing. It turned out Lucy didn't mind knitting. It was actually kind of relaxing, even though it wasn't easy. It took her mind off the really hard stuff. She'd taken to practicing her seed stitches before bed each night, head bowed, eyes on her needlework in the dim lighting of her room. Without realizing it, it became a soothing part of her evening routine. But she wouldn't be doing that anymore. Not when it came with the hassle of a pity party.

It seemed Eudora had finally given up by the time Lucy checked out the customer she'd been helping. The woman bought a copy of Steven Rowley's latest for herself, and after consulting with Lucy, two Tracy Deonn titles for her teenage daughter. Afterward, Lucy ducked around the register and into the back to grab her lunch. Somehow Eudora and Alfred had snuck past her.

"We missed you today," Eudora said, looking up from the project table. Lucy groaned inwardly and went around to the butler's pantry where Leah kept a mini fridge for their lunches. The studio was adjacent, and so Eudora kept talking. "I know it's hard to join the group while you're on duty, but I was hoping to give you that yarn before I left."

Still bent in the fridge, Lucy cursed quietly under her breath. Could the woman be any nicer? Now she'd have to talk to her. She emerged with her lunch. Sure enough Eudora had set the ball of yarn on the table between them.

"You didn't have to do that for me."

"I wanted to. How's your needle work coming?"

Lucy shrugged. "It's coming." The ball of yarn was sitting there, yearning to be touched. Lucy could tell how soft it would feel against her skin. But she was still mad.

Eudora must have read her mind. "This wool was dyed with the petals of Iris blooms. I get it from a farm who raises their own alpacas. Isn't it lovely?"

She could feel Eudora studying her as she stared at the wool. There was no way she could not accept it. Sure enough, the wool was supple and soft in her hand when she picked it up. She felt her mood become a little more supple, too. "Thank you."

"You are welcome, Lucy Hart." Eudora looked at her hard. "I realize now that your sister is Ella Hart. I hope she's doing alright."

Lucy squeezed the yarn in her hand. "I figured as much."

"I hope it's okay that I shared that with Leah. It's important the people you work with understand."

Lucy didn't need any more understanding. What she needed was space. And for people to stop asking her about her family. She almost set the yarn back down.

"I can tell I've upset you," Eudora said, suddenly. "I'm sorry. I have a bad habit of sticking my nose in, my husband, Milton, used to tell me all the time."

Lucy wanted to tell her Milton was right. Instead she said, "My lunch break is ending. I should go eat." They always ate at the project table, but Lucy took her lunch out to the storefront. She knew Eudora was disappointed, but just as she was about to forgive her, she had to go and bring up Ella. Lucy needed some air.

Outside the day was bright and the sidewalk busy. Tourists lingered across the way at the overlook, taking photos. Dog walkers passed, along with the usual stroller-pushing young parents and chatty toddlers. Lucy ate her turkey sandwich slowly, savoring the sun. She wasn't going to the beach this summer, nor was she hanging out in town. The one bonfire Reya had mentioned, she'd skipped. Those were the things she did with Ella. It seemed impossible to go to them without her.

On her way back in she was surprised to see a tall platform ladder set up by one of the front windows. Brad stared down at her from the upper rungs. "The things I do for this woman." Lucy watched as he strung tiny paper lanterns across the front window. They were pale blue and delicate, in the shape of little beehives. When he finished the first string, Lucy passed him another from the box on the floor, this one the color of wheat.

"Handmade by a woman in Provincetown who does dinner party decor," he said before Lucy could ask. "They'll sell fast."

Lucy had no doubt. It gave her an idea. Ella would love them. She selected a blue string; the price tag was about four hours' pay for work, but after hesitating she held on to it. "Mind if I save this by the register?"

Brad nodded appreciatively. "Get them while they last. There's a whole box I still haven't unpacked. If you could put them out on display, that would be great." He indicated a spot he'd cleared on the front table.

One thing she loved was going through new merchandise. Leah selected some of the prettiest wares from local craftspeople, things Lucy would never think to buy for herself, but they proved hard to resist. She had just settled the last package of lanterns into a pretty display basket when the bell jangled over the front door.

Jep Parsons stood in the doorway, looking ruffled. "Can I talk to you?"

Lucy glanced around. The store was quiet and thankfully there was no sign of Leah or Brad. "I'm *working*," she said. How many times was he going to pull this stunt? Then, under her breath, "I gave her the note, so let it go."

"That's not why I'm here." Jep's eyes were drilling holes into hers. "We need to talk. Like right now."

Had he not just heard what she said? "I can't." At that moment Leah emerged from her office.

"Hello there," she said, looking between the two. Lucy wanted the floor to open up right then and there. Leah had seen Jep before. She'd gone so far as to mistake him for Lucy's boyfriend.

Jep cleared his throat. "Sorry to interrupt, but is it alright if I speak to Lucy really quick?" God, he was ballsy.

Lucy began to protest, but Leah cut her off. "Of course!" Then, looking sympathetically at Lucy, "Go ahead, take as long as you need."

Damn Eudora. Lucy had no choice but to follow Jep outside. By then, she was livid. She stormed around the side of the house, out of sight of the shop front. "What are you doing here? You're going to get me fired."

But this time Jep looked even madder than she felt. "Your family is suing me?"

Lucy froze. Her parents had said they'd filed the suit. Jep must have just found out. "It's not personal!" she said, hearing just how ridiculous it sounded. Of course it was personal to him.

"Do you know a marshal came to the garage yesterday? Served me papers in front of my dad and all our customers." Jep's eyes were wild with the hurt of it.

"It's because of the hospital bills," she tried to explain. Though she didn't have to. It wasn't her job and what Jep did was the reason he was in this predicament in the first place.

"I'm going to lose everything! My dad's business. My work. And now *her*."

Her. Lucy flinched. Among everything he was losing, Ella counted. In spite of all Jep Parsons had done to her family, Lucy felt for him. He was just another dumb, flawed human and he was falling apart, right there in front of her.

"How else do they pay all those bills? What if she doesn't get better?" Lucy asked. "They had no choice."

"Well, now I have no choice, either."

It sounded like a threat. Lucy crossed her arms, bracing herself. "What's that supposed to mean?"

"You know why I sent her that note? I wasn't going to tell you or anyone else, but now I have to." Jep stepped so close to her that she could smell his shampoo. His voice wavered, just above her ear. "It was Ella."

"What was Ella?"

"She was the one driving my car that night."

"No." Lucy stepped back against the side of the house, the full effect of his words radiating through her. "Don't you dare."

"It's true," he insisted. "I let her drive my car home after the party, but I had no idea she was drunk." He glanced nervously around, but no one was there to hear.

"You're just saying that," Lucy hissed. "You're saying that because we're suing you. Because you're scared."

"I am scared! But it's still the truth." Jep grabbed her hands in his own. "You have to tell your parents, so they call off this suit."

"Are you crazy?" She tried to tug her hands free, but Jep held on tighter. Fear started to course through her like a current.

"I swear," Jep went on. "I'll still take the blame to protect Ella, but I can't lose the garage. It's my family's business. My grandfather started that garage, and my father passed it down to me. Please don't do that to them."

"You're lying. I don't believe one word." Lucy jerked her hands free and stalked toward the sidewalk. She had to get away from him, from his disgusting lies.

Jep followed. "I took the fall for her."

"No, you didn't. You're blaming her now to cover your ass."

"Don't you get it? That's why I wanted you to give her the note! I didn't want her to tell the truth because she'd be arrested. Because she'd have a record, and then Tufts would find out."

Lucy spun around to face him. "What does Tufts have to do with anything?"

"They'd take her scholarship away! She'd lose *everything* she's worked for."

"Hasn't she already?" Lucy wanted to scream. What he was saying was outrageous. The police had never said anything different. Nor had the accident report, or the lawyers. Jep was lying.

Lucy blazed around the corner of the house and down the sidewalk, shoving past the tourists coming toward them. She didn't care. Jep Parsons was a lying piece of crap. He'd almost killed her sister. Now he was trying to take her down with him.

The sound of footsteps reverberated behind her, and Jep pulled up alongside her just as she reached the shop door. She reached for the handle, but he grabbed for it first, holding it closed.

"Lucy, please." His breath came in gasps. "Tell your parents to call off the suit. It wasn't me."

Eudora appeared, eyes wide with alarm on the other side of the glass. When she tugged the door open, Jep let go. Lucy surged inside. Only then did she stop and turn around. Jep Parsons was gone.

Leah

Book business aside, there was a multitude of personal business at the Sandy Page, and Leah had no one to share it with. Brad was enmeshed in the beginnings of love, from the high of a first date to the low of saying goodbye to Ethan who was returning to Boston. Lucy, whose family tragedy she'd just learned of, was heavy on her mind. Eudora, who'd been the most unsettled of all, now seemed to be the only one relatively at ease. As for herself, Leah dealt with strain the only way she knew how that summer: new projects. Turning the kitchen area into a little café was her latest coping mechanism. Normally she'd be happy to have Luke back in the mix to assist, but after the reunion her feelings about him were complicated and confusing. It had taken a couple days to get up the courage to call him and ask if he'd be willing to take on one more project at the shop. There was no mention of the reunion. Or Holly Houston. Their call was businesslike and brief, but he agreed to come by. By then, Leah didn't know if that was good news or not.

It didn't help that her ex, Greg, had reached out again. She'd let his calls over the weekend go straight to voicemail. Whatever he had to say, he could leave a message. Only he didn't. Instead, he called again that morning as she drove into work. She took the first rotary on Route 28 sharply, as her phone rang. Then the next. What Greg wanted was not important to her anymore. But as she headed down Main Street and stopped for a pedestrian crossing, she gave in. Something about the last few days had left her raw, ready for a fight. Greg was a perfect opponent.

"What?" she said, answering.

"Leah? It's me."

"I know who it is," she barked. "Why do you keep calling?"

"I need to talk to you." He paused. "Is now a good time?"

The man had such nerve. They were done. She was trying to get on with her life. "There is never a good time. What is it?"

Greg hesitated. "Maybe I should call back when you sound less busy. It's kind of important."

There was nothing he could say that would ever again register on Leah's list of importance. "Please just say whatever it is. I'm almost at work."

"I left Rebekah."

After everything, it was the last thing she expected.

"Did you hear what I said?" he asked, when she didn't answer.

"You left, or she did?" As soon as the words were out, Leah realized it shouldn't matter. She was not interested in getting into the weeds. It was Greg's mess, Greg's life, and she wanted no part of it.

"I did," he said adamantly. "Because I still love you."

This time Leah pulled over. She swung into the parking lot for Tale of the Cod and leaned back in the driver's seat. "Greg."

"I do, Leah. I still love you, and I want us to get back together. I want our life back."

His voice filled her car, but she could not let the words get into her head. She'd worked too hard that summer to rid herself of his broken promises.

"Can I come see you?"

"No. I need to stop you right there." Leah looked around her, at the tourists starting to fill the sidewalks in their cheery summer garb, at the young family sitting on the bench by Buffy's Ice Cream, all of it juxtaposed against the dread that was filling her. "This is too much. It's outrageous."

"If we could just sit down and talk . . . "

She had to cut him off before he uttered another crazy word. "You made your choices, Greg."

"I never left you for her! I realize now that Rebekah was just a knee-jerk reaction to our breakup. To help me get through it."

"Get through *what*?" Leah wanted to hit the steering wheel. "I was the one who lost her job, who went down in flames over the scandal with Luna's book. I was the one who lost everything, not you!" She stopped to catch her breath. "And what did you do, instead of supporting me through it? You had second thoughts! You called off our wedding."

"And you left Boston. You packed up and left without giving us time to maybe figure things out."

"Because you faltered. How could I marry someone who faltered? When I needed him most?" She was shouting now, and people outside the car were turning to look. Leah took a deep breath. "I don't want to revisit things, Greg. This is crazy."

"Leah, please, it's not crazy—"

"It is. You're reeling from your breakup with Rebekah or whatever the hell is going on back there, and you're just grasping at straws. I won't be your straw, Greg. Goodbye."

The shop was just around the corner, at the end of Main, but it took Leah several minutes to collect herself. In the short drive until she parked her car out front, she'd gone from outrage to near hysteria. Who did Greg think he was? *What* was he thinking? For an insane moment she wondered what had happened between him and Rebekah, then she chided herself. None of it mattered. On her way into the shop, she began to laugh. The ridiculousness of it all had gotten to her. She was still laughing when she unlocked the door and flicked on the lights. Across the room, a head popped up from one of the armchairs. Leah dropped her bag and screamed.

"It's me!" Brad bolted upright looking equally alarmed. A blanket slipped from his lap. "Sorry, it's just me."

"Jesus, Brad, you scared me to death!"

"I didn't mean to." He rubbed his eyes and looked at his watch. "I must have fallen back to sleep."

"Did you sleep here all night?" Leah lowered herself into the chair opposite Brad, studying him. He looked terrible, his eyes lined by dark circles. His seersucker shirt, which she realized he must've worn for his goodbye dinner with Ethan, was badly creased.

Brad looked down at his hands. "My grandmother kicked me out."

"Oh, Brad."

She made coffee. Since there would be none of Maria's pastries, she rummaged through the fridge and found a sleeve of bagels. She toasted one, slathering it with extra cream cheese, and brought all of it out to the storefront on a little tray.

"Eat," she ordered. For once Brad did not complain about the carbs.

When he'd devoured the bagel and finished the coffee, he was ready to talk.

"How did she find out?" Leah asked softly.

"Ethan and I went out to dinner last night, before he left." He smiled sadly. "It was so nice. We went to STARS at Chatham Bars. Everything was perfect."

She waited for him to go on.

"The thing is, I never expected an Ethan in my life. My goal for this summer was to earn some money for grad school and see my grandma. I wasn't even looking for someone new."

"They say that's when it happens."

"Last night at dinner, we talked. About making this work long term." Brad's eyes shone. "We're both so surprised to have stumbled into each other, and we don't want to let go."

"That's beautiful, Brad. It's what you deserve."

"I was so happy on the drive home. I wasn't even sad Ethan was leaving. We made a commitment. In a few short months, I'd be back in the city with him. I was just so . . ."

"Happy?" Leah could feel it emanating from him just in the telling. But then his face fell.

"When I got home, it was late. My grandmother always goes to bed early, but there was a light on in the parlor. She had waited up for me." Brad let out a long breath. "Right away, I knew why."

"What did she say?"

"She was worked up. The second I opened the door she hopped up out of her chair. I could see her cheeks were flushed, like she'd been pacing. Straightaway she asked me if I had been out with Ethan."

"She knew."

Brad nodded. "When I told her yes, she told me that she did not like me hanging out with him. That he was a sinner."

"Oh, Brad. What did you say?"

"I told her I guess that made me one, too." He put his head in his hands. "She told me to get out. That she never wanted to see me again." His voice broke. "That I was dead to her."

Leah rose and wrapped her arms around Brad. Here was one of the kindest, funniest, most generous hearts she'd known, and his own grandmother had turned him away. When she let go, she looked him in the eye. "You're going through a lot, but you can't stay here," she told him.

"I know." Brad stood up, gathering his blanket and pillow. "I'll find a place, don't worry."

"No, that's not what I meant," Leah said. "I meant, you can't stay here at the shop. I want you to stay with me. At my house."

She could see him beginning to object. "I mean it. I could use the company."

He was so worn out, Brad did not argue "Thank you, Leah."

"Where's your stuff?"

"Outside. In my car."

"I want you to take the morning off and go to the house. Take a shower, then try to get a nap."

"But Luke is coming in, and we've got coffee and bakery vendors scheduled."

"Which I will handle." She smiled at him. "You're good, but you're not irreplaceable."

To her relief, Brad smiled back. "Yes I am." She gave him her key, directions to the house, and sent him out the door.

Greg's call had thrown her, but walking in on Brad had sent her spinning. Despite the café space being nothing more than a sketchy concept and an ugly seventies kitchen, she'd lined up meetings with a few local food vendors. She was so deep in thought she didn't hear Luke come in the front door.

He found her staring blankly at her laptop in her office. "You alright?" he asked.

Leah jumped. How she wanted to divulge the blows of the morning, but it was not the time and Luke was not her person. "Just busy and distracted," she lied.

She followed him to the kitchen, trying to get her head in the game.

"Well, it's just as ugly as I remembered it," he said. Looking into his blue eyes she was reminded of the last time they spoke, leaning against the railing at Wequassett. How handsome he looked, how his words had stung. "So, what's the plan in here?"

He pulled out a pad and it snapped her back to attention. "I want to set up a little café area in the back corner of the store, with a few tables and chairs for customers. Since the kitchen already has a window cutout that looks into the store. I wondered if we could open it up into a doorway?" she asked.

"What are you planning to offer?"

"Coffee, muffins, light café fare."

"Are you looking to do a commercial kitchen?"

"Goodness, no. We'll be selling prepared goods sourced elsewhere. I need to keep it simple."

Luke looked around, calculating what that meant for his involvement. "So, counter space and storage. Refrigerator, but no stove?"

"Exactly."

He opened and closed a few cabinets, ran his hand along the old Formica counters. "You can replace the counters cheaply if you go with laminate. The floors seem solid, just need a cleaning." For a few concerning moments, he turned the sink handle on and off and then crawled underneath. "You may want new fixtures for aesthetics, but the plumbing works."

"Good."

He stood up. "Keeping the layout?"

"Yes?"

"It's cheaper and faster."

"Then yes."

She waited while he inspected the rest of the room. "Should be easy enough. I'll open up the window from the kitchen to the storefront and turn it into a proper door. Other than that, it's largely cosmetic. Maybe a week?"

"Seriously?" She couldn't believe it. The kitchen was distressingly dated if operational, but she'd expected something major to crop up. Mold. Water damage. Broken pipes.

Luke's phone dinged audibly in his pocket, but he ignored it. "What're you doing about permits?" he asked.

"I've applied for a food vendor license. It means an inspection by the health department."

Luke raised his eyebrows. "You get bored easily, don't you?"

His ribbing was friendly and familiar. It comforted her from that morning's upsets and allayed some of her worries about their friendship. "Not with everything," she said.

If he heard he didn't show it, already focused on the notes he was making. She waited while he took a few measurements before returning to where she stood in the doorway. "I think with some fresh paint, a little shoring up, and some new fittings you should be good to go. You're in luck," he added. "There was a water leak at my current site which set it back two weeks. So I happen to be freed up." Luke shook his head. "Flooded the homeowner's entire first floor."

"That's fantastic!" she blurted. "I mean, the fact that you're available."

His eyes crinkled. "I know what you meant."

Talking to him was so easy; she liked the way they bantered. But there were things nagging at her. She was still dying to know why he'd driven off with Holly on reunion night. If it meant what it looked like, and if he'd seen her since. But they were standing in an old kitchen in her commercial rental with a notepad of business ideas between them, and that was all she had a right to. "When can you start?"

Luke's phone dinged again. This time he pulled it out of his pocket and glanced at it. From the look on his face, Leah knew it wasn't a work message. The message made him laugh, leaving her with the distinct feeling of being left out of a conversation. "Excuse me for a second." He stepped aside, his face turning from hers along with his attention. The whoosh of his reply filled the space between them. When he looked up again, she could already see their conversation was over.

"Sorry about that. What were you saying?"

"Nothing," she said. He'd come when he could. And whenever that was, she'd let him in to work. Because that's what this was about, she reminded herself. No matter the swell of relief she got in his presence or the way her dark mood had lifted. In the end, it was just business.

Luke

He had not expected anything new to arise from the high school reunion. That was the thing about reunions—you knew exactly what you were going to get. There were the varsity guys, from whatever team, most of whom had expanded their careers and families along with their waistbands. (The women seemed to fare better than the men.) There were those who peaked in high school whose glory days were behind them. The nerds who'd found their stride safely outside of the cafeteria and now ran companies or headed hospitals when they weren't traveling between first and second homes. Then there were the late bloomers everyone overlooked in the halls but who now turned heads. Some people surprised you, most people tracked where you expected. Luke only went for the memories, all of which he understood were well in the rearview mirror. Which is why he was surprised to strike up something new with someone long-forgotten.

Holly had been on the periphery of his group of friends in high school, and had been a last-minute ask for the prom. He was a senior and she a junior. After a night of dancing and a few stolen kisses, they dated casually through the summer and parted ways when he went to college. When she tapped him on the shoulder at the bar, it was probably the first time he'd seen or thought of her since. They shared a few drinks. They danced. At the end of the night, when she was too tipsy to drive, she joked that he'd need to give her a ride home just as he did after the prom.

Luke still wasn't sure what to make of it. From what she'd shared, Holly was freshly divorced and back from Michigan, where she'd gone to college, met her husband, and stayed. It had only been three months since she'd been back, around the same time Leah returned, which was kind of funny when he thought about it. Unlike Leah, Holly didn't know what she wanted to do now that she was back.

"What did you do in Michigan?" Luke had asked.

"My husband works for Google, so."

"You mean ex-husband?"

"Right." Luke took that to mean she hadn't needed to work, and more notably, the reality of being divorced had perhaps not fully landed on her. From experience he tended to avoid entangling himself in other people's transitions. But she was an old friend, he reasoned. Plus, she was fun. Holly laughed easily, could talk to anyone, and had clearly taken good care of herself. There was no denying she was an attractive woman. When he dropped her off at her mother's house after the reunion, she'd been the one to lean across the front seat of his truck and kiss him. The next day she texted to ask if he wanted to go to the beach. Work being what it was, he didn't have disposable time during the middle of a summer day. When she asked if he'd like to meet for a drink at the Squire, he said he'd get back to her after he checked his schedule. The truth was, beyond Scout, his evenings were wide open; he was just buying time to think. As the day went on, he found himself thinking, *Why not?*

Leah was the why not, he realized, when he stopped by the Sandy Page. Standing in her shop once again and listening to her ideas about the café, Luke was reminded why he kept finding himself drawn back to her. Despite his work demands, he somehow managed to squeeze her harebrained projects in. More surprising, her harebrained projects seemed to turn out just fine. She was confounding at times and pushy at others, but he liked that she held herself to even higher standards than she did him. When he was at the Sandy Page, he felt at home. He liked watching how personally she interacted with her customers, how she leaned in close when listening and threw her head back to laugh that wild laugh of hers. He liked how at home she made her staff feel, how much of a regular Eudora Shipman had become, and how the shy girl Lucy seemed to trail Leah like a lost puppy. Now, standing in the ugly old kitchen as she prattled on about café countertops, he found himself reeling back to the night at Harding's Beach: to the sand dunes and the sunset and her warm full lips. It was going to be hard to come back and finish another project for her, but he knew he would. He also knew he had to find something or someone else to invest his headspace in, because Leah Powell had made herself clear.

During his visit at the Sandy Page, Holly had texted him more than once. On the way home he called her.

"So, are you meeting me tonight or not?" she asked. Her tone was rich with flirtation, and he found himself smiling even as he sat in traffic.

"As it turns out, I am."

Eudora

The café work was interfering with the knitters and the painters, and the handful of little kids who'd come in with their grandmothers to craft. Though Eudora was still coming to grips with the added noise and activity, Leah's Sandy Studio had opened its doors to all for an official crafting hour. It was just as Leah wanted. For a small fee, people of all ages came in with projects of all kinds during hours which she listed as "open studio." Thankfully, the sessions were just three times a week, Monday, Wednesday, and Friday, with a dedicated end time. Dedicated end times mattered, especially when glitter and little hands were involved. It also allowed Eudora to protect the sanctity of her knitting group and enjoy quieter moments with her regulars on Tuesdays and Thursdays. The thing was, many of the knitters came in for all of it. They staked out their chairs in the corner by the good window, the kids and young parents took over the big table, and the artists of other mediums spread out around the perimeter. Leah had found three art easels at an elementary school tag sale. Plus, news of the café got out. Nothing drove local foot traffic like gossip and nosiness.

Though it was still a week from opening, reviews on the café were already mixed.

"What does Chatham Perk have to say about this?" Eudora overheard a middle-aged woman ask Leah at the register.

"Actually, I'm a regular at Chatham Perk myself," Leah told her. "They recommended suppliers for me." Leah smiled warmly at the woman, who did not smile back. "Our café will have a small-scale offering to complement the bookshop, not to compete with anyone else. It's nice when small businesses work together, don't you think?"

Eudora could understand the negativity some people assigned to change, but she would never get why some people just liked to stir the pot. It reminded her of the two gossipy women she'd overheard talking about the Sandy Page at the start of the summer at the library book club she'd failed to stay for. How far she'd come since then!

Despite the constant hum of background construction, it was nice to see Luke back in the shop. He was the one person Alfred sort of liked, and the little dog seemed to enjoy tailing him through the store, though Eudora suspected Alfred might operate from his own cache of nosiness. For a misguided minute, Scout was permitted in the shop as well, but the chaos of the chase that ensued caused a display table to tip over and the youngsters in the children's section to go wild. Scout was subsequently confined to the kitchen with Luke.

Amidst all the café construction, Eudora found herself most

distracted by her coworkers, whose personal lives appeared to be undergoing a dismantling of their own. There was Lucy, who'd burst back into the shop after talking to that teenage boy who'd been lurking about. Then there was Brad, who'd gone solemn and serious, the usual bright light of his disposition all but extinguished. How Eudora would like a word with that grandmother! Finally, there was Leah, who had her business hat on but whose smile didn't quite make it to her eyes these days. Trouble was afoot, so Eudora set up camp in the studio. She cleaned paint spills and swept glitter and replenished supplies when Leah wasn't looking.

"Oh gosh, you don't have to do that!" Leah kept saying. But someone did.

By the end of the week, not much had changed on those fronts. Brad was residing with Leah and not speaking with his grandmother. Lucy was still hauling an invisible basket of misery around, reading the story time books with a flat tone and refusing Eudora's invitations to knit. Leah had absconded to her office, making occasional appearances in the kitchen doorway while Luke worked, and then retreating behind her closed door. The only happy person seemed to be Luke. He was more gregarious than ever, despite the long hours. A handful of times Eudora could swear she heard the sound of whistling coming from the kitchen.

All week she tried to stay out of his way, but by the end of it, she peeked behind the tarp covering the kitchen doorway. Luke had all but finished.

The spacious old kitchen had been neatly divided in two. Behind a wide counter was the food service, and in front of it was the seating. Two old-fashioned display cases flanked the service counter. The old wide plank floorboards were polished and four cute little tables, mismatched and salvaged, as was Leah's signature style, were set out for customers.

"What do you think?" Leah joined her in the doorway.

"I think I'm in the wrong house," Eudora said with wonder.

"Take a tour," Leah said. It was the first time she'd looked happy all week.

Eudora walked behind the counter to the kitchen area. Gone were the cracked and faded green laminate counters. Sleek faux granite worktops stretched the length of each wall. The cabinets had been sanded and the ugly decorative scrollwork stripped, the cabinet faces now painted a deep navy, both classic and coastal. The walls were a hushed gray that evoked fog coming in off the bay. All about were pops of lobster red: an old-fashioned enamel-faced refrigerator, coffee-making equipment, blenders, and other small appliances.

"It's so inviting," Eudora gushed. She spun around to face Leah. "You did all this!"

Leah shrugged half-heartedly. "With Luke. And, of course, the team."

"You have amassed quite a team here, my dear. I hope you know that."

"I'm very lucky," Leah said, but she didn't sound like she felt very lucky. Perhaps she was just exhausted. Eudora suspected it was more, though.

"Are you alright, dear?" she asked. "It's been a long, hard week."

Leah grimaced. "Did you ever second guess yourself over a really big decision, and wonder if you made the wrong choice?"

Eudora glanced around the cozy little café, the glittering new space practically humming. Already she could feel it filling with customers, smell the freshly brewed coffee. "I can assure you, this decision was not wrong."

"It's not this, it's personal." She shook her head as if dismissing the thought. "Never mind, it's nothing. You're right—it's been a long week."

It occurred to Eudora that Leah was having second thoughts about the men in her life; there were only two she knew of, but it didn't matter. "I was married a long time to a wonderful man. And though we enjoyed many happy times together, some of them right here in this old house, there were times we both struggled."

"But you stayed together, and you were mostly happy?"

It was Eudora's turn to shrug. "We were in the same boat. As you age, you realize life is not just about the good weather days— the days your health is strong or there's money in the bank or a new baby is on the way. It's full of the other kind. And it's how you steer the boat through those days that matters most."

Leah looked away, and for a moment Eudora feared her analogy may have been lost. But when she turned back, Eudora understood. She waited while Leah swiped the tear from her cheek. "What if you got out of the boat?" Leah asked.

"Then I guess you have to ask yourself a question."

"You mean, will he let me back in?"

"No." Eudora shook her head. "Are you sure you want to?"

Lucy

On her one morning to sleep in, there was sudden banging on her bedroom door. Lucy looked up to see her mother's face silhouetted in the morning light streaming through the doorway. "She's talking!"

"What?" Lucy blinked, rubbing the sleep from her eyes, trying to understand.

"You sister! She's talking. Get up, we're going to Spaulding."

Her parents were both taking their breakfast standing in the kitchen. Her mother wasn't even eating, so much as pacing around with her still-full coffee cup. If Ella was talking, this changed everything. It meant she could tell them how she was feeling, what she was thinking. It meant Lucy could talk to her about the accident, about what Jep said. It meant she was back.

"So the hospital called and said Ella started talking, just like that?" Lucy asked. The doctors had said the brain was mysterious, but to wake up talking was nearly a miracle. She popped a bagel into the toaster.

"Not exactly," her mother said. "Her speech therapist, Karen, said she had good news. Ella's articulation is stronger."

"Wait. So she's still not talking?"

Her mother was still pacing, talking fast. Lucy wondered just how much coffee she'd had. "When I called for my usual update, Karen said her speech was more intelligible today."

"So they didn't call us. You called them," Lucy clarified.

Her mother looked hurt. "What difference does it make?"

It made a lot of difference. The optimism her mother had blasted her with in her bedroom doorway moments ago seeped out of her. Lucy looked at her father, who leaned into evidence over emotion, always pushing the doctors and therapists for proof of any improvement. "They said your sister is articulating," he said. "This is excellent!"

So there was no miracle necessitating waking Lucy up and racing off to Spaulding. She yanked her bagel out of the toaster and buttered it, even though it was too early to be hungry. "Sorry, but I still don't get what's so excellent about it?"

Her mother spun around like Lucy had slapped her. "How dare you? Your sister is finally talking, and you want to stand around and argue about it? You can't be happy for her? For all of us?"

Lucy reeled back. "That's not what I said! I am happy, but you guys made it sound like the hospital called to say she was all better now. Like she could talk to us, tell us what happened."

"Alright, enough!" her father interjected. "It's early, and we're all tired. Let's go to the hospital and see for ourselves. Lucy, eat your bagel in the car."

On the drive to Spaulding Lucy's mind skittered from her last run-in with Jep to the way her mother acted in the kitchen that morning. She was tired of living on the edge, everyone's emotions raw and unpredictable.

She was also tired of being the sole keeper of information. Lucy had not done as Jep had asked. She hadn't even told Reya what he'd said the other day. First, she didn't believe him. Sure, Ella went to parties and drank, but she would never have gotten behind the wheel drunk; she was too smart, her future too bright. Her whole life Ella had worked hard to get to where she was. Tufts loomed on her horizon, along with her future. Ironically, it was the same future Jep claimed he was trying to protect.

What a joke. No one would take the blame for someone else's accident, especially one that ended with his girlfriend seriously injured, and his classic car totaled. Especially in a small town where everyone knows your business and your family, too. Even if it wasn't a prestigious college scholarship, Jep had his own future to lose. Unlike Ella, his family business was right there in Chatham, where everyone would know who he was and what he'd done. The ramifications for his garage were not small. It didn't make sense that he'd take the fall.

What did make sense was the timing: Jep was coming forward now with this claim because her family had sued him. He was running scared. This was about him saving his own tail, not protecting Ella. Lucy fumed, her indignation spinning along with the wheels of their family car on the highway. Her sister had a right to know what Jep was saying: she had a right to set the record straight. But it left Lucy with a burning question: At what cost? One thing she'd learned that summer was there was no black-and-white when it came to doing what you thought was right. People were influenced all the time, their reasons colored gray; by their beliefs, by their fears, by greed. If Lucy told Ella what Jep had accused her of, it would crush her, and right at a time when she was finally demonstrating measurable signs of healing. It made Lucy wonder if telling her parents was the better choice. It made her wonder if she should just keep her mouth shut and say nothing at all.

Her father had barely turned off the car engine when her mother threw the passenger door ajar. "Come on," she urged them, hurrying around to open Lucy's door. "Let's go, let's go."

It was funny the things that resonated with her parents when it came to signs of Ella returning to them. For her father, it had been the fact that Ella could walk again. The physicality of her sister rising up on her own, no matter how shaky, and putting one foot in front of the other had marked a turning point in his own healing. For her mother, she'd been holding out all summer for words. Ella being able to communicate with them again was the sign her mother counted dearest. No one had asked Lucy what sign she was holding out hope for. If they had, she would tell them it was something she was *still* waiting for.

As they rounded the corner to Ella's room, Dr. Forrester was standing in the hallway. She motioned to them. "Good morning!" she said, coming over. "Exciting changes today."

"Yes!" Lucy's mother kept turning toward Ella's room. She did not want to be held up by whatever Dr. Forrester had to say. "I can't wait to see her."

"If I may have a word first?" Dr. Forrester's expression grew more serious. "I know you're eager to see her, so I won't keep you. Let's remember that Ella's articulation is coming back. She won't speak as fluently and clearly as she once did, at least not at first. It's important we give her time and adjust our expectations."

Lucy's father wanted to know more. "Are you saying she won't ever regain full speech?"

"Not at all, in fact the signs are promising. Karen, the speech therapist, will be in shortly to talk more with you and offer a clear explanation of what we can look forward to." Dr. Forrester nodded to the doorway. "Go on, I'm sure she'll be happy to see you."

For all their eagerness to arrive, Lucy's parents hesitated on the threshold of the door. Lucy understood. There had been losses and gains all summer. High hopes and dashed dreams. She squeezed between her parents and entered first.

"Hey there, Ella," she said.

Ella was watching something on TV, and her head snapped in her family's direction, a smile spreading across her face. Lucy felt her parents press in close on either side, like bookends.

"Hi," Ella said, her voice raspy but strong.

Lucy's mother burst into tears.

They stayed the morning at Spaulding. From the strained attempts at conversation, it became clear quickly that Ella's speech was still very limited; she spoke only a few words, most in isolation. Certain sounds were easier than others. But Lucy's parents were overjoyed. When Danny took Ella for PT, Karen, the speech pathologist, came to speak to them about the new development.

"The brain is a miraculous organ," she told them happily.

"It's what we've been waiting for," Lucy's mother said. "What changed?"

Karen shrugged. "Speech can return in weeks or months, sometimes longer. We don't always know why. In Ella's case, as you know she's been dealing with dysarthria. That involves muscle control weakness from damage to the nerves or brain, which is why she's had difficulty articulating."

"Does this mean she's over it now?"

"Unfortunately, it doesn't work that way," Karen said sympathetically. "It's a motor speech disorder, and that requires time and continued therapy. The good news is her gains are strong."

Lucy's father cleared his throat. "Ella is supposed to be at Tufts in September." Hadn't her father just seen what she had seen? It was both heartbreaking and infuriating. He was asking Karen for assurances she couldn't give.

"Mr. Hart, Ella has suffered a traumatic injury. She's young, and the neuroplasticity of her brain is in our favor. What lies ahead looks promising, but every individual responds differently. It's something the team will discuss with you and Dr. Forrester at our weekly."

Lucy knew those weekly meetings too well, and she'd opted out. She blamed it on work, but the truth was she purposely scheduled shifts at the Sandy Page on those days. Sitting around a table with the team under the glare of the fluorescent lights was too painful. There were endless reports: OT, PT, speech, physiatrists. No one ever had answers. And yet her father just kept asking for miracles.

"But she's walking again!" her father reminded Karen. "You saw her leave with Danny. And her speech is coming back. So it's still possible she could attend school, right?"

The hope on his face was too much. Lucy excused herself.

"Where are you going?" her mother asked.

"Coffee." Lucy didn't drink coffee. The last thing she heard Karen say was, "Let's try and take things one day at a time."

It was exhausting, the grip her parents had on hope. Maybe it was better than the opposite, Lucy reasoned. At least they weren't drowning in depression, taking to their beds. But still. They refused to come to terms with what Lucy felt all along in her bones. There would be no packing of the car that August. Lucy and her family would not drive up the Mass Pike or decorate a dorm room or say a tearful goodbye in the campus parking lot. Maybe that would happen next year. Maybe it would never happen at all. For now, they were stuck here; the only drive for certain was the daily commute to and from Spaulding Rehab.

Only when Lucy knew Ella's PT was over did she return to her room. Lunch was brought in, and Lucy's mom produced sandwiches she must have made and packed before Lucy even woke up that morning. Ella was able to feed herself independently. At least Lucy's mom no longer cut up her food the way she used to, even when the OT had insisted they not. Lucy watched Ella take a few bites of macaroni and cheese and a sip of her apple juice before turning her attention to her own turkey sandwich. She would try to be more like her parents; she would try to believe life would return to normal.

They were eating in silence when Ella began talking. It wasn't the kind of talking Lucy had expected. It was garbled, maybe because of her still developing articulation, or maybe because she was crying, Lucy realized with a start.

"Darling? What is it?" Her mother hopped up, leaning over the bed.

Ella looked at her mother through a stream of tears. Her lunch tray tipped precariously on her lap. Lucy grabbed it just in time.

Ella repeated herself a second time, then a third. By then Lucy understood.

"I'm sorry," Ella cried, looking between her parents.

"Honey, no! There's nothing to be sorry for," their mother said.

"It's alright," their father said. "Everything is going to be okay."

But Ella would not stop. Her words were slurred but her meaning distinct. "I'm sorry," she cried. "I'm sorry. I'm so sorry."

No one noticed Lucy slip out into the hall for the second time that afternoon. She had to. The clues were tumbling at her, too fast to hang on to.

Jep Parson's words: *She was the one driving.* Ella's gold bracelet, found on the driver's side of the car. The note: *Please don't tell.* The broken look on her sister's face each time Lucy cheered her on. Clues, all of them.

Clues that Lucy had unwittingly collected all summer, like sea glass washed ashore. As Ella's slurred apology warbled out to the hall, no one was sorrier than Lucy Hart.

Leah

What she probably needed was a mental health day, but instead she was hosting the café's grand opening. The problem was, no one was feeling particularly grand.

"I think you should aim for a soft opening," Brad suggested flatly, back at her house. He was lounging on the couch in gym shorts and a frayed T-shirt, two things she would never have believed Brad owned, except for the fact he'd worn them two days in a row. Since his grandmother had kicked him out, Brad had slid into a despair that was at odds with everything Leah knew about him. When not working, he ate junk food, took long naps, and binge-watched Netflix. The only sign of old Brad came through the walls late at night when Ethan called. They talked for hours on the phone. "Or you could just open the café with no hoopla, and let word get out organically." She could tell that was Brad's preference.

Leah wasn't in the mood for hoopla, either, but after all the hard work and investment, she couldn't just give up now. Greg's call begging to get back together had haunted her. That, and Luke. Despite the fact the café depended on him finishing the job, having him back at the shop had been unbearable. All evidence pointed to him becoming involved with Holly Houston. And that depressed her. It made her wonder if she'd missed out on something she didn't know she'd needed. It made her wonder if feeling *anything* about Luke and Holly was just a rebound response to Greg; Greg and his ridiculous claims of love returned. What Leah wanted to yell back at him was, *Where* did it go in the first place? As if love could take a holiday, or get misplaced like keys, or run away like a dog. (In that vein, she wondered: *Where* did Rebekah go?)

Despite her conflicted mood, the café needed to open. A soft opening sounded nice, like a gentle landing, a down comforter. She settled for a midweek date, set the time for three o'clock and posted an announcement online. When that felt uninspired, she hung up a few flyers in the store window. It was hardly a publicity campaign, but it was what she could manage.

Luckily, Brad came back to life as the opening loomed, but they weren't quite on the same page with aesthetics. "It's very French bistro, I'll give you that," he said, scrutinizing the room. "But dear God, not one more red tchotchke." He snatched a ceramic lobster saltshaker off a table. "It's like a crustacean invasion."

"They're accessories," Leah told him. "They're part of my coastal New England color palette."

"Which is starting to feel more like a Midwestern Fourth of July."

After rounding up the better part of her red decor and shoving it in the closet, Brad got to work rearranging the tables she'd just finished positioning. Leah waited until he was done before rescuing her red *tchotchkes* from the closet and dragging the tables back into their original places. Together they experimented with the newly delivered espresso machine, which intimidated her but delighted him. They set up the coffee carafes and stocked the fridge with dairy and oat milks, whipping cream, and simple syrups. Orders were finalized for the baked goods.

By midweek it was time to open to the public. Coastal Grains made their first fresh bakery delivery. As soon as Lucy arranged the goods in the display case, it began to feel like a café. There were cheese Danish, croissants, bagels, and blueberry muffins. For heartier fare, Leah had decided to add puff pastries of spinach and cheddar, and ham and Gruyère to their order. Their lower Cape coffee vendor, Sacred Grounds, suggested they start with a breakfast blend, a dark roast, and an espresso, all fair trade and organic, roasted in micro-batches for the freshest grounds. Coffees could be ordered hot, cold brew, or iced. Menus were printed on thick sand-colored cardstock with little navy seashells embossed at the borders. Lucy and Brad took turns writing out a store menu on an oversized chalkboard Leah had discovered at a schoolhouse auction. They were ready.

There would be no ribbon cutting, but Eudora suggested they keep the tarp over the entrance to the kitchen. "Nothing like a little mystery," she said.

Just before three o'clock people started trickling in, and when a small group had amassed Leah gathered everyone by the tarped doorway. There were about twenty guests, most of them faces she recognized as story time and studio regulars. A few were new. A few were neighbors, like Willet Smith. Seeing all of them renewed her spirits, reminding her why she was doing this.

"I want to thank each and every one of you for being here and being part of the Sandy Page family," she said, in welcome.

A round of applause and murmurs of approval reverberated through the group.

"For those of you who've been with us since opening day, I guess you could say a lot has happened. What began as a new bookstore in an old house has taken on a life of its own." As she spoke, a few stragglers joined. Leah was heartened to see Luke among them. When he caught her eye, he smiled. "From books to a community art studio, and today, to our little corner café, my wish is that all of you find something here that makes you feel at home." Leah turned to Brad, who was standing to the side. "Shall we?"

With a flourish, Brad whisked the tarp away revealing the sparkling café space behind it. Lucy waved from behind the display counter inside. People clapped. The little crowd surged forward, and Leah found herself swept to the side in its wake.

A warm hand reached out and steadied her. "Congratulations," Luke said. He was dressed up in a crisp white linen shirt and freshly shaven.

"Thanks for coming," Leah said. "And for all of this." She turned, taking it all in. "It's incredible."

"It sure is. You and your crazy ideas." He was shaking his head, but the way he looked at her made her feel like all of it was worth doing, even if she wasn't quite sure how it would turn out.

Eudora waved to them from the café counter. "Come in and enjoy! You two earned it."

It reminded Leah of something she'd set aside. "I wasn't sure if you'd come today, but I wanted to give you this." Leah retrieved a small plate from the framed window Luke had enlarged between the kitchen and the shop and held it out to him.

"For me?" He lifted the red napkin to find a ham and Gruyère pastry, still warm.

"I wanted you to be the first person served." She could feel herself start to choke up, but she pulled herself together.

Luke took a big bite of the pastry, closing his eyes with pleasure. "Damn that's good. Thank you." Watching him enjoy the food, surrounded by the buzz of customers, Leah felt something inside her shift. After a week when nothing felt right, this small moment did.

It gave her an idea. "I know it's last minute, but is there any chance you might want to . . ." Leah was going with her gut and about to ask him to meet her for a drink that evening, when someone called Luke's name from the front of the shop.

They both turned to see Holly Houston. "I was waiting for you outside."

Leah's stomach dropped. The nice outfit and the fresh shave hadn't been for the opening, after all. Luke already had plans. He turned to her now. "Holly, you remember Leah?"

"Hi," she said, glancing around. "Cute store."

"Thank you," Leah said. "And welcome to the café opening."

Holly was dressed in a white summer dress, her hair pulled back in a sleek ponytail. She leaned against Luke. "We should go. I don't want to be late."

Luke looked apologetically at Leah. "Congratulations, again. Glad I made it."

"Me, too," Leah told him.

He began to pop the rest of the pastry in his mouth when Holly noticed. "Don't ruin your appetite. We've got reservations." Then she pecked him on the cheek. "I'll wait outside."

"Right." For an awkward moment Luke stood there, looking around for a trash can.

"Let me," Leah said. Before he could object, she took the plate from his hands. "Holly's waiting."

Leah watched them leave, as Holly slipped her arm into his and as Luke held the door for her on the way out. "How is it?" Brad came up beside her, looking at Luke's half-eaten pastry.

"I don't know. It wasn't mine."

It was a success and it was over. Leah should've felt pleased, but by the time she locked up it was seven-thirty and what she was feeling was restless and frustrated. All evening, customers came up to her commenting on how wonderful it was to have a café in the bookshop, how nice it was to bring their grandchildren to story time, their friends to a Paint and Sip. While Leah registered these interactions as the gifts they were, they just didn't make it to her heart.

Between Luke and Holly's burgeoning relationship, and

Greg's request to get back together, Leah felt like the punching bag at her old gym; swinging between blows and forever chained in place. She needed a reprieve.

Instead of going home, she decided to take a walk. At the corner of Main Street she took a hard left into the thick of the village and the tourists. She passed the residence of a children's author, whose tidy little roadside barn boasted a set of transom windows, each one filled with curiosities and old toys, a wooden sign that read IMAGINE affixed over its sliding doors. The night was still young. It was good to lose herself in the crowd; the long line outside Buffy's Ice Cream shop, the couples holding hands, the late shoppers with their bags. When she got to the doors of the Chatham Squire, she went in.

At the narrow bar by the front windows, Leah grabbed a stool and ordered her favorite summer drink, a Painkiller. How apropos, she thought. The tropical concoction went down too easily; she ordered another. The barstools faced the street, proffering up the perfect Americana view of the boutiques and galleries across the way, the sidewalk strollers, the window boxes teeming with flowers. The restaurant was noisy, filled with sunburned families and mouthwatering aromas. This time when the bartender inquired, she ordered a half dozen oysters, a bowl of New England clam chowder, and another Painkiller. *Chatham is heaven,* she thought, stirring her clam chowder. How lucky she was to be here. How lucky she was to have her little shop, despite the constant grind.

Between courses and cocktails, however, she found her resolve wavering. Soon the season would end, and the summer bustle would wrap up. The sidewalks would still. Almost all the shops and galleries closed down for the winter, and the village became a bit of a ghost town. No doubt it would impact revenue at the Sandy Page, which was barely a fledgling. Brad would go back to school, and Lucy, too. She pictured herself and Eudora sitting in the empty shop with Alfred the dog. She might have to take up knitting. Winter would be lonely and long. What if the shop faltered?

When the bartender came by to offer the check, she asked for another drink. And a basket of bread. Why not?

She'd resolved to keep her phone off for the night, but as the Painkiller's initial buzz handed the reins over to a fresh wave of despair she pulled it from her bag. Greg had texted, again. *Leah, we can do this. Think of the life we planned. It's still ours for the taking.*

For the taking. Hadn't he taken from her, when she was at her lowest? Greg had always been a stand-up guy, a loyal partner. She even believed that Greg hadn't sought out Rebekah; she was just a piece of his past who happened to reappear when times were tough. The fact Leah wrestled with most was that when things got ugly for her, Greg hadn't been gutsy enough to see her through. He hadn't been there for her.

Still, she could not deny the years they had together; they were good years. They had a secure future, even without her old job at Morgan. Boston afforded them cultural stimulation that the sleepy Cape could not: theater, museums, restaurants, Fenway. What had she done since returning to Chatham except slave away in the bookstore? Here she had no friends, no personal life outside of work.

However, to even consider Greg's request meant to consider letting go of the Sandy Page. Questions spiraled through her head. Was she willing to walk away from everything she'd just begun? No, Greg would have to come to her, at least at first. That thought gave her further pause; did that mean she was considering Greg's offer? Leah took another swallow of her drink.

As it always did, the Squire got busier as the evening went on. The empty stools around her had filled. Surrounded by the commotion of families in the restaurant and patrons at the bar, Leah was still alone. It made her wonder. It made her worry. She pushed the unfinished cocktail away from her. She needed to go home. The long walk back to her car at the shop would sober her up, she figured. When she stood, the bar swayed sharply in front of her. Leah sat back down hard. She'd had more to drink than she'd realized, those damn Painkillers. To her mortification, the bartender leaned in. "Would you like me to call an Uber?" he asked gently.

She could feel her cheeks flush. "My friend is coming," she said, forcing a smile. She texted Brad to please come get her. When she looked up, a tall glass of water and more bread sat before her. "Thanks," she said, feeling sheepish.

When she'd finished the water, and still didn't feel any better, she checked her phone. Brad had not replied. If anything, she felt woozier than before—how she'd like a straw to suck out the last two drinks as quickly as she'd sucked them down. When she called Brad it went straight to voicemail. She'd have to get an Uber. But first, she needed to use the bathroom.

Leah took one look at the line of little kids outside the restaurant restroom and cut through to the tavern, on the other side.

It took all her concentration not to wobble. Live music met her in the dark hallway between the two establishments, and the crowd shifted instantly from parents holding toddler hands to college-age kids gripping pints of beer. Once upon a time, she used to be part of this crowd. It was louder and the noise denser over here, but at least the restroom line was short. On her way out, a young woman bumped against her and almost knocked Leah down. "Sorry!" the girl said, reaching out. It was embarrassing, but it was nothing compared to the shame she felt when she looked up. Coming out of the other restroom at the same time was Luke. He'd seen the whole thing.

"Leah. You okay?"

"I'm fine," she said, but her slurred words were obvious even to her ears. She needed to get out of there.

"Are you here alone?" he asked.

Leah propped herself against the wall, hoping to appear less drunk. Clearly it had the opposite effect. "What makes you think I'm alone?" she asked, glancing past him for any sign of Holly Houston. She didn't like the implication. She liked even less that he likely was not.

At least Luke looked appropriately reprimanded. "Nothing. I'm only asking because I want to make sure you get home safe."

"Who says I'm going home?" It had been so long since she'd been in this bad shape, she'd forgotten how stubborn it made her.

Luke glanced behind him and sighed like he was between a rock and a hard place.

"Looking for someone?" Leah asked. Somewhere in that crowd Holly Houston was standing alone with two drinks.

"Do me a favor." Luke placed both hands on her shoulders. "Stay here, be quiet, and don't move, alright?"

Leah did not appreciate being told what to do, but she was in no condition to do otherwise. Luke disappeared into the thick of the tavern crowd. A moment later, he returned, looking grim.

"Trouble in paradise?"

Luke ignored the cheeky comment and grabbed her hand. "Let's go."

"Wait. Where are we going?"

"Home." His grip was strong and warm, and she felt her insolence give way. She allowed Luke to lead her back down the narrow hallway and out through the restaurant to the sidewalk. As soon as they hit the fresh air outside, Leah felt steadier.

"Where's your car?" he asked, glancing up and down Main Street.

"Back at the shop."

"Good. It can stay there until tomorrow. I'll drive you." Luke seemed intent on getting her home, and suddenly she didn't want his help. He was on a date. He would probably be coming right back here to finish it. And she did not want to think about how his date would end.

"Look, I can get an Uber," she told him, straightening. "Brad is back at the house, so I can call him, too."

This got his attention. "Brad is at your place?"

"He's staying with me now. His grandmother asked him to leave."

"That's really nice of you," he said.

"I'm a nice girl." The words were out of her mouth before her brain could catch them.

Luke's eyes crinkled with laughter. "I know you are. It's another reason I'd feel better driving you home, myself. C'mon, I'm parked up by the church."

The church was at the opposite end of Main Street. Leah trailed behind Luke on the sidewalk. Several times he stopped so she could catch up. Finally, after she bumped against a passerby, he wrapped an arm around her waist and they walked together.

"Sorry it's so far. Town was crowded tonight."

"I don't mind," she said. In truth, she wished he'd parked a mile away, or ten. Pressed against Luke's side like that, the alcohol humming through her veins and all her predicaments with it, Leah felt time slow. They passed the chamber of commerce booth where she worked one summer in college; past Yankee Ingenuity, her father's favorite shop of curiosities; the Eldredge Library where her mother used to take her as a child. She had so many memories here, and Luke was among them.

When they finally reached his truck, he held the door for her and helped her in. Suddenly Leah was so tired, her eyelids so heavy.

"I'm just going to rest my head a little," she said, curling up on the bench seat.

"You do that." Luke climbed into the driver's side and started the engine.

As they rolled down Main Street, Leah lay very still, her head resting next to Luke's thigh. From that position she could see the signs and awnings of the buildings they passed, the gentle glow of the streetlamps, and Luke's strong jaw, set in concentration. Her eyes fluttered with fatigue, but she fought it: she didn't want to miss any of it. And then a thought jerked her out of her reverie. "Are you going back after you drop me off?"

"Back where?"

"The Squire. Isn't Holly waiting for you?"

Luke put on the indicator and she felt herself slide gently against him as they made the wide turn around the rotary. "Not tonight."

Leah almost felt bad for him. "Is she upset you left with me?"

"Holly will be fine," he said, finally.

Leah thought about that. "Holly is lucky." Had she said it aloud, or just thought it? Luke didn't say a word. Maybe it was just a thought. Maybe she should close her eyes and give in.

The sky grew dark as they left Main Street behind. When they turned again, up Old Queen Anne, Leah knew she was almost home. The scenery from where she lay became treetops and leafy branches, silhouetted against sky. Her eyelids grew pleasantly heavy. So, too, did the warm hand she realized was resting on her head.

When she woke up the next morning, Leah was safe in her bed, the blankets pulled up to her chin, her clothes from the night before still on. There was a piece of paper folded on her bedside table. Leah squinted at it in the early light.

She reached for it. *Good night Leah Powell.*

Eudora

After the initial opening party, the café developed some immediate regulars. True, Eudora was one of them. So was Willet Smith, who was always trying to strike up a conversation with her. In fact, he would wait by the front door before they opened each day, which Leah found charming and Brad found exasperating. "That man," he muttered. "Here for anything, as long as it isn't a book."

Eudora felt Leah's gaze land on her. "I think Willet is here for more than baked goods," she suggested. "What are your thoughts on the matter, Eudora?"

Well. Eudora didn't know anything about that, nor was she going to dignify it. "I think I have some knitting to get to. My group will be in shortly."

"Willet's in the café, if you'd like some company," Leah added.

As far as company went, Willet Smith was not as grumpy as he looked, once you got to know him, and that's exactly what had happened that summer. Sometimes when he brought in vegetables, he'd sit down at the project table in the studio and watch what everyone was doing. At first it annoyed Eudora; those seats were for customers. There was enough room for all, however. Plus, Willet always left a bag of mixed vegetables for each staff member; she noticed hers was heavier on the heirlooms she so favored.

She found her way into the café. Immediately Willet looked up. "Can I buy you a coffee?" he asked. "The mocha latte sounded like a whole lot of fuss to me, but it's actually not terrible."

"Thank you, but I think I'll have a cup of tea."

Willet stood, reaching around for his wallet. "No, no," Eudora said, noticing his cup was empty. "This one's on me."

She ordered a tea for herself and another latte for Willet, then joined him at the little red table for two by the window. Predictably, Willet needed to warm up with a weather commentary. "Looks to be another hot one," he said, rubbing the stubble on his chin. Milton was such a careful shaver, not scruffy like Willet. Still, it suited him somehow.

"Yes, my Shasta daisies are loving it. As are my coneflowers."

Willet considered this. "Those are pretty, but you can't eat flowers."

"I don't feel the need to eat everything I plant," she told him. "Life is also about beauty."

"Beauty." He rolled the word around on his tongue. "Beauty is nice, too." The way he was looking at her made her shift in her seat. Where was Lucy with that tea?

Willet cleared his throat. "I read in the news that there's going to be an art show this weekend. That artist you mentioned the other day that you like so much—Amy Ross is her name?"

Eudora was surprised. She'd forgotten all about the conversation she'd had with one of her knitters a while ago; Willet must've been listening. "Why, yes, I enjoy her watercolors immensely."

"Well, she's coming to the Cape in August." He unfolded a newspaper clipping and slid it across the table to her.

Eudora scanned the article. "She's coming to Provincetown! How did I miss this?" Eudora had two pieces by Amy hanging in her living room. Milton had once brought her to an opening in Sandwich, where they purchased their first piece, a watercolor of Chatham Bay. "It's been years since I've been to one of her shows."

Willet cleared his throat. "Would you like to go with me?"

"With you?" Luckily, Lucy arrived with their beverages. It gave Eudora a moment to collect her thoughts. She busied herself stirring sugar into her tea. Eudora never took sugar in her tea. As Willet waited, she added more. "That might be nice," she said, finally. When she looked at him through the steam of their mugs, his face fell.

"But you don't want to go."

"No! It's just that I need to check my calendar. And Provincetown is kind of far."

"Just an hour," he said. "I can drive."

If Willet drove the way he walked, as she suspected he did, it would likely take even longer. What he didn't understand was that every minute out and about equated to anxiety rising. Eudora didn't do anything an hour outside of her house, except for the Sandy Page, which didn't count. Driving made her anxious, and being a passenger was possibly worse. If her anxiety flared, she'd have the added burden of disappointing Willet. No, it was too much to even consider. "I'll take a look and let you know," she said, sipping her tea. It was horribly sweet. She would have to dump it out, just as she'd have to find a way to politely dump Willet's offer.

"Well, the offer stands. Just let me know." Willet finished his mocha latte and bid her goodbye. "Enjoy the summer squash. I left you a bag at the register."

Eudora waved goodbye, a lump already forming in her stomach.

When knitting group started, she was cheered by the sight of Lucy in the studio doorway. She held a small canvas bag. "Is it alright if I join today?"

Eudora had thought the girl would never ask. As the other knitters arrived and settled in, Lucy shared the progress on the scarf she'd started with Eudora weeks ago. "My goodness, you've been knitting all this time?" There was enough length to wrap around an elephant's neck.

"I never stopped," Lucy said shyly. "I just didn't have time for the group."

"Well, I'm glad you're back," Eudora told her. She knew Lucy had needed time to forgive her, and she didn't blame her. Eudora had let her guidance counselor hat weigh heavier on her head than her good sense. Lucy's family news had never been hers to share, and even though she'd done so with good intentions, she felt bad. "And I owe you an apology. I should not have shared your family business with Leah. What I should have done was ask you, first."

Lucy nodded shyly. "It's okay."

"No, it's not. I was a busybody, trying to help out where I wasn't asked. From now I will keep my big mouth shut until you ask for it."

From the look on Lucy's face, it was unclear how this made her feel. "Deal," she said, finally. The word filled Eudora's chest with more gratitude than she'd felt all summer.

When knitting group wrapped up, Lucy lingered. "Do you need help with anything else?" Eudora asked, nodding at her needlework.

Lucy bit her lip. "Actually, yes."

Eudora sat down beside her.

"You know about my sister, Ella. I was wondering if you could help me with something."

"What do you need, honey?"

She could see Lucy was afraid to ask. And she was unprepared for the question that followed. "I need to visit Ella this afternoon. Would give me a ride?"

Two requests for car rides had come in the same morning. Eudora planned to say no to one, but there was no way she could say no to the other. Despite the fact Lucy's sister was all the way over at Spaulding Rehabilitation Hospital, and despite the fact Eudora was afraid to drive anywhere these days, she agreed to pick Lucy up at five.

"I'll meet you by the curb," Lucy told her. And then she did something just as unexpected. She leaned over and gave Eudora a hug.

Eudora needed to go home and lie down. If she was going

to make this work, she needed to prepare herself. It was really no different than one of her rescue dogs needing a ride, she told herself. It would take the life out of her, and might likely require several days of recuperation after, but she would do it. Lucy Hart needed her.

She was so frazzled she drifted right by the register without her knitting materials. "Oh no. My bag!"

"I'll get it," Brad offered. He returned, and as he handed it over the newspaper clipping sailed out and onto the floor. He bent to retrieve it.

"Ooh, an art opening. Are you going?"

Eudora shook her head and shoved the clipping deep into her bag. "It's just something Willet shared this with me today."

Leah was studying her curiously. "Are you feeling alright?"

She could not risk letting on what Lucy had asked of her. "Yes, just a little rattled. Willet invited me to go with him to the opening." Oh Lord. In trying to keep one cat in the bag, she'd released another.

Brad seized upon this. "Willet asked you on a date?"

"Goodness, no. He overheard me mention the artist, is all."

A huge smile spread across Brad's face. "Is it possible Willet Smith is a romantic?"

"Oh, I don't think so." Eudora could feel the deep blush that followed flash across her cheeks like wildfire. "It's not like that."

"Well, he doesn't strike me as an art connoisseur." Brad chuckled. "Though, I guess you never know. You should go. Together."

Leah leaned across the counter. "I think it's nice, Eudora. That you two have a friendship."

Is that what it was? She supposed so. A friendship wasn't so terrible; at least it wasn't as terrifying as a date. Still, there was the matter of the distance and the drive. And the crowd that would be there. But she didn't want to unload all that on Leah and Brad. Her nerves were already ablaze with the task before her that afternoon and she needed to get home. Besides, a customer had just come in. The bell jangled once, then twice as the front door opened and closed.

Whoever it was, Leah did not look happy. Eudora turned to see for herself. A young man, dressed more for a business meeting than a day at the Cape, stood in the doorway. He looked very handsome, his face friendly. Eudora glanced back at Leah.

Leah froze behind the register. She crossed her arms. "What are *you* doing here?"

Lucy

The last thing she wanted was to involve anyone else in her business, but there was no way around it. She did not want her parents to know she was going to see Ella. And none of her friends had licenses. Eudora Shipman had given her a ride once before. It turned out she was willing to do it again.

When work ended, she texted her mom that she was staying late. Then she hurried out to the curb where Mrs. Shipman was already waiting. When Lucy slid into the passenger seat Alfred yipped and barked himself into a frenzy from the back, but it was Mrs. Shipman who looked worse. Lucy's memory swung hard to the nail-biting drive home the last time, and she wondered if she'd made a huge mistake.

"You sure you're okay with this, Mrs. Shipman?"

The old woman nodded hard, took a rattling breath, and put the car roughly in drive. "Here we go."

The drive wasn't deadly exactly, but there were moments.

Mrs. Shipman was nervous, and it wasn't just the sheen on her pale forehead or the death grip on the steering wheel. After a few hard stops and sharp turns, they swung onto Route 6 and things evened out in the slow lane. It was a snail's pace, and there were some honks, but eventually they pulled up to Spaulding. Lucy let out her breath the moment Mrs. Shipman put the car in park. She hadn't realized she'd been holding it.

"Thank you so much," she told Mrs. Shipman.

"You are welcome." She pulled a tissue from her oversized purse and dabbed her head, then reached for another. "Sorry, I get a little jumpy on the highway."

"You did great," Lucy told her. That seemed to help. "Do you want to come in?" It hadn't occurred to her what to do with Mrs. Shipman once they got there. It was too hot to leave her in the car, and too rude, too. Plus, there was the matter of Alfred, who snarled when Lucy turned to look at him.

"It would be good to get out. Don't worry. Alfred has a therapy dog vest, so they'll let him in."

Lucy could not imagine Alfred providing any sense of calm to anyone, but then it dawned on her: he did for Mrs. Shipman.

The three of them checked in at the front desk, and Mrs. Shipman settled into a chair in the waiting area. "We'll be right here."

"I won't be long," Lucy promised.

When she got to Ella's room, Lucy hesitated in the doorway. All this time Ella had been trying to heal and her parents were wracked with worry and the daily commute back and forth, Lucy had been saddled with her own grief and worry. People's lives had been upended. With the pending lawsuit, lives were about to be upended even more. And if Lucy held the key to making something right out of all the wrong that had happened that summer, she needed to use it. Even if it meant upsetting her family in doing so.

She knocked lightly on the door and Ella looked up. "Lucy!" Her voice was still gravelly from lack of use, but her expression was bright.

"Hey there." Lucy went and sat on the edge of the bed. "How're you doing today?"

In the last week, color had returned to Ella's cheeks, and clarity to her expression. She looked more and more like her old self and it made Lucy brave.

"I'm good," Ella said, with some effort. "Mom and Dad?" She looked to the door.

Lucy shook her head. "It's just me today. I got a ride, with a friend." She winked. "Don't tell Mom or Dad."

Ella laughed softly and Lucy did, too. It felt good to share a sisterly secret again. "I came today because there's something I need to know." Lucy reached into her pocket. "Do you remember when I brought you that note from Jep?"

Ella turned to her side table, to the copy of *Anne of Green Gables*. Lucy watched as she flipped through the book. There, in the middle, was the folded note from Jep.

"Love note–bookmark?" Lucy asked.

Ella winced. "I miss him."

"That's why I'm here." She handed Ella the other half of the note, the part she'd torn from the bottom. "I'm sorry I kept this from you. I didn't know what it meant, and I was worried it would upset you."

Heart in her throat, Lucy waited as Ella read the entirety of Jep's message for the first time.

Ella's eyes flicked over the message once more, then back at Lucy. Neither of them spoke.

Lucy cleared her throat. "Ella, does that mean what I think it does?"

Ella let out a long breath. She pulled the other half of the note from the pages of her book and lay both on her lap, one atop the other. Then she read the words aloud, slowly and sadly, "I-love-you-Ella. P.S. Please-don't-tell."

When she looked up again, Lucy had her answer. "You were the one driving the car that night."

Ella did not cry. This time her voice did not waver. "Yes."

"Jep took the blame for you."

"He did?" Ella's face crumpled.

"Mom and Dad don't know. The police don't know. Jep told everyone that he was the one driving."

"Why?" Ella threw up her hands, her voice cracking. "Why would he?"

"To protect you."

In one sudden motion, Ella flipped her covers back. She swung her legs over the side of the bed like she was going to run out of there.

"Wait!" Lucy stood, placing both hands on her sister's shoulders, as if she could stop her. Ella was stronger now, and she leaned into Lucy hard. "Ella, wait. Listen. This is why I didn't tell you." She pressed her forehead to her sister's and held her. "I will help you tell the truth. But this isn't going to help."

Her eyes had filled with tears, but Ella was listening. Lucy felt her soften as she spoke.

"Is that why you keep saying you're sorry?"

Between hiccups of tears, Ella nodded.

"Then let's tell Mom and Dad the truth. I'll help you, alright?"

"Jep." Ella squeezed Lucy's arm with her fingers. "I-want-Jep." She sank back down onto her bed.

"I'll get him," Lucy promised. This time Ella let Lucy slide her legs back under the covers. "But first I'm going to tell Mom and Dad. They need to know. Okay?"

Ella slumped against her pillows and nodded. She looked like a broken little bird again.

Lucy could not tell her sister about the lawsuit. Not today. The note had already been too much.

"Don't worry. Mom and Dad won't be mad. Maybe this is good. Maybe they'll let Jep come visit you now." Even as she said these things, Lucy could not help but wonder. Their parents would not be mad. But they'd be gutted.

When her sister finally settled, Lucy kissed her on the cheek and smoothed the hair from her face. "Get some rest. I'll be back tomorrow."

"With Jep?" Ella sat up.

"I'll do my best," Lucy told her, glancing back at the door. She didn't want to risk upsetting Ella any more, but she couldn't keep Eudora waiting longer, either.

To her relief, Ella sank back against her pillows again. "Jep," she said. "Promise."

"Promise."

Ella had no way of knowing Jep had been banned from Spaulding, at her parents' insistence. Lucy doubted that what she was about to tell them would change their minds. Still, a promise between sisters was a promise.

As she hurried down the hall to Mrs. Shipman, Lucy had an urgent list ahead of her. At the top, always, was Ella.

It was a quiet ride back to Chatham. "Is your sister doing well?" Mrs. Shipman asked.

"Yes, thank you," Lucy replied. "She'll be even better tomorrow."

After Mrs. Shipman dropped her back at the bookstore, Lucy rode home as fast as she could. Inside the house was cool and dark, a welcome respite to the beads of perspiration on her face.

"Mom? Dad?" she called. No one answered. Before she went to find them, Lucy ran upstairs to Ella's bedroom. She found what she needed tucked away in the jewelry box.

Back downstairs the kitchen was empty, but there were signs of dinner preparations underway. Lucy found them outside, on the patio, the grill smoking and her father sitting in a patio chair with a beer. Lucy could not remember the last time she'd seen him enjoy one.

"Hey," she said, stepping outside to join them.

"Oh good, you're back in time for supper!" Her mother came over and kissed her cheek. "You worked late today."

Her father looked up. "Steaks for dinner," he said, happily.

Lucy took a seat opposite her father at the patio table. "There's something I have to tell you guys."

"How was work?" her mother asked, lifting the lid of the grill to inspect the meat.

"Mom, can you come sit with us?" Lucy asked.

Her father set his bottle down. "What's wrong?" His senses had been sharpened by the accident, able to cut through minutiae like a blade. "Tell me."

"Lucy?" Her mother joined them, looking worried.

"It's about the accident," Lucy began.

Both her parents' faces went dark. The accident was a topic they avoided. "What about it?"

"Jep wasn't the one driving."

"What?" Her mother shook her head, as if Lucy was speaking a language she did not understand.

But her father did. "Nonsense. Of course he drove. He drank, and then he drove."

"No, Dad. He didn't."

"Then who did?" her mother asked. And then it dawned on her what Lucy was trying to say. "Not Ella."

"Yes, Mom. Ella. I went to see her today." She looked between her parents. "I'm sorry I didn't tell you, but I had to ask her alone."

"No!" Her father pounded the patio table with his fist. "The police report says so. The lawyers say so." He stood up. "Even Jep Parsons said he did."

In the face of her father's rage, Lucy swallowed. She had to tell the truth. "Did Ella say he did?"

"Honey, your sister has a traumatic brain injury. Whatever she said to you today, she's mistaken. Or confused."

Lucy shook her head. "She's not confused, Mom. She remembers that night and she's able to talk now."

"Then why hasn't she told us?" her father asked.

"It never occurred to her to tell us who was driving because she thought we already knew." Lucy turned to her mother. "That's why she keeps saying she's sorry. She's sorry because she's the one who crashed the car."

Her parents went still.

"I went to Parsons's Garage and looked at the Mustang," Lucy admitted.

"You did what?" her father said.

"I needed to see it for myself. And I found this, on the floor of the car." Lucy reached into her pocket and handed her mother Ella's broken gold bracelet.

"Her graduation bracelet."

"It was under the steering wheel. On the driver's-side floor." Lucy looked between her parents. "She'll tell you herself, when you see her tomorrow."

"Only because she's trying to protect that boyfriend!"

"No, Dad. He's been the one protecting her. Jep knew if she was given a DUI she'd have a record. He didn't want her to lose her scholarship or her spot at Tufts. Don't you see?"

Her father sat down.

"This can't be true." Lucy's mother pressed the bracelet to her heart. "How can this be true?"

"I'm sorry," Lucy told them. She sat beside her father, wrung out by the words. "I didn't want to worry you with this until I was sure. You have to call off the lawsuit. It's not right."

"What is right anymore?" Lucy's father cradled his hands in his head.

The truth was out, but somehow it felt worse. The three of them sat at the table, the acrid smoke of the grill filling the silence between them.

Leah

As much as it pained her to see him again, Greg looked good to her in the same way your childhood home looks good when you make the turn into your driveway after being away a long time. As he took a seat across from her at the Beach House Grill, she instinctively shielded her eyes as though the sun was in them. This was no time for nostalgia.

At the store he'd begged her to go somewhere to talk. "Can you please hear me out? I swear, I'll leave if you still want me to. But hear me out first."

There was no way she was taking him back to her house: too personal. There was no way they could talk in the store: too many curious ears. As it was, Brad was practically hovering outside her office after she'd dragged Greg into it. "Let me take you out for lunch," Greg pleaded. "I found a nice place where we can talk. Like old times."

Leah was not in the mood for old times; she could barely manage to keep up with the new times. "Fine," she'd said, just to get him out of the shop. The Beach House Grill was a special place, even with an ex. Nestled in the sand dunes, the swanky outdoor venue sat right on the beach at Chatham Bars Inn. It was popular among the summer crowd, but when the server brought them menus, Leah only had eyes for Greg. She wasn't hungry; she was angry.

"You can't just show up like this," she told him.

"What else was I supposed to do, Leah?" He looked genuinely distressed, and despite his tailored appearance, there were deep rims beneath his eyes. "You wouldn't take my calls. You ignored all my texts."

There was no use dancing around. "What happened with Rebekah?"

Greg sank in his chair. "I ended things with her. She's not the one I want to spend the rest of my life with."

"Well, neither was I. You said you had a change of heart, if I recall. Then Rebekah came back on the scene. Now she's gone and you're here." Leah paused. "You're having a pretty indecisive summer, Greg. It's a wonder you could pick out that shirt you're wearing."

Greg shifted uncomfortably in his seat. "I screwed up."

"You sure did."

"I know, and I'm sorry."

"I lost my job and you called off the wedding."

"It wasn't just about your job, Leah. We could never get things off the ground. Come on, you must've felt it, too." When he reached across the table for her hand Leah slid it into her lap.

"What do you mean?"

"Let's start with the wedding. We've been engaged for three years."

"And that's my fault?"

"No, but that's on both of us. We spent so long planning the wedding, trying to pick the right date, the right venue, that nothing ended up getting planned. It made me think you had cold feet."

"Then why didn't you ask me?"

"Because then your mom died, so things naturally went on hold."

Leah looked out at the harbor, at the boats on their moorings, the water like pale blue glass.

"It was a tough time," he added. "I didn't want to push you."

"It *was* a tough time," she said.

"I know," he said. "And just when I thought things were getting back to normal, when we could finally move forward together, your job blew up at Morgan."

"That wasn't my fault," Leah barked. The couple at the next table looked over, but Leah didn't care. "Maybe I should have seen it coming with Luna, but I don't know how I could have. Her story seemed legitimate." She leaned in, the hurt still fresh in her voice. "I worked *so hard* to get where I was at Morgan. Losing that job killed me."

"I'd never seen you so down." Greg sat back in his seat, looking both resigned and sorry. "I started to think that there would never be a time we'd get married or find our way back. I got scared, and I screwed up. I should have waited for you, Leah."

"Instead you opened the door—*our* old door—to Rebekah."

Greg stared into his lap. "It's a mistake I will never stop regretting. I'm so sorry."

The server interrupted and they composed themselves. Leah ordered an iced tea, and Greg ordered scallop rolls for both of them.

"I don't want one," she told him.

"Then you can have mine." It was a joke they used to share. Whatever Greg ordered she always ended up stealing and eating, even though she claimed she wasn't hungry. In spite of herself, she smiled.

"Tell me about the store," Greg said. "It looked incredible. I'd love to go back and see more of it."

Reluctantly, she did. The store was so dear to her heart, she couldn't resist. Greg listened intently, chiming in with meaningful questions. He knew her so well. It was kind of nice not to have to explain herself; for better or worse, it reinforced their shared history.

Their food and drinks came. Leah ended up taking a bite of the scallop roll, and then another, which Greg did not point out but clearly it pleased him. They ate in amicable silence, which she was reminded was also a nice thing. It took a long time to develop that kind of ease with someone.

When they were done, Greg paid. "Would you like to grab a drink at the bar?"

"No, thanks. Besides, I had kind of a big night the other night." It just came out, naturally, but she could see the questions it raised in his mind.

"I have no right to ask you . . . "

"Then don't," she said, cutting him off.

"Alright," Greg said, nodding. "Fair enough." He paused, glancing out at the water view as if choosing his next words carefully. "Then let me ask you this. Will you please reconsider our future? I'm asking for a second chance, Leah. For both of us."

The harbor was so calm, at odds with the swell of emotions that seeing Greg had raised. Leah shook her head, but she didn't say no. "My head is in a different place, Greg. I've started over. I'm home now, with my shop." She let that sink in.

"I've thought about that. With my job, I can pretty much work remotely. So what if I had to commute into the city now and then?"

"You'd live here?" She couldn't believe he'd even thought this so far through, let alone come back to her with the proposal.

"I would. Of course I would—if it meant getting you back." This time when he reached for her hand, Leah didn't pull away. "Please, Leah. Just think about it."

"I need to get back to work," she told him. "And you should get on the road before traffic gets bad."

"Actually, I'm staying here tonight." He nodded across the street, toward the inn. "Tonight and tomorrow are wide open, in case you'd like to join me."

Leah was taken aback. Greg never took days off. He'd shown up, here in Chatham. And now he was staying the night. Leah wasn't sure if the gesture was intrusive or romantic. "I really should get back to the store."

When he dropped her off, Greg ran around the side of the car and held the door for her. He did not try to follow her in. "You know where to find me," he said. Then, without warning, he pulled her in tight and kissed her passionately on the lips.

Luke

Summers in Chatham turned slowly like May leaves unfurling on branches, like a tide rising beneath a waxing moon. At first the turn of season was a slow bloom, and then suddenly you found yourself in the thick of it. Hydrangeas burst forth along picket fences, the village swarmed with tourists, and the heat drove everyone to the shore. The frantic onset was no different than the surge of uncertainty Luke felt as August rolled in, and for the life of him he could not get his head straight.

He began rising earlier and taking longer runs on the beach with Scout. Some days he worked late in his boathouse shop, just to keep his mind and hands busy. Some days he abandoned whatever project was on his worktable, dragging his kayak down the embankment into Oyster Pond and paddling for hours instead. No matter how exhausted his limbs, he could not quiet the thoughts in his mind.

Until he reconnected with Holly, Luke was at a point where he'd decided summer would be survivable only as long as he remained single. And then she came along, like a trinket washing up on the beach. They began spending his limited free time together. He found himself enjoying her company. It wasn't just her easy laugh or playful nature. Holly made time for him whenever he had it to give. It was so effortless, in fact, that Luke began to wonder if that might indicate a problem. While his ego was certainly not suffering the attention, his conscience began to. What did Holly have to offer him, other than easy company? It was early, but there was never any conflict. Not once did he feel pushed or challenged. Whenever he suggested places to go, she readily agreed. If he asked what she wanted to do, she deferred to him. When he asked her where she pictured herself once the summer ended, she shrugged and said she'd figure it out eventually. While Holly went with the flow, it was something he was finding less and less desirable.

Though he knew better than to compare, he couldn't help it. By contrast, Leah was a riptide: strong but unpredictable. It was easy to get swept along. It was also undeniably alluring. She'd driven him crazy at times and driven him away at others. Still, that summer he'd felt a connection that surpassed mere childhood history. It stayed with him even after she made clear her boundaries, even after he'd given up. Until the other night at the Squire. When Luke saw Leah propped up against the wall like that, he knew something had changed. The decision to take her home was the right one, even if he'd paid for it with Holly. The two had been talking about taking a trip to the Vineyard, but since that night Holly had stopped speaking to him.

Luke wasn't too worried about that, though. What worried

him was what Leah said on the drive home. As soon as she clambered into the cab, she'd curled up on the seat beside him. The whole way home he drove extra slow, so as not to rouse her. At some point she started rambling, something he'd grown used to, but this time it seemed the alcohol had lifted the mask of her inhibitions. Leah had wondered aloud if Holly was waiting for him back at the Squire. She'd asked him if Holly was upset. When he told her Holly would be fine, Leah said that Holly was lucky. *Lucky.*

It stayed with him all night, after he helped her inside and handed her over to Brad. After the two of them got her upstairs and tucked her into bed. It was with him still, now.

Had Leah Powell had a change of heart? Maybe she was able to finally consider life outside her bookshop. Maybe that life might involve him. And if it didn't, maybe he could finally get some answers to the questions that had chased him all summer. Their conversation was not over; he needed to go see her.

All morning in his workshop Luke struggled to concentrate on the wood pieces he was shaping on the lathe; twice, he almost nicked himself. Before he lost a finger, he turned off the machine and closed up the boathouse. After a quick shower and shave, he called Scout.

"C'mon boy," he said, holding the truck door open. Scout bounded across the front yard and leaped onto the truck seat, eager for whatever adventure was coming. Luke rubbed his head. "What I'd give for half your optimism."

There were no parking spots, so Luke parked across the street in the Lighthouse Beach lot. He didn't care if he got a ticket.

Scout at his side, he jogged toward the Sandy Page shop. As soon as they hit the crosswalk, Luke halted.

A sleek blue BMW was parked in front of the Sandy Page, right behind Leah's car. Right where he usually parked his truck. Two people stood beside it. One was Leah. The other was someone Luke hadn't seen since her mother's funeral but recognized straightaway: her old fiancé, Greg.

Scout had seen Leah, too. He pulled at his leash, whining and wagging with excitement. Luke barely noticed. Nor did he notice the cars that kept slowing to let him cross the street. He was too transfixed by the sight of Leah with Greg.

Heart in his throat, Luke waited on the other side of the street. He watched while Leah and Greg talked. He was still watching as Greg pulled her in close and kissed her on the lips.

Scout whined again.

"No," Luke said firmly, holding Scout back. Luke turned in the direction he'd come from. He had his answer.

Lucy

It wasn't easy breaking your parents' hearts. But then, Lucy supposed, they'd already been broken that summer. The night she told her parents the truth about the accident brought back all the hurt. At first her father could not, would not, believe her. Her mother tried in vain to make sense of it. It wasn't their fault. Lucy herself had struggled to believe what had revealed itself slowly to her, all summer long, like honey spilling out of a jar. It took a visit to Spaulding the next day for the strange new information to make its way to reason. Followed by another visit to the attorneys' office. And later, when Lucy thought her parents hadn't an ounce left in them, a trip to the police station to speak with the investigating officer. That was not the last visit they had to make, however.

The last visit came the following day when everyone had had a chance to sleep on the hard new truths that had found them. Lucy's father sat at the breakfast table looking resolved, if still weary. He had a conversation ahead of him that he'd sworn he would never have. Change is hard. Changing your mind about someone is even harder.

Lucy rode to Parsons's Garage with her father. They found Mr. Parsons in the small office ringing up a client at the register. He didn't see them, so they sat together on the old plastic chairs by the window where people waited for their cars to be serviced. While they sat, Lucy stole a look at her father. She did not know what it was like to be a parent, but looking at him now, there were signs. Her father's hands were clasped tightly, but that didn't keep them still. His jaw was set, something she and Ella had long attributed to sternness, but now there was the slightest tremble in it. Her father was afraid.

Until that summer Lucy had not considered how frightening it must be to be a parent. Terrifying, even. Until then she'd thought a parent's biggest job was to feed their kids, clothe them, love them. Get them to school. Bake birthday cakes. Teach them to drive. Send them away to college, if they could. That was hard work, but it wasn't terrifying.

What was terrifying, at times, was being a teenager. Fitting in. Finding friends. Keeping friends. Covering up pimples. Living in a body that is always morphing in ways you don't fully understand. Your first kiss. Your first failed test. Hiding under desks during active shooter drills. Saying no to the pot someone offers you at a party. Saying yes. Flying under the radar of bullies. Getting on the radar of the popular crowd. Every day there was something to manage, to avoid, to cultivate. All of it, terrifying.

As Mr. Parsons thanked his customer and said goodbye, Lucy's father shifted uncomfortably in the seat beside her. What he was about to do would not be easy. He was there to introduce himself. To apologize. To try to make sense of a senseless situation between two families in a small town one summer night. She realized her father was terrified by the love he had for Ella and Lucy. Because when you loved someone that much, there was so much to lose.

When her father rose from his seat, Lucy rose, too. She walked with him, right up to Mr. Parsons at the counter. And when her father introduced himself, his voice strong and clear, Lucy reached over and grabbed his hand. She squeezed it, as hard as she could, willing him all the bravery she had in her young brave bones.

Later, as Lucy and her mother drove to Spaulding, they talked. Lucy felt the layers of the summer peeling away as they did, like the outer petals of a peony curled dry by the sun. With each word spoken, a sun-scarred petal fell away until what was left was still beautiful, if reduced.

They talked about easier things, like summer coming to a close and school starting again. They talked about the harder things, too; the difficult phone call made to Tufts informing them of Ella's DUI. As a result, there were new uncertainties. Ella's academic scholarship would now go under review. It turned out that Jep Parsons's desire to protect her had not been wrong.

This fresh hurdle seemed too much. After all, how much could one person endure? "Can't the lawyers do something? Can't you and Dad write a letter?"

"We will help her however we can, but I don't know that it will make a difference. We'll have to wait and see."

It didn't sit right with Lucy. "It doesn't seem fair."

"Ella made a choice that night," her mother said sadly. "Things could have been worse."

"But she's suffered so much already." It was like that dark game they used to play on the playground when the teachers weren't looking, when someone twisted your wrist until you called mercy. Yes, Ella had made a choice. But at what point would someone cry mercy?

Her mother glanced over at her in the passenger seat. In the golden light at that hour the tiredness about her eyes was softened, the worry lines blurred. "Your sister has fought hard to get to this point. Whatever happens, we will help her through the rest."

That was one thing no one could take away. Ella was returning to them, bit by bit. She was speaking and walking, showering herself, able to take stairs. The smallest things that were no longer small at all, and that signaled big hope. Hope, Lucy realized, was everything.

On the way into the hospital, her mother stopped at the physiatrist's office. Lucy went ahead without her, unafraid as she had been when Ella first came here. She said hello to Danny, who was walking another patient down the hall. She waved to Dr. Forrester. Soon Ella would be coming home. Lucy had never thought there would be so many wonderful people she hoped to never see again.

At Ella's door, a familiar sound stopped her in her tracks. Lucy stopped on the threshold, listening. It was Ella speaking, her voice high and bright. She was talking animatedly like she used to on the phone with a friend or with Lucy when she had juicy news to share. Lucy peered inside.

Ella was not alone. Jep Parsons sat on the edge of her bed. Behind them sunlight spilled through the hospital window like a glittering golden shroud. Their heads were bowed together the way people do when sharing stories. Or secrets. Or love. Between them, something rested on the blanket. Lucy squinted, realizing it was their hands, clasped together.

As the late-day sun made its weary climb outside the sky shifted, casting the two of them in momentary shadow. Lovebird silhouettes, face to face, hand in hand. Lucy smiled to herself and walked back down the hallway, the way she'd come.

Leah

G irls need their fathers," her mother had told her. It was said near the end, when her health was failing and their days together were growing shorter. Leah knew she meant it as comfort, that her father would look after her. Their family had always been close; ironically, it was after her mother passed away when distance crept in between them. As if, somehow, her absence left a crack too jagged to be closed, as if she'd been the ribbon that tied them all together. Leah had read plenty of books on loss. She knew how the distance found them: it was her grief, it was her father's guilt for surviving, and for later remarrying. It was a lot of things. Though they gathered for holidays and talked occasionally, for the most part Leah tried not to need her father. That night, however, after Greg showed up, Leah needed grounding.

Greg's surprise visit had rattled her more than she'd thought possible. When she first looked up and saw him standing in her shop she was livid. How dare he just show up like that? Later, seated across the table from him at the grill she'd realized she actually wanted to hear him out. As much as she'd moved on that summer, their ending had been abrupt and there was still need for closure. She'd listened to Greg, head spinning as she did. She'd agreed to consider his proposal, despite all her misgivings. One thing about Greg was that his timing was impeccable. He'd managed to catch her in a moment of uncertainty, even if he didn't realize it. Her life in Chatham, which she'd just started to settle into, was suddenly feeling *unsettled* again. And there was Greg, right on time. When he kissed her like that in front of the bookstore it was the final blow.

"What are you doing?" she'd cried, reeling back.

"I'm sorry," he said, "but I still love you."

A disconcerting surge of old feelings rushed her: the familiar press of his lips, the comforting scent of his aftershave. Even the handsome face that looked back at her, his gaze ripe with hope. The memories hit Leah hard on the sidewalk, as did the possibility that she could have all of this back. If she wanted it.

It was a scene ripped straight from the page of a romance novel, no different than one of the titles sitting on the front table inside her shop, mere steps away: old lovers standing beneath a streetlamp. Leah holding her ground in front of her new shop, symbolic of her solo start. And Greg, climbing out of pages past and inserting himself smack-dab into her latest chapter. Two characters at the intersection of past and present; and yet instead of feeling like serendipity, it felt like a car crash.

Now Greg was staying at Chatham Bars Inn, awaiting her decision. Luke was still heavy on her mind. And Leah found herself suddenly needing her father. It was just as her mother had said.

"What a nice surprise," her dad said, when he answered her call. "I've been following the shop online, on the Facebook."

His comment chipped at any distance between them and made her laugh. "You're on Facebook, Dad?"

"I am now. It's the only way I can keep up with you. How is business?"

"Busy."

"Good. And you?"

"Also busy. But I'm hanging in there."

There was a pause on the other end. "You sound a little down, honey. Is everything alright?" She did not want to unload all her troubles on her father.

"It's been a long week. I just wanted to hear your voice."

"Well, that's an awfully nice thing for a father to hear." She could tell he was smiling. "How about I do the talking for once?"

He told her about his garden and about a nest of robin eggs he'd discovered over the front door, things that were beautiful to imagine and easy on the ears. His voice was soft and gentle, like him, and the lilt of it took her back to childhood when her life felt soft and gentle, too. After they chatted awhile, there was one last thing he wanted to tell her.

"You know, honey, I don't say it enough perhaps, but I am very proud of you. Of both you and your brother." Even on the other end of the phone, she could hear the catch in his voice.

"I know you are, Dad."

"There are no guarantees in life," he went on. "We know that better than most, don't we?"

"We do," she said sadly.

"But that never stopped you. Since you were a little girl, you always went after what you wanted. Whatever is bothering you, follow that gut of yours. I have no doubt you'll be alright."

It was the sharpest connection she'd felt with her father in longer than she could recall, and she wished suddenly she'd done this more often. It was not hard to pick up the phone. She would try to do that more. "Thanks, Dad," she managed. "That's an awfully nice thing for a daughter to hear."

When she hung up, Leah grabbed her purse and keys. It was time for a conversation of another kind.

Greg met her in front of the Chatham Bars Inn, as she'd requested. Leah had chosen two Adirondack chairs, off to the side and with a view of the fishing boats coming in to the pier.

The moment Greg sat down, she could tell he knew. Still, he was brave enough to ask for himself. "So did you have a chance to think about what I said?"

"I did." She turned to face him. "I'm sorry, but I don't see a future for us, Greg. Not anymore."

He closed his eyes and leaned back in his chair. "At least you were quick about it," he said glumly.

"I wasn't quick," she told him. "I already knew." She reached across the space between the two chairs and took his hand. "I've changed, after everything that happened. I like being back here, and I like where my life is going."

"It's only been a few months, Leah. Where is your life going?"

She shrugged, turning her gaze back to the water. "I don't know. But I can't wait to find out."

When she left the hotel, Leah went straight home to her

couch. Telling Greg was one thing, but the reverberations that followed were another. "I know we broke things off months ago, but today feels so final," she said, sinking onto the cushion next to Brad.

He wrapped an arm around her. "But it's what you want, right?"

"It is. I just feel so . . . alone."

"You're not alone. You're stuck with me." Brad, still nursing his own hurts from his grandmother, looked to be staying with her until he went back to Boston. Which was too soon, as far as Leah was concerned.

"Summer is ending. You'll be leaving soon, too," she said. And then she started to cry. In large hiccupping cries, she gave in. It wasn't about Greg, or Brad leaving, or even the uncertainty of the bookshop's future when tourist season came to a close. It was that Leah had been going so hard for so long, and yet there was no sign of any of it getting any easier.

Brad held on as she cried, and didn't even make a peep when she wiped her nose on the sleeve of his linen shirt.

"All I have is a shop," she said, sniffling. "A stupid little shop full of books and trinkets and strange if wonderful people."

"Can I tell you something?" Brad asked.

"It better not be that I owe you a new shirt. I can barely make payroll."

Brad shook his head. "That stupid little shop is a pretty big deal, Leah."

"It's been so much work."

"Yes, and think about what's come out of that."

"Blood, sweat, and tears?"

He shook his head. "It's a place where people come to gather. To escape, to learn. It's where I met Ethan. And when my vovó kicked me out, it's where I had a safe place to land."

"I know." She wiped her nose. "It's how I reconnected with Luke, too."

"See? Fixing up that old house spun some magic."

"Well, Luke gets credit for the fixing part. He's been a good friend."

"Leah, I think he's more than that."

She made a face.

"When he brought you home the other night, I saw the way he carried you upstairs and tucked you in," Brad told her. "It wasn't like a friend."

"What's that supposed to mean?"

"It means he did it with care. He adjusted your covers just so, smoothed your hair on the pillow. It was actually very sweet."

Other than being helped inside, Leah had little recollection of that part of the night. What she did recall was feeling safe. Now she knew why. "I didn't know any of that."

"Well, you do now. And you can thank your stupid little shop for that, too."

She blew her nose and smiled. "It's not that stupid."

"No, it's not. Even all the strange people who come in with tomatoes and dogs and their sticky kids. It's its own little community. People aren't going to let that go, now that they're part of it."

"Thank you," she said. It was the nicest thing Brad had ever said.

"You're welcome. Now, can we at least order food while we wallow? I'm starving."

As they sat on the couch, a box of Kleenex between them and Chinese food on the way, Leah thought about what Brad said. She thought about the captain's daughters who opened the inn, who Brad swore still traipsed up and down the upstairs halls. She imagined the general store, and all the people who found what they needed in there to take care of their families. And of the gallery, that hosted artists and brought art to the village. The house had had a life long before she'd even envisioned her bookshop; Leah was just another part of its history. When she finally climbed the stairs to her room that night, she slept soundly for the first time all week.

The next morning, Leah drove out to Oyster Pond. She couldn't stop thinking back to what Brad said, about how Luke carried her up to bed and tucked her in. About all the things he'd done for her that summer. An envelope with a payment inside it sat on the passenger seat beside her; but it wasn't the reason she was driving over there.

To her dismay, Luke's truck was not in the driveway. Still, she parked and walked around to the boathouse, hoping. At the very least, she could leave the check there. But when she rounded the corner of the house, the workshop was closed up, the windows dark and the yard quiet. She must have missed him.

The Oyster Pond River glistened in the morning light. Luke's red kayak lay on its side along the bank. There was such beauty here in the wildness of the salt marsh, the shorebirds calling, and the river streaking out to Nantucket Sound. It was hard to believe one person could own all of this.

She was walking around the side of the house, when a truck pulled into the driveway. Only it wasn't Luke's. A young man parked and got out. "May I help you?" he asked when he saw her.

"I'm a friend of Luke's," she said, holding up the envelope. "Just dropping something off for him."

"You may want to hang on to it until he comes back."

"Comes back?" Leah asked.

The guy nodded. "He just left for a week." He lowered the tailgate of his truck and pulled a table saw out. "I'm helping to finish up a job for him, since he had to leave in such a hurry."

"A hurry?" This gave her pause. "Do you know where he went?"

"The Vineyard."

Leah swallowed hard. When he was working on her café, he'd mentioned that Holly wanted to go to the Vineyard. Leah hadn't liked the sound of it even then.

She shoved the envelope in her back pocket. She was too late.

"If it's really important, you may still be able to catch him," the guy added.

"He hasn't left yet?"

"Not sure, but he mentioned stopping at the marina to grab his fishing gear."

"Which one?"

"The Landing."

"Thanks!" Leah hopped in her car and reversed quickly out

of the driveway. The marina was just around the corner. Leah drove as fast as she dared through the rabbit warren of streets. A school bus pulled in front of her at the last intersection and stopped.

Leah waited, heart pounding. She was so close.

In front of her the bus flipped open its stop sign. It took forever for two small kids to get off, dressed in swimsuits, wet towels dragging behind them. They were sea camp kids, like she and her brother had been years ago. It made Leah think of James, living in Duxbury with his family. Of her father, down in New Jersey. Of Luke who'd stayed, and herself, who'd come back.

As the bus lights blinked before her, Leah thought about what she was doing. As her father said, there were no guarantees in life. There was no guarantee Luke was still at the marina. Even if he were, Holly was sure to be with him. He was leaving for the Vineyard, after all. It's what Holly had wanted. If that was the case, hadn't Luke already made his choice?

Leah thought back to the phone call with her father. How he said she always went after what she wanted. Is that what she was doing?

Finally the school bus closed its stop sign and the blinking lights went off. It turned off at the next street. The road ahead was clear. The marina was just half a mile up, on the left. Leah proceeded, trusting her gut. When she got to the turnoff for the marina, she kept going straight. Tears in her eyes, she kept going all the way back to the shop.

Everyone

Goodbyes are always hard. August had slipped past them, like a New England breeze coming in off the coast. There were author visits and book signings. There were story hours and children's tea parties. Paint and Sip had become a weekly event. The knitting group almost took over. There were children sticky with sunscreen, fresh off the beach, and young mothers with weary smiles. There were grandparents with younger generations in tow, who'd been coming to Chatham for decades and wanted to see the old inn/store/gallery that had now become a bookshop. The café hummed with activity. Willet Smith's grilled tomato and cheese paninis were now a menu staple. Finally, *finally*, Brad had sold Willet a book. Of course, it was about gardening.

With the last ribbons of summer unspooling, it was time for Brad to return to Boston for graduate school. He'd packed his things, all still at Leah's house, and would be driving up the Mass Pike early the following morning. Ethan had come back to help him. Eudora, who had taken years to make a new friend, now struggled with how to say farewell to two. She'd been walking around the store weepy-eyed with Alfred all day.

By evening, Leah turned the *Open* sign to *Closed*. It was time for the party. Everyone got to work. A cake was procured from the café and set atop a glass stand on the front table, usually reserved for beach reads, and now cleared for the guests. There were trays of lemon cookies and tiny strawberry cheesecakes. Plates of skewered shrimp and diminutive puffs of crab. Platters of roasted eggplant and tomato and squash, all from Willet's garden. Crackers and fruit and cheese.

Lucy, who they never ever saw dress up, emerged from the back in a breezy pastel blue slip dress.

"What?" she said when Brad did a double take.

"Nothing. You look grown up."

"What he means," Leah corrected, "is that you look very pretty."

Lucy, because she knew how much Brad liked children, had suggested a final teddy bear tea party send-off for adults. It was too perfect for even Brad to eschew. At the appropriate hour, guests arrived in their summer best. Leah poured champagne into teacups. Eudora and Willet and the knitters all came. Brad, the guest of honor, disappeared into the back to change. He returned, strolling through the shop in a navy seersucker suit. When the knitters laid eyes on him there was an uproarious round of applause, so he did an encore spin of the room.

For the very first time that summer, Lucy's family visited the store. Ella had been recently released from the rehab hospital. She was slight and fair, a less vivid portrait of her sister, reminding Eudora of a delicate fledgling. Looking at the sisters standing together, she had never seen anything so beautiful.

A handful of neighbors turned patrons turned friends joined the festivities. The owner of the Candy Manor who'd made their specialty Sandy Page saltwater taffies arrived. The baker who provided their goods. Two coiffed women of a certain age who'd started a book club called the Coastal Grandmothers. Jep Parsons was the last one in the door, and this time he did not lurk about like an intruder. Eudora couldn't help but notice he stood right beside the Harts.

Leah, who'd been dreading the event all week, stuck to the periphery of the party. To her relief, everyone seemed to be having a grand time, talking and laughing, passing plates and clinking cups. At one point, someone put on music and Brad and Ethan danced. Others joined. Someone broke a teacup. Cake was served and more champagne poured. The night wore on and when the schoolhouse lights dimmed, along with the sky outside, the party did not stop.

At some point the front door opened. The bell jangled overhead, but the partygoers were too deep in their celebrations to hear. No one paid attention to the late guest, moving through the crowd. Nor the platter of baked pastries she added to the table. Brad was speaking with a guest when Leah saw the woman approach and tap him gingerly on the shoulder.

Maria had come. When Brad turned and saw his grandmother's face, Leah could not see what his expression looked like, because her own eyes swelled with tears. What she did see was the hug he gave his grandmother, and the way the older woman held on tight to her grandson. It was a fresh chapter that both were finally ready to turn the page to.

Leah was pretty sure no one noticed her slip out the front door, and it was just as she wanted. The people inside, her people, she realized, deserved to have the fun. How far they'd all come that summer, from strangers to staff to friends. The Sandy Page had sprung from dubious beginnings, a flimsy *For Rent* sign in a window, a foolish notion during an uncertain time in a young woman's life. And yet, in some small way, it had saved them all.

Inside the party went on, beneath the watchful eyes of the Harding sisters' portrait. Once again, Leah was on the outside looking in the window, just as she had on that first summer night she stopped here. As she watched her friends celebrate, she felt someone come up from behind.

"Leah?"

When she turned, Luke Nickerson stood in front of her.

"I thought you were in the Vineyard," she said, trying to hide her surprise.

"I was. I came back early."

Leah studied his face, the strong lines she'd grown so used to that summer. The blue eyes, reflected in the light streaming from the window.

"Did you and Holly have fun?"

Luke shook his head. "No."

"Oh. I'm sorry to hear that." She wasn't sorry, but it would be rude not to say so.

"No," he said, still shaking his head. "I mean Holly wasn't with me."

"What?" Leah faltered. "But I thought . . . "

"I was on a fishing trip. I needed to get away for a few days, to clear my head."

The rush of her relief almost caused Leah to sway in its wake. "A fishing trip."

Luke glanced past her, through the window. "Looks like a good party."

"Brad's leaving tomorrow."

"I know, Eudora called me. I came to say goodbye."

"He'll be happy to see you." She did not say what seeing him did to her. Nor did she say how happy she felt that he was back.

"It must be hard to see Brad go. I know how close you two became."

Leah smiled sadly and leaned against the doorway. "It seems I've said a lot of goodbyes lately."

"Is Greg not here tonight?"

"Greg?" Leah shook her head in confusion.

"I saw you two together," Luke admitted. She could see it pained him to say it, and suddenly she understood.

"Wait. Is that why you left so suddenly? Is *that* why you had to clear your head?"

When he didn't answer, Leah rushed to find the words. There had been too many misunderstandings, the words in all the wrong places. "Luke, Greg is gone. There is nothing be-tween us."

"But I saw you two kissing."

"That wasn't a kiss. That was Greg showing up to ask me for a second chance. A chance I said no to." She studied his face, waiting for the truth to settle in. "I went to your house the next day, looking for you."

"You and Greg are over?" She could tell he didn't quite believe it. Just as she couldn't believe he'd gone on a fishing trip alone. To clear his head, because of her.

"End of chapter," she said, pointing up at the bookshop sign he had made.

Luke shook his head. "Leah Powell."

"What?"

He smiled. "You have been nothing but trouble since the day you came back."

"And yet, here you are." It was her turn to smile.

Luke reached for her, wrapping his arms around her waist. Pulling her in tight. "Here I am."

When his lips pressed against hers, they were warm and full of desire, like the night in the dunes. And this time, something more. Certainty, she decided.

She threw her arms around his neck. She'd not been more certain of anything that summer.

The shop door opened and they hopped apart. Eudora appeared in the doorway. "What're you two doing out here?" Looking between them, suddenly she understood. "Oh my. Another little party."

Leah grabbed Luke's hand and pulled him inside. Into the music and past the smiling guests, around the shelves Luke had built, through the crowd of people she had built, and toward the faces she now counted as family. The house hummed with chatter, the old boards creaked beneath all the feet and Leah felt the joy seeping through the walls. The house was happy again, and so was she.

Leah did not know what lay ahead for the Sandy Page, or for her, for that matter. The summer crowds of Chatham had been kind to her and her little shop. There was no telling what winter would bring with its gray days and biting winds. The sidewalks would empty, and most of the big houses, too. Soon, the summer homes would be shuttered for the season, the boutiques closed, the gallery windows dark. Greg was gone, taking with him the pages she thought they'd write, and that was alright. It was time to renew, once more. To staff the shop and fill the shelves.

All her life Leah had loved stories; she'd devoured novels as a child, studied literature in college. She'd thrown herself into the world of publishing, the same world that would later spit her out. And yet she'd never strayed.

Words mattered to her. They mattered on the page, and in promises made. They mattered on a note ripped from a pad of paper and written by the hand of a teenage lover. Words mattered between friends, in the apologies made or the feelings declared. All of her life, Leah realized, she'd surrounded herself with words. Just that summer, stories had been written right in front of her. The story of two sisters, a secret held between them. The story of two young men, falling in love. The story of a widow braving her fears to find connection. The story of an old house brought back to life. All around Leah and on the shelves of her shop were stories unfolding. As the season turned, Leah would be here. The next chapter was hers to write.

Acknowledgments

Thanks must always be given, and when sending a book out into the world there are many to thank. To my brilliant editor, Emily Bestler of Emily Bestler Books, I am so grateful for this, our ninth title together! With yet another in the works, I consider it my good fortune to have always had your eyes on the page and your thoughts in the margins. It must also be shared what love I have for Susan Ginsburg, of Writer's House, who I count as both agent and friend. I am eternally grateful to have you in my corner and on the other end of the phone!

The talented team at EBB has their handprints all over this book. Tremendous thanks to publishers Libby McGuire and Dana Trocker, to senior managing editor Paige Lytle and managing editor assistant Shelby Pumphrey for all their work on this novel. Gratitude to publicist Sierra Swanson, whose enthusiasm is inspiring and to marketing specialist, Zakiya Jamal, who is always at the ready and on her toes! The covers grow dreamier each year, and are the magic of art director Jimmy Iacobelli and art designer Claire Sullivan. You outdo yourselves with each title! Finally, thank you to Hydia Scott-Riley who takes all the calls and answers all the emails with wit and humor (and patience!) with every book we work on. It's a joy to work with such good people.

I never take for granted that readers have limited time and endless options, so thank you to you, my reader, if this book finds itself in your hands! Thank you for putting the word out, for coming to meet me on tour, for the emails and kind reviews. In this digital age, reviews and followers and word of mouth mean everything to an author. After a long winter writing in my home office, it's such a privilege to meet you on the road and in the bookstores! Please keep sharing and I will keep writing. In that vein, I am convinced that the most wonderful people on the planet are bookstore people. They just are. Thank you to all my Indie booksellers who welcome me back, summer after summer, and introduce me to your book people and make room for my title on your shelves. Bringing books and people together is a particular kind of magic, and it's no secret that the people who work in this field carry wands. Thank you especially to the dynamic mother-daughter team Caitlin Doggart-Bernal and Joanne Doggart who make me feel like family. The Sandy Page Bookshop is a fictional haven, but the real deal is their creation, Where the Sidewalk Ends, on Main Street in Chatham, and it was no small inspiration for this story.

As inspirations go, Eudora's canine rescue efforts in this novel hail from some of the biggest-hearted and most enduring individuals I've had the good fortune to know in my years of animal rescue work. I especially want to thank Kathy Wetmore of Houston Shaggy Dog Rescue for never turning away the saddest and most difficult cases at the shelter and on the streets. The rescue group in this book is fictional, but is inspired by a very real network of tireless and marvelous people from Texas to New England, some of who've helped deliver my own rescue dogs home to me in Connecticut. As all my books have been written with one dog or other under my desk, it felt overdue to include the cause in this one. It's one dear to my heart.

The ultimate thanks must always go to my family and friends for all their love and support through these many pages.

Thank you to dear friend and eagle eye editor, Amy Caraluzzi, who buoys both the word and this writer.

To my family, educators and parents extraordinaire Marlene and Barry Roberts, for putting books in my hands and taking me to the library since I could toddle. To my brother, Jesse, for letting me read Roald Dahl aloud in the back of the car and sharing your Encyclopedia Brown's on those long trips to Canada each summer. To John, for believing both in what I do and who I am. And to Grace and Finley, of whom I am fiercely proud and with whom I will always float on my back at Hardings, make the stir fry, take the call, walk beside. You are the light.